Ankush Saikia was born in Tezpur, Assam in 1975 and grew up in Madison, Wisconsin; Assam; and Shillong, Meghalaya. He has worked in journalism and publishing in New Delhi, and is currently based in Shillong in North-East India. Saikia is the author of eight previous books including *The Forest Beneath the Mountains*, *The Girl From Nongrim Hills*, and the Detective Arjun Arora series. *Tears of the Dragon* is the fourth book in the Arjun Arora series. He was shortlisted for the Outlook/Picador-India non-fiction writing competition in 2005, and was one of the recipients of the Shanghai Writers' Association's 2018 fellowships. His articles and longform stories (mostly on North-East India) have appeared in *FountainInk* magazine, *Scroll.in*, *The Indian Express*, *The Hindu*, and *Hindustan Times*, among others.

ALSO BY ANKUSH SAIKIA

Jet City Woman
Spotting Veron and Other Stories
Red River, Blue Hills
The Girl From Nongrim Hills
Dead Meat (Arjun Arora 1)
Remember Death (Arjun Arora 2)
More Bodies Will Fall (Arjun Arora 3)
The Forest Beneath the Mountains

TEARS OF THE DRAGON

AN ARJUN ARORA MYSTERY

ANKUSH SAIKIA

SPEAKING TIGER

SPEAKING TIGER BOOKS LLP
125A, Ground Floor, Shahpur Jat, near Asiad Village,
New Delhi 110049

Published by Speaking Tiger Books in paperback 2023

ISBN: 978-93-5447-449-1
eISBN: 978-93-5447-468-2

10 9 8 7 6 5 4 3 2 1

Typeset in EB Garamond by SŪRYA, New Delhi
Printed at Chaman Enterprises, New Delhi

'This is my investigation,
It's not a public inquiry'

—Mark Knopfler, *Private Investigations*

'I didn't want to infect younger generations—dreaming the glorious dreams I too had dreamed when I was young—with the loneliness that came to torment me.'

—Lu Xun, Preface to *Outcry*, Beijing 1922

1

London, 2004

Rohit Vats came out of Aldgate East tube station and pulled the jacket hood over his head. January, and it was freezing, and now a persistent drizzle fell from a low grey sky. He walked quickly to the nearby bus stop, hands shoved into his jacket pockets, his head bent down. There was a pub before the bus stop, and he saw through its glass-fronted doors a pudgy English youth in shirtsleeves laughing along with a blonde in a purple cardigan, half-drunk pints on the table before them. A double-decker bus crossed him and pulled up at the stop ahead, and he hurried to join the queue entering it: blacks and Chinese and Bangladeshis.

He swiped his Oyster card and made his way to the upper deck as the bus turned onto Whitechapel. There were two empty seats at the back and he gratefully sank into one, placing the box with the pastries on the other seat. The windows were fogged up and the rest of the passengers sat silent and alone. As the bus went up Commercial Road, he wiped away the condensation on the glass with his jacket sleeve and looked down at the grimy off-licences and graffitied walls and boarded-up shopfronts.

His thoughts turned, as they often did, to his native Delhi, where he had grown up, and where his family was. It was almost Lohri, when his family and relatives would get together at night and make a bonfire in front of their house before dinner. A spasm of homesickness so strong passed through him that he gripped the edge of the seat before him. Growing up, like so many of his friends, he had wanted to leave: America, the UK, Australia. He was here now, in London, and found himself wishing that he could go back. But loans had been taken and needed to be paid off before he could return.

The couple in the pub, seen through the glass, laughing, was a glimpse of another world, one he now knew he couldn't become a part of. Worse than that knowledge, and worse than the cold, was the loneliness. He took out his phone and checked the messages. No word from Xiaomei yet. What could have happened to her? The uncertainty gnawed at him, and the closer he got to her apartment the more anxious he grew.

Her name was Vivien, but in the short time they had known each other, Rohit had progressed to using her nickname. He had met her at a Pakistani-run off-licence in Limehouse near the old docks. He was there with an Indian friend to meet a classmate from his university who was from Mumbai. Rohit had been looking at the various brands of beer on display in the large visi-coolers, confused for choice, when she had approached him, a short girl with a pert face wearing a black jacket with a fur hood and pulling along a small suitcase from which she sold pirated CDs and DVDs. He had bought a recent Hollywood movie from her for a pound and a half, and asked her if she could get him a new Hindi film, to which she said she would try, and gave him her number.

She never could arrange for that DVD, but he called her a couple of times, and they had started calling and texting each other, and then had gone out a couple of times, to McDonalds and the Turkish and Pakistani burger shops on Commercial Road, close to where she stayed in Limehouse with a Chinese family in a council flat. There was something vibrant about her buried under her heavy clothes, and she was interested in India. She said she was from Hong Kong, and spoke English well, and the two of them, out of loneliness and a shared sense of gloom about the city, came closer. He called her one Saturday for dinner to the student flat in Brixton he shared with two other boys, cooked roti and dal for her, and then she had stayed the night.

They didn't discuss the future, they were just getting through. When they talked, Rohit shared his life in Delhi with her; in her, though, he sensed something she held back: it was always the barest details she gave him. There was some problem in her family: that was what he thought. Of late, though, her normally lively self had become somewhat withdrawn. He felt there were times she was avoiding him, and at other times a phone call which she answered in Chinese would turn her moody and see her leave his company early. After she hadn't replied to his messages, he decided one morning to go see her at the flat.

The pastries he had bought on the way weren't just a suitor's gift; they were a modest way to say thank you as well. Though small there was something fierce within her and he had gotten a glimpse of it one evening when a group of white teenagers had started troubling him outside a store, heckling him and then pushing him around as a 'bloody Paki'. Vivien was inside, buying some crisps. She had come out, swung her handbag and hit one of them and given them such a tongue lashing that they had in the end backed away, laughing to cover up their embarrassment. He had thanked her, but she hadn't noticed, so furious had she been. 'I learnt to fight since I was a child,' she later told him.

The council apartment block rose up at the end of a field behind a line of off-licences and fried chicken and fish-and-chips shops. Rohit made his way along the cemented path bisecting the field, stray rubbish lying around on the wet, muddy grass. Two tall women who looked like Somalis passed him by, talking in their own language. From somewhere in the upper levels of the building came shouts and loud hip hop music. He looked up nervously as he got closer: the area he and his roommates stayed in was rough, but nothing like this.

The entrance had spray-painted graffiti and a group of black youth who were smoking something that smelt like weed. Thankfully they didn't bother him as he got into the elevator. Xiaomei or Vivien's flat was on the seventh floor, and as he went along the open corridor, the cold air stung his face. From somewhere came the smell of onions frying, maybe an African or Indian family. Tower of Babel: the phrase popped up in his mind unbidden. Number 712 was down at one end, and as he approached it, he could hear voices raised in argument.

Rohit came closer, the box of pastries in one hand. Then he stopped. The voices were Chinese, shrill and angry: Xiaomei's voice, another female voice, and a deeper male voice. He took the last few steps. Past the glazed kitchen window the front door was half open, cardboard cartons beside it which for a moment reminded him of the enclosed rear of their Delhi house. Without thinking, he pushed the door open. Inside he saw Xiaomei, her aunt, and a tall Chinese youth. Xiaomei was in an old grey sweatshirt, her hair left loose, her face puffy as if she hadn't slept well.

'Rohit!' she exclaimed, and a pained look came over her face.

The youth looked at Rohit, then at Xiaomei, and said something roughly in Chinese.

Xiaomei replied equally roughly, then stepped outside.

'What are you doing here?' she asked.

'I'm sorry, but I didn't hear from you for so many days...' Rohit trailed off.

The youth inside the flat had stepped outside too. His hair was cropped close to his skull, Rohit saw, and there was a scar on his right cheekbone. The aunt, from inside, yelled at both of them in Chinese.

'You shouldn't have come here,' Xiaomei said in a sad voice, even as the youth laid a hand on her shoulder and tried to pull her back inside.

Sadness and anger coursed through Rohit, and he stepped forward and wrenched the large hand off her shoulder. The youth snarled and drew his fist back and punched Rohit, sending him staggering. Xiaomei turned and blocked him and started shouting at him.

'Who are you?' the youth yelled at him in English. 'Get out!'

The aunt had started shouting again, and Xiaomei turned to Rohit, tears running down her face now.

'Leave! Please leave!'

'What? Why...'

'Just leave!' she shouted.

He took a step back, bewildered, the fight gone out of him now. The youth grinned.

'Go, just go!' she went on. 'You'll get to know later. I promise.'

The aunt had come out now, and started shouting at him. Rohit retreated. Xiaomei's tearful face met his, then she turned away, pushing the youth inside.

Rohit turned and walked back to the lift. What sounded like a pressure cooker whistle went off inside someone's kitchen. They have those here, a part of him thought absentmindedly. By the time he reached the elevator and turned to look, there was no one at the end of the cold open corridor. The hip hop music was still booming from somewhere above him. Only when he stepped into the elevator did he realize that he was still holding the box of pastries.

2

India, 2014

Assam–Arunachal Pradesh border. North-east India.

The hunter lying in wait in the fork of the tree trunk raised his head, suddenly alert. There was a faint downward breeze from the forested slope behind him, and he had picked up a familiar old smell, a mix of damp fur and rotting meat. He waited patiently, his eyes fixed on the grassy patch below him along which the tiger was sure to pass. He wiped each hand in turn on his threadbare jeans and gripped the AK series rifle firmly. Years ago, as a teenager when he had accompanied his father in these forests, they would only have a double-barrel shotgun or an old Czech rifle with them, sometimes just a bow and arrow with aconite-tipped poison arrows. Still, having the AK was a comfort. If the tiger decided to jump up at him, he had protection.

The weapon had been given to him by a member of a group from neighbouring Assam; they sheltered here in the forests of Arunachal as well, but didn't bother the hunter's people. The skin and bones the hunter would harvest at the group's camp in the forests—his tribe weren't supposed to kill the tiger as it was supposed to be their kin, but he needed money, for himself and his family, and those stories told by the old people in their village meant nothing to him. The boys from the group would probably eat the meat, but the hunter would draw the line at that. What would happen to the skin and bones after he'd been paid for them he didn't know, but he had an idea that the leader of the group in the area would be passing it on to someone else. The hunter had heard that there was great demand for things like that in China. Maybe after this he could kill a bear: how much would they pay him for the bile and paws?

A deep, low growl made him forget whatever he was thinking of. For a moment he felt panic, then he calmed himself. He was high up on the tree with an automatic rifle in his hands. A few seconds later the immense bulk of the tiger passed by below, its muscles rolling within its striped skin as the legs moved smoothly and quietly on padded feet. In spite of himself, the hunter felt his panic returning. Then he took a deep breath and cocked the rifle. The tiger stopped and turned his head to look up; the hunter raised the weapon and took aim.

Tezpur, Assam. North-east India.

The couple had reached the town on the banks of the Brahmaputra earlier that day in a Sumo taxi from further up the North Bank region, and now, as evening fell, they waited in a tea stall near the ASTC station for their night bus to Siliguri. They were a young couple, the boy with a crewcut and the girl in a new sari, and anyone asking the boy for his ID would have been confidently shown one that said he was a member of a paramilitary organization which guarded the country's Himalayan borders.

They came from two villages on either side of a river running down to the Assam plains from the hills of Arunachal, and they had seen the forests disappearing along the foothills as they had grown up. Their forefathers had migrated long ago from parts of north India and Nepal, but they spoke only Assamese now and that was their sole identity.

Beside them on their bench were two pieces of luggage: a suitcase and an airbag, both worn with use. The boy's uncle, who lived in a nearby town and who supplied sand and stones from the river to contractors, had been clear on that point: take your parents' old luggage so that it won't attract attention. The uncle had arranged it: following a phone call from someone in Guwahati, he had been contacted by a youth from the armed group in the forests. A gunny sack had been handed over and a few bundles of soiled notes had exchanged hands.

And now the contents of the sack were in the suitcase, wrapped in plastic and covered with clothes. A risk, but the boy wanted the money, and he knew his uncle to be a careful man, not one prone to shooting his mouth off. They were to stay the night in a hotel in Siliguri where a Bengali man would be staying too: he would collect the packet and money would be transferred online into the boy's account from Guwahati. It would go into the nest egg for his own house, supplemented by whatever extra he made from smugglers operating up on the border.

As he sat drinking tea from a chipped glass in the tea stall, the boy wondered where the package would end up. Kolkata, and then? He had heard there was high demand in places like Hong Kong and China for that kind of stuff. Like the fungus the smugglers hired villagers near the border to dig up from the high meadows during summer. In his wife's village there was a poacher who paid people for the *keku xap* or tokay gecko, and it was said he boiled pangolins alive to take out their scales—and later ate their meat. Anyway, where it ended up was none of his concern, only that he would get paid.

'Do you want anything to eat?' he asked his wife. 'A chop? A paratha?'

She shook her head. 'I'll have dinner when the bus stops for the night.'

He nodded. She would return alone by the same bus after he left for his posting up in the mountains. On a sudden impulse he reached across the narrow table and squeezed her hand.

'Two years, three at the most, okay? Then we'll have our own cemented house. And a child too, to keep you busy.'

She giggled and looked down, a smile on her face, and he felt an ache in his heart. A bus drew up nearby and the conductor started shouting. He looked outside, then got to his feet.

'Our bus has come,' he said to his wife. 'Let's go put our bags inside.'

Kolkata, West Bengal.

The Scorpio with the commercial number plate entered the side street, leaving the evening traffic behind. It made a couple of turns, and crossed the new mosque finished with tiles and glazed glass. Another turn, and the driver could make out sacks filled with animal hair stacked outside small rooms at the bottom of raw-brick buildings, and parked trucks with red-coloured pools of blood about their tyres.

The young driver parked opposite the biryani restaurant as he had been asked and dialled the number. This area made him nervous: he wanted to finish the business and get paid and leave. He was a quiet boy from a lower-middle class home in south Dum Dum, studious too, but that hadn't led him anywhere and now he found himself driving someone else's car as a taxi. Still, compared to some boys he knew he was lucky. And it would be good to have some extra money to give his father, for repairs to the house and his mother's medicines.

Five minutes later a short man in a grimy kurta pyjama appeared beside his window. The man looked up and down the street, then motioned for him to get out.

'Come on, hurry up and give me the stuff.'

He got down and opened the rear door and took out an ordinary looking black duffel bag. The man took it from him.

'What about my money?' he asked.

'Wait here in the car,' the man hissed. 'The malik has to see it first.'

The man in the kurta pyjama hurried along on sandaled

feet, past the trucks being emptied of their loads of raw cowhides and the rooms inside where men were bent over turning goat hair into shoe brushes. He went down a narrow alley, then turned this way and that, past small kebab shops and general stores, till he came to the building with the guard beside the high black gate. He held up the bag, and the guard nodded and opened a small side gate.

The malik was in a room at the back, seated at a table and going through names and amounts in a diary in his small neat handwriting. The handwriting was the product of a madrassa in a village lost in the vastness of Rajasthan's Barmer district, and it was one of the reasons of his success as he had journeyed over the years from Rajasthan to Assam to West Bengal. He was a slim man dressed ordinarily in trousers and a half-shirt, nothing flashy. Only the expensive Chinese smartphone beside the diary hinted at what he was worth.

His nephew—from the same village—was packing the current consignment of pangolin scales and pieces of elephant tusk and tiger bones into cardboard cartons which would end up inside shipping containers with other goods. Soon the containers would be aboard a ship sailing for Hong Kong. There was a knock on the door, and the man with the bag entered. The malik stood up and came around the table as the man set down the bag and opened it, and took out from under a blanket a plastic-wrapped package. The nephew helped the man open the package, and they took out the tiger skin from inside and unfolded it. Within it were the bones and the claws. A musty rotting stench filled the room but none of the men noticed it.

The malik squatted down and inspected the still damp hide and the striped fur on the other side, and the yellowish bones. He looked up at his nephew and smiled.

'Almost 15 feet long, and more than hundred pieces of bone,' he said. 'Just as they had said.'

'The driver's waiting outside,' the man who'd brought the bag said.

The malik nodded, went to the table and used a key to unlock a drawer from which he took out a small bundle of 500-rupee notes.

'Give him this,' he told the man. 'And tell him to forget that he ever came here.'

After he'd left with the bag the malik went back to the remains of animal which had been shot about ten days ago in North-east India. His nephew was watching him, and ventured a question: 'So the consignment is leaving next week?'

'Yes. As planned. After we've cleaned this skin.'

'And you're going to Bangkok, I heard?'

The malik looked up, nodded.

'Take me along with you. I want to learn more. You're meeting the Chinese fellow, aren't you? The big boss!'

The malik smiled, and said, 'Patience my boy. Do you know how long it took me to get here? When it's time, you'll get to go.'

He picked up an incisor tooth, curved and yellow, the outer enamel worn in places from cracking open bones. He placed the tooth on the table, took a photo of it with his phone, then opened the WeChat app and sent the photo to the contact he had saved as 'Big Boss'.

'How much will we get for that? In China?' the nephew asked.

'Just this tooth? It will easily fetch more than 2000 US dollars in Shanghai.'

'They have real money, don't they? What will you be having this time with big boss?'

The malik smiled at this. 'Last time he made me have pangolin cooked in rice wine. Who knows what he'll feed me this time? Bat soup or snake wine maybe. Some of these tiger bones will go into making tiger wine.'

'Will you get some for me?'

The malik laughed and returned to the accounts in his diary. 'Taste it yourself when you go. Now finish the packing.'

3

Bangkok, Thailand. 2014.

Sheng Li, the man whom Muhammad Khan, the malik in Kolkata, called the Big Boss, stood in the sun on the stern of a passenger ferry, his feet placed apart. Li was tall and well built, his straight black hair flecked with grey cropped close to his skull, and a scar on his right cheekbone just under his Alexander McQueen sunglasses. The breeze on his face and the sunlight on the glittering water, here and there by the bank the spires of a *wat* or the façade of a luxury hotel or designer mall, the occasional brick warehouse from the old days now crumbling by the riverside, long-tail boats and ferries churning up the water's surface: he liked it here upon the Chao Phraya river.

The rear end of old wooden houses and run-down buildings, their paint faded by the sun and the damp, appeared to his right, and the ferry started moving toward them: the jetty for Chinatown, or Yaowarat, was just ahead. As the ferry pulled in and a rope was thrown over the capstan, Li joined the few people who stepped off. He picked up a smell of moss and mud from the brown-coloured water slapping against the riverbank; it reminded him of Hong Kong and his childhood, the restaurant his parents ran on Quarry Bay.

He walked quickly, and soon the ferry stop and the street-food vendors were left behind and he was striding past warehouses and wholesale shops: sacks of rice, cartons of pearl barley, open containers heaped with slices of dried wood-apple and dried roselle flower; just a few of the items traded here. Workers carried sacks and bales in and out of the warehouses, while some of them were out in the streets eating or smoking or playing cards. When he came here, he preferred entering the area from the riverside; not only was his office nearby, he also avoided the main road with the traffic and tourists. In his dark suit minus a tie and patent leather shoes he looked like any other prosperous trader here in Yaowarat, maybe a merchant's son, only the items he handled were slightly different.

At a small temple down a side street people were burning incense and praying, and he took a detour to light a few joss sticks and say a prayer for his children. As he came out, he saw an elderly couple step out of a black Bentley and walk toward the modest temple: some family connection perhaps, he thought. Many Chinese now lived on the outskirts of the Thai capital, but they kept their old properties here out of nostalgia, and more: the area was prime real estate.

Li crossed the road, went past a truck being loaded with sacks, looked around quickly and entered another side street. The nondescript blue door with a tiny rectangle of glazed one-way glass was in the shadows of buildings rising up on either side. A red Chinese decoration hung from the lintel for good luck, and in a corner of the recessed doorway was a small black surveillance camera. Beside the door was a discreet bronze plaque which said 'Phoenix Trading'. He knocked. It was very quiet here away from the crowds of the main road. A long-haired receptionist in a brown dress came and opened the door. She was a gentle, efficient girl, of Chinese descent as well. She went and sat down behind her desk in the small room, cluttered with all manner of office material.

'Colonel Wattana is waiting for you,' she said.

Li nodded, and handed her a plastic folder with some documents.

'And someone came looking for you a few days ago. An Indian man.'

'Indian?' Li frowned. 'Who? What did you tell him?'

'I don't know who he was. I told him you were away and I didn't know when you would be back.'

'Did he say who he was? What he wanted?'

'No. He was just looking for you.'

He nodded, and then opened a door beside the receptionist's desk and stepped into the second room. It was actually an old warehouse, filled now with boxes and cartons and wooden crates, plastic-wrapped bundles lying around. A dry, musty smell mixed with various fragrances from dried herbs and plants filled the air. In a far corner two of his workers were sorting and cleaning a heap of pangolin scales which would ultimately find their way to the cities of China.

'Welcome back to Thailand,' a gravelly voice called out from a small cabin in the left corner.

Made of plywood and glass, its door was open, and inside it were a safe and a wooden cabinet against the wall and a desk and chairs. In one of the chairs sat a lean figure in the grey uniform of an officer of the Royal Metropolitan Police. There was a cigarette in his hand and a glossy magazine lay open beside him on the desk.

Li sat down behind the desk. He squirted out some sanitizer from a plastic bottle and rubbed his hands. Colonel Wattana idly flipped over the pages of the magazine as he smoked.

'You had something for me?' Li said.

The colonel nodded and put out his cigarette in an old glass ashtray. He reached between his feet for a black drawstring bag from which he took out a small silk bag; this he opened and turned its mouth over the table. Out tumbled a few red rubies, the kind known as 'pigeon's blood' in the trade. Li let out a low whistle. He took one and held it up, admiring the light.

'Straight from a mine in Kachin,' Wattana said. 'You were supposed to show me something too?'

Li got up and went to the safe bolted to the wall, turned the combination dial and opened the heavy door, and from within it took out a greyish lump rising up to a point at one end. The colonel took it from him and turned it around in his hands.

'A beauty!' he exclaimed. 'How much does it weigh?'

'Almost a kilo and a half,' Li said.

He closed the door of the safe, returned to his chair and lit a cigarette from Wattana's pack lying on the table.

'From where?' the colonel asked, checking the rhino horn closely now.

'Assam. Near Myanmar. They still have lots of animals there.'

The colonel nodded in agreement. He set down the horn beside the rubies and lit another cigarette.

'How did it get here?' he asked.

'Khan shipped it out for us,' Li said. 'He'll be sending the skin and bones of a wild tiger soon.'

'And the cordyceps fungus?'

'That too.'

'I sometimes wonder, when it all runs out, animals, birds, trees, what do we do then?' the colonel asked through a cloud of smoke.

Li shrugged. 'We'll be old men by then. Let's make some money while we can.'

The officer pointed to an advertisement in the open magazine.

'Look at this seaside villa. I want something like that. And a pretty young thing inside it to look after me.'

He chuckled at this, and Li studied the officer's dark pockmarked face. He would have to get rid of this fellow one day. He needed him for the moment, both as a partner and for running the operation smoothly. But he would have to be got rid of in the long run. Other partners could be found, less intrusive ones.

'By the way,' Wattana piped up, flicking through the magazine again. 'Meiling told me someone came looking for you. An Indian.' He looked up. 'You know him?'

Li shook his head. 'She just told me too.'

'One of Khan's men?'

'I don't think so. Khan is coming himself in a few days.'

'Hmm. I wonder who it could have been? You better look into it.'

After the colonel had taken his leave, and after the workers had left and he had shut the safe, Li came out and locked the door to the warehouse.

'This Indian fellow you said was looking for me,' he said to the receptionist, 'he must be on the camera footage?'

'Yes sir.'

'Can you get it for me?'

The girl searched for the camera feed within the subfolders of a desktop folder.

'How did you know he was an Indian?' Li asked.

'Oh, just the way he looked and spoke. Here he is.'

She paused the video clip of the fair-complexioned man in a black polo tee standing outside their office door. Li leaned closer to the computer screen, frowning.

'Do you know him?' Meiling asked.

Li looked at her and drew back, then looked at the screen again. 'No. I don't.'

He made for the door. 'Close up once you're done, all right?'

'Yes Mr Li.'

The door opened and closed, and Meiling sat looking at the grainy colour image before her. The boss knew the man, she could feel it, from the way he had tensed up. So who was this Indian fellow?

Sheng Li came out of his office and took a right; up ahead were a couple of printers and a Chinese bookshop. He took a left at a crossing and then he was in a small street full of shoe wholesale shops, workers packing and unpacking all manner of footwear outside them while the owners did the accounts. He ducked into a small restaurant with an exterior of cracked white tiles, took a seat along a table fixed to the wall, and asked one of the waiters for a beer and chilli crab.

The cold Singha came first, and he drank from it amid the hubbub of voices. That face, from all those years ago, how was it possible? How could he have turned up here? Could he have been sent by ... no, that was an absurd idea. One person might know something about it. He took out his cell phone and dialled a number in Kolkata, India: a number belonging to Muhammad Khan.

4

New Delhi. 2014.

'Do you know something, beta?' said Madan Arora from his hospital bed. 'I don't think you know this. Your brother was supposed to have been named Arjun. Me and your mother had decided upon the name. We were expecting a beautiful baby. But he didn't survive. He came out stillborn.' The old man sniffed and looked at his gnarled hands on his lap. 'That was when I was posted in Tezpur. Assam. We had a road and bridge contract near the Arunachal border.'

Arjun Arora, sitting in a chair beside the bed, looked up from the *Hindustan Times* he had been reading.

'Mother told me about him once, but I didn't know about the name,' he said.

'Maybe we should have given you another name.'

'I don't mind the name,' Arjun said. 'But why are you telling me this now?'

'I don't know. Maybe because I feel like it's time for me to go.'

'What are you talking about? You'll get better, and then you'll go home.'

Madan Arora nodded absently, his eyes fixed in the

middle distance. Arjun looked at his father's craggy side-profile, still imposing, topped with white hair which had only recently started thinning. The old man was right, he thought, it *had* been a long innings: pre-Partition Punjab, Delhi, Kolkata, all over North-east India, being shot in the kneecap in Manipur, and then back in Delhi for more than twenty-five years.

His father had never been a very communicative person, but today, with the afternoon sun pouring into the hospital room, he seemed to be in a talkative mood. Maybe he was feeling better. It was just an ordinary respiratory infection, but at his age, there were complications to everything.

'Do you know where we come from?' he asked. 'We Aroras?'

'No, I don't,' Arjun said. He knew, but he wanted to give his father a chance to talk.

'Our ancestors were traders from Multan,' Madan Arora said. 'They would take caravans of rice, sugar and spices across the Hindu Kush mountains to Central Asia, and return with horses. Then they had to move to Sind. And ultimately to Delhi in 1947.'

The old man fell silent for a while.

'I dreamed about your grandmother last night,' Arora senior went on. '*My* mother. I wonder how she managed, all of us children, moving from Delhi to Calcutta. You never met her, did you?'

'No, I didn't.' Arjun folded up the newspaper. Maybe it would do them both good to talk about this.

'We travelled by train from Delhi, it was packed with people. We only had roti and achar to eat, which mother would give us. At the stations we would get down to fill our lotas with water.' The old man sighed and looked up at the ceiling. 'Everyone was still talking about the killings during Partition. We children were scared. Then came Calcutta. All five of us were living in a room on the third floor of a building and mother would cook in the corridor outside.'

'You all were staying in Bara Bazar then?'

'At the end of Boro Bazar,' his father said, using the Bengali pronunciation, 'not too far from Jorasanko, the old house of the Tagores.'

'Did you like it there?'

'The first year we had a good time. We didn't have school and roamed around all day. There was a group of boys. Your uncle Balbir was our leader. By that time there were refugees from East Pakistan too, living on the footpaths, they didn't have food to eat or clothes to wear. We saw a family lying dead once, mother, father, three children, they were like skeletons.' He fell silent for a while, as if seeing those skeletal bodies again. 'My father got a job with a transporter who was from Punjab. He would leave in the morning and come back at night. How much they sacrificed for us, Ma and Babuji.'

'And what would you all do?'

'We played cricket in the streets with a ball made of rags, wandered around Boro Bazar and Posto Bazar, went and bathed in the Hooghly ghats on hot days. No one had any money but we were happy. But then once...' his father frowned and paused.

'What happened?'

'Balbir had a friend. A Bihari boy who was older than

us, his parents were no more. He was a good swimmer. We used to go to the Jagannath Ghat near Posto Bazar. Once another group of boys challenged your uncle's friend to swim across the Hooghly. For 2 annas. It was during the rainy season and the river was swollen. He jumped in and started swimming. We were all sure he would be able to cross, but when he got to the middle he started struggling, and then a while later he disappeared, taken away by the river. I still remember that day. It started raining. No one said anything after that, and we all went home. Taken away by the river, just for 2 annas. Now what was his name?'

As his father tried to recall the name of the young swimmer who had been washed away in the Hooghly decades ago, Arjun heard the door open and close behind him.

'You aren't sleeping?' Gita Arora asked as she came around his bed.

'How much will I sleep. I want to go home.'

For a moment he seemed to Arjun to be a small boy again, frightened and confused by the world outside.

'We'll go home soon, don't worry,' said his wife. 'Be patient.'

Arjun got up and helped his mother take out the tiffin carrier, some fruits and two bedsheets from the bag she was carrying.

'Have you eaten?' she asked.

'I had something in the canteen downstairs.'

His phone beeped with a message, and he took it out of the pocket of his jeans. It was a message from Bunty Chawla: MEET ME AT 8PM. He turned to the window and looked out at the identical hospital building outside, his face grim all of a sudden. His mother noticed, and asked him if everything was all right.

'Work. I have to meet a client this evening. I'll come tomorrow.'

'Get some mousambi juice when you come, it's almost over.'

'Okay, Ma.'

He turned toward the bed, and saw that his father was asleep, his head slightly angled across the white pillow. Arjun felt a great tenderness for this man who used to thrash him within an inch of his life when he had been in school, or rather in those various schools across the North East. The other boys had beaten him too, till he had learned how to stand up for himself.

'I hope you didn't tire him out, talking to him,' his mother said.

'He was talking about his childhood. In Calcutta. Someone drowning in the Hooghly river.'

His mother sighed. 'That's all he was doing lately, talking about the past.'

As Arjun stood there a moment with his hand on the side railing of the bed, looking down at the sleeping man, he thought of what he had to do that night. A line from somewhere, maybe one of those Christian schools in the hills, came to his mind: 'Forgive me, Father, for I have sinned.' There would be no forgiveness for him though.

The sun was going down by the time he left the hospital after settling a couple of his father's bills. As he slowly made his way homeward, he was only vaguely aware of the traffic and the lengthening shadows amid the dust and smoke. The twilight of his father's life. He was thinking of his mother's words just before he had left the hospital room. She was, he realized, far less sentimental than Arjun or his father, whereas it should have been the other way around. Had she always been that way, or was it a by-product of having turned her back on her family to marry his father? She had never spoken about those things as far as he could recall. He supposed it was only his father and himself who were haunted by ghosts of the past.

5

'Really, what kind of a person are you? You were shot, you almost died, you were in a coma, you're still taking medicines and doing physiotherapy, isn't that enough for you?'

'You know, you're worse than a wife,' Arjun Arora muttered in the shadowy interior of the car as he carefully poured whisky into a half-empty bottle of mineral water.

'Hah!' Bunty Chawla exclaimed. 'Listen to the expert on wives.'

Arjun put the cap on the half bottle and put it down at his feet, then shook the water bottle and took a swig. The mix burned its way down his throat and he offered the bottle to Bunty, who, in spite of his objections, took it and had a drink.

'Aaah, this is bloody strong,' he said, then asked, 'How's your father now?'

'Better. Should be going home soon.'

'You should stay with them. It'll be good for him.'

'He needs his space, I need mine.'

'Well, you know better. Chalo, open the glove compartment.'

Arjun opened it. Inside was a rag wrapped around

something. He took out the cloth and unwrapped it: within it was a pistol, none too impressive looking with the discoloured metal, and a black cylindrical metal tube. He took out a pair of rubber gloves from the light windcheater he was wearing and put them on.

'Couldn't get anything better than this,' Bunty said.

'I hope it doesn't blow up in my hand,' Arjun said, examining the silencer.

'Arre bhai, it's not that bad. I tested it up on my balcony.'

Arjun screwed on the silencer, then ejected the magazine and checked that.

'Two bullets,' Bunty said. 'One shot, two if necessary, okay? Then get rid of it.'

'I know,' Arjun said, unscrewing the silencer and putting it and the gun back into the glove compartment wrapped in the rag. 'Here, pass the whisky.'

Bunty handed him the plastic bottle and then started the Hyundai i10, a vehicle he usually kept at home.

'You're sure about this?' he asked, his hand on the gear shaft.

'100 per cent,' Arjun said, and took a large gulp of whisky.

'Then we better get moving, *kancha*.'

The car eased out from under the row of trees beside the road. Up ahead were hulking concrete buildings from the 1980s, which, along with the yellow streetlights and the gritty air, held in them memories of Delhi that went into the bones of both men. Somewhere in one of these buildings were the offices of a state hydropower company which

Arjun had visited once in connection with a case. Now there appeared to their left the brown-coloured poorly-lit commercial buildings of Bhikaji Cama Place, a warren of offices with eateries at the bottom.

'Devinder Properties, fourth floor, left-hand side, end of the corridor,' Bunty said, even as he turned left onto the service lane running parallel to Africa Avenue.

'Yes, I remember,' Arjun said.

He opened the glove compartment and took out the gun and shoved it down the waistband of his jeans at the back, then took the silencer and put it into his right front pocket where his cigarettes were. They passed a couple of cars which were still parked along the dusty lane, and Bunty slowed down along a darkened stretch and then stopped. Arjun took off the gloves and put them into a pocket of his jacket, then reached behind for a cap he had brought along and pulled it on low. He opened the door and got down.

'Be careful,' Bunty said to him. 'And call me afterwards.'

With that he drove off, toward the flyover ahead on the Ring Road. Arjun quickly walked past the cars and the screen of trees and between two buildings till he came out in one of the dismal-looking squares between the buildings of Bhikaji Cama Place, here he took a right and walked between another set of buildings to the next square. A few stragglers with office bags or computer backpacks were leaving their offices. In a ground-floor north Indian restaurant the workers were making rotis at the outdoor tandoor. He sat down on the raised border around a dry patch where once flowers might have grown and lit a cigarette and opened a news site on his phone: just another anonymous city dweller. Only from where he sat, he had a clear view of the entrance of the building before him.

Arjun discretely looked around him: a man and a woman sitting together and talking in low voices, a couple of jolly office workers who seemed to be having a drink mixed in soft drink bottles. He brought his attention back to what was before him. The previous year, after he had returned from Nagaland and Manipur in connection with the murder of Amenla Longkumer, he had been shot at and left for dead by Prem Tanwar, on the instructions of the murderer. After he had woken from the coma, Arjun had told Bunty Chawla about who had shot him. Chawla had then made enquiries on his own and in a few weeks had managed to find out that every Wednesday night DCP Prem Tanwar came from his residence in the police lines at Hauz Khas to the office of a property dealer in Bhikaji Cama, for a couple of drinks and card games with his friend Devinder Jaiswal. Arjun thought about that night a couple of months ago, going out into the evening to get into his car, and being shot down. Like always the rage slowly built up within him: nobody would do that to him and get away. That was why he told the police he hadn't seen who had shot him as it had been dark.

He was halfway through his second cigarette when he saw a familiar figure of medium height and wiry build walking along the colonnade at the bottom of the building, talking on his phone. Prem Tanwar was dressed in dark trousers and a maroon shirt and looked every inch the shady playboy he was. Arjun got up and followed as the policeman entered the building. He reached the entrance and walked quickly along the corridor till he reached the staircase. It was dimly lit and stuffy as he went up the stairs. No CCTV cameras, he noted with relief. Tanwar's footsteps and voice rang out above him: 'Yes baby, I'm almost there. Open the bottle and pour me a drink, ha ha!' Was there another person in the office? As he climbed the steps Arjun put on the gloves, then took out a bandana from the back pocket of his jeans and tied it across his face. The corridors running off on either side at each landing stood empty and forlorn. By the time he was going up to the fourth floor he saw Tanwar taking a left above him.

This was it. He could feel the adrenaline flooding through him, his heart beating fast, just like during the old days when he had been in the army, going on operations in the jungle. Arjun came to the landing and turned left onto the darkened corridor. 'Tanwar,' he called out, and the person in front of him stopped, and turned around. The office on the right at the end of the corridor was lighted, and as Arjun took out the gun and screwed on the silencer he absently wondered why a property dealer would pick such a hidden location: shady places for shady deals possibly. Two more steps and he raised the gun and only now was the DCP able to see clearly.

'Sisterfucker, who are you trying...'

He fell silent as Arjun tugged on the bandana to show him his face.

'Tanwar you motherfucker,' Arjun said quietly, 'you should have finished me off when you had the chance.'

'Arora please!' the other man exclaimed in terror. 'I'll tell you what...'

Two pops, a double tap to the chest and the head, just as he had been taught, and Tanwar fell to the floor. Arjun went up to the body. The second bullet had smashed through the right eye socket and exited through the head. He heard a door handle turning, and pulled up the mask and looked up. A slim girl in a red sari came out of the property dealer's office, and advanced hesitantly down the corridor. When she realized what had happened she brought her hands up to her face. Arjun held up the gun so that she could see it, and raised a finger to his lips. She nodded, and he backed away till he came out to the landing, where he turned around and walked down.

He took off the cap and put the gun and the silencer into it, followed by the bandana and jacket, and then put the cap into a black plastic garbage bag he took out from his pockets, followed by the gloves. He tied the bag and walked unhurriedly out of the building, not crossing anyone till he was out in the darkness of the square, headed up towards the Engineers India Limited building and the Ring Road flyover beyond it.

Adjacent to the EIL building and below the flyover was the entrance for the underpass to the Bhikaji Cama Metro station, with several autorickshaws and hire cabs outside the entrance. Arjun took an auto for Sarojini Market. He lit a cigarette as the auto headed in a north-westerly direction through the glare and smog of the Delhi night. Vengeance is mine, he thought, but what difference did it make? As the auto turned left at a deserted crossing in Sarojini Nagar amid the blocks of central government quarters, Arjun casually tossed the plastic bag into a roadside drain. He felt a sudden anxiety about his father, lying in his hospital bed. He got down near the market and walked over to the Sarojini Nagar Metro Station from where he got onto the eastbound line, travelling under the city to South Extension and then to Lajpat Nagar, where he exited from the station high above on the pillars and came down and got another auto for CR Park.

Before and after the Moolchand flyover the hijras and whores and rent boys were waiting for customers who came in cars, and further up ahead on Josip Tito Marg was the traffic crossing where he had thwarted a would-be bike-borne killer almost two years ago. It was suddenly chilly as they crossed the forested Siri Fort stretch, then came the stench of the drain before Panchsheel Enclave. The auto took a left from under the Chirag Delhi flyover, and he got down across the road from the Savitri flyover, crossed over to his wine shop in the commercial complex, which was about to close, and walked home with a bottle of Blender's Pride whisky.

6

The persistent chiming of the doorbell slowly amplified within his consciousness till he came awake. As he opened his eyes, he became aware of the pounding in his head and the nausea.

'Fucking bloody hell,' he muttered as he stumbled out of the bedroom and made his way to the front door.

The sitting room was bright and hot; the curtains were pulled open, so was the balcony door, and there was the previous night's Blender's Pride bottle and a glass on the coffee table. He didn't bother with the keyhole and yanked the door open. The woman standing there involuntarily flinched, and for a moment Arjun Arora saw himself through her eyes: unshaven, bleary eyed, wearing only a pair of boxers and a vest and reeking of whisky.

'How can I help you?'

'Uh, Arjun Arora?'

'Yes. What do you want?'

His blunt reply further flustered her.

'I'm Kadambari Vats. Your secretary ... she told me to come here. I mean, I had gone there. To your office.' She added helplessly, 'It's about a case. I was given your name.'

'Can you give me two minutes, please? Yes?'

Arjun half-shut the door and went and took the whisky bottle and the glass to the kitchen. He drank a glass of water, then went to the bathroom attached to his bedroom where he washed his face and sprayed some deodorant under his arms, and on an afterthought sprayed a little into his mouth as well, which he then rinsed with water. In the bedroom he hastily pulled on the previous day's trousers and half shirt, stepped into his leather sandals and returned to the door. How many days had it been since he'd gone to the detective agency? His receptionist Liza was trying to send him a message. He took a deep breath and opened the door.

'Come in.'

She smiled a quick nervous smile and stepped inside. Long hair still smelling of shampoo, maroon salwar kameez, pretty in a chubby way. There would be a husband and children at home he guessed. In the sitting room she sat on the sofa opposite the wall-mounted large screen television. Arjun pointed to the ceiling fan.

'Will that do? Or do you need the air conditioner?'

'I'm fine, thanks. Can we get down to business?'

'Sure. Can I make us some tea first?'

He saw her hesitating, perhaps wondering if it would be polite to say no. She *was* in a hurry. Arjun said, 'My brain won't work till I've had my first cup,' and this time she nodded.

As he waited for the tea to brew, he discretely looked back into the sitting room. Kadambari Vats was on the edge of the sofa wringing her hands and frowning at the glass top of the coffee table. She seemed to be in some distress. Turning, his eyes fell on the whisky bottle on an upper shelf. There was about a 100 ml left in it. Not yet, he told himself.

He took two mugs of tea on a polished bamboo tray which he placed on the table, and then sat in a chair at a right angle to the sofa, facing the open balcony door. The wall clock showed it was almost half-past ten. He couldn't remember what time he had gone to bed, only that he hadn't eaten anything since a plate of veg momos the previous evening after buying the bottle at the nearby Savitri wine shop.

'I've added milk and sugar in both,' he said, handing her a cup. 'If you don't ...'

'Oh it's fine, no problem.'

'So what brings you here, Mrs Kadambari Vats. I'm assuming it's Mrs?'

'Yes, it is. You can call me Pinky.' She cleared her throat and swallowed, then said, 'It's about my husband, Rohit. He's dead. I mean, he was killed. In Kolkata.'

Arjun felt a sudden throbbing pain at the back of his head. Another dead body, the last thing he needed in his present state. He drank his tea and asked, 'When did this happen?'

'Two weeks ago. They found his body in a dirty canal in a place called Garfa. What a name. Garfa!'

She bent her head and started sobbing softly. While he waited for her to recover, Arjun got himself a pen and a small notebook from among the odds and ends on his dining table. The throbbing in his head hadn't gone away. He found himself wishing he had poured some whisky into his tea.

Pinky blew her nose with a handkerchief and dabbed her eyes with the back of a fair hand before looking up.

'Sorry,' she said. 'It just happens sometimes.'

'It's okay,' Arjun said, suddenly moved. 'Now tell me what happened. Starting with your husband's personal details. Name, age, profession.'

'His name is, I mean, was, Rohit Vats. Was, right?' she pleaded.

Varun nodded, and she continued, this time more in control of herself.

'Rohit Vats. Age 34. He was from Delhi. So am I. He was working for Pure Life, it's a pharmaceutical company. A month ago, he went to China on a business trip. He was there for ten days. When he returned there was something different about him. I mean, he seemed to be somewhere else mentally. At the time I just thought *ki chalo*, work and all that, and I didn't ask him anything. A week after that he left on a business trip. Mumbai, he told me. The first three days he called me as usual, morning and night. On the fourth day, he made a short call in the morning, but there was no call at night. I called around midnight but his phone was switched off.'

Here she paused to gather herself and take a sip of tea. In his notebook, Arjun wrote CHINA in capitals followed by a question mark.

'In the morning I tried calling again. This time there was a message from the phone company in a language I couldn't understand. Then I remembered something and had our maid Mala didi listen to it. She told me it was in their language, Bengali, and that it said the phone was switched off. I took our son to school, then went to my office. I kept calling but every time it was the same message in English or Bengali: his phone was switched off. By the time it was evening I was really worried. I mean, why would the phone message be in Bengali if he was in Mumbai? So I called Rohit's boss, Pankaj. He told me,' here she took a deep breath before continuing, 'he told me that Rohit had applied for a week's leave after he had got back from China. So he was actually on holiday. After this I went with my father and filed a missing persons report at the Def Col police station.'

Pinky paused again to drink her tea. Arjun was quickly scribbling down a few points in the notebook.

'They sent out a missing person notice to the police forces across the country with a photo of Rohit I had given them. They also called the Kolkata police and gave them his mobile phone number. Within two days I got the news from the SHO at the Garfa thana. Rohit's body had been found in Kolkata. So my father and I went to Kolkata. I left our kids with my mother. There we found out that Rohit's body had been recovered from a nullah in the Garfa area. On the morning of the day I had found out that he had taken leave from office. The body was kept in a morgue. Katapukur, that was the name of the place. They did an autopsy.'

Shc took a deep breath before going on.

'According to it he had been killed by manual strangulation: there were marks around his neck. There was no mud in his lungs, which meant he had been killed and then thrown ... thrown into the canal. We decided to cremate the body. The morgue authorities sent it to Kalighat, that was where it was done. And so far the Kolkata police haven't found out anything.'

She shook her head sadly, then lowered her head and started sobbing softly again. Arjun looked at her, then put down the notebook and went out to the balcony to light a cigarette.

7

He stayed out there, shading his eyes against the bright sun as he smoked. Down below in the B block park the stage was being set up for next month's Durga puja celebrations. His head still throbbed, but Arjun was also intrigued by the story the woman was telling him. A low cough, and then she called out his name: 'Mr Arora?'

He went back inside and sat down and she resumed her account.

'The worst part ... the worst part is that I didn't even get to say goodbye to him. He had left early in the morning for the airport, before I was up. And why did he have to make up that story about going to Mumbai on work?' She took another sip of her tea and turned the cup around in her hands. 'And now there's a problem with the insurance.'

She looked up at him, her eyes dry now but slightly red. Her eyebrows hadn't been done, and she had probably put on weight after marriage and motherhood, but there was still something of the fresh-faced college girl about her. Had she not been enough for Rohit Vats?

'Suspicious death?' Arjun asked.

She nodded. 'He had put in quite a lot of money into a policy, to provide for me and the children in case anything happened to him.'

'How many children do you have?'

'Two. Son and daughter. He's six and she's three. They're with my parents at the moment. I've had to lie to them you know, saying he'll be back. What else can I tell them?'

For a moment Arjun thought she might start crying again, but she held herself together.

'My job doesn't pay enough,' she said, 'I only joined work again last year after I took a break for a few years. Because of the kids. I mean, the insurance is important for us. But the Kolkata cops had filed an FIR, and now the insurance company says since it's a suspicious death they'll need a case closure report from the police. But the police haven't got anything so far ... which is why I came to you.'

'Did the police ask for money? To close the case and inform the insurance company?'

'No. And the insurance company found out that he lied about going to Mumbai.'

'Any idea why he might have gone to Kolkata?'

She shook her head. 'I never heard him mention it too, you know. I mean, he had nothing to do with the eastern market. In his job,' she explained.

'Did he have any friends there? Family?' Arjun asked, and for a moment remembered his father's story about the boy who had been swept away by the Hooghly.

'No, not that I know of. I asked in his office too, no one knew why he might have gone there.'

'And the four of you were staying with his parents?'

'Yes, in their house in Defence Colony.' She looked down again, picking at a thread of her kurta. 'We were happy, you know...'

So was I, once, Arjun thought. He asked, 'And how did you come to my agency?'

'My father-in-law suggested that I come see you. A person he knows, some Chawla, had told him about you.'

'Bunty Chawla,' Arjun said. Bunty had certainly spread his name across Delhi. 'Mrs Vats, Pinky, what do you think might have happened? Please don't try to, you know, hide anything.'

'I don't know really ... who would want to kill Rohit?'

'Was there another woman?'

She flinched and looked away then, a kind of grimace on her face.

'Pinky?'

She sighed and said, 'Ranjana Ganguly, she was a colleague of his. They were friendly. I asked him about her once, but he said they were just friends. Still ... I mean, women have their intuition. There was no ... *proof*, however. So ...' She looked at him, and added, 'Her husband is a big shot in the Ministry of Railways. Subir Ganguly.'

'You know the husband?'

'I met him once at an office party in South Ex. A Pure Life party.'

Arjun noted that down, looked through what he had written so far, then put the notebook down on the table.

'Pinky, I have to be honest, this seems ... complicated. Kolkata. China. Where do I even start?'

'But ... I mean, talk to his colleagues, his friends.'

'What I meant was I'll probably have to go to those places.'

'Oh ... don't worry about that. You'll be paid. You have

my word. It might take some time but you'll be paid. I want to know what happened.'

Arjun nodded. 'Give me some time to decide.'

A look of disappointment came over her face. 'I came here because I was told you're the best. I need my husband's name to be cleared, for my sake and for my children.'

'I understand that. But like I said...'

'Do you know what the ACP from the Kolkata Police told me? That they need to be sure there isn't a criminal angle to Rohit's death. I mean, I knew Rohit! Whatever else he might have been, he wasn't a criminal.'

'Give me some time to think this over. I'll let you know by tomorrow. All right?'

Mrs Vats looked at him for a while, shook her head, and got to her feet.

'You're my last chance Mr Arora. If you say no, I don't know where else I can go.'

'I'll take your number,' he said.

On her way out she stopped before the cane bookcase. It was stuffed with magazines and old CDs below, and above, books and a couple of mementoes, including one from his old Rajput regiment.

'You were in the army?' she asked.

'Yes. I took voluntary retirement.'

'Rohit's father was in the army as well. He was captured by the Chinese during 1962 and kept for a couple of months as a prisoner-of-war.'

'Really? Where was he posted then?'

'Arunachal Pradesh. You should come talk to him.'

With that she walked toward the front door. Arjun

closed the door behind her then took the tea cups to the kitchen where he rinsed them, poured the remaining whiskey into his cup, added some water, and took it out to the balcony where he lit another cigarette. His headache had worsened, and he drank his hair-of-the-dog with relief.

Diagonally across from his flat, on the road bisecting the large and small parks in B block, he saw through the trees Mrs Vats—Pinky—walking past a banana-seller's cart and looking at her phone. Then she stopped, looked up and down, and crossed the road to where a man was waiting beside a white sedan, smoking. They spoke, and she got in from the other side. The man tossed away his cigarette, looked in the direction of Arjun's flat, got into the car and drove off. Who was he?

Arjun drank the rest of his whiskey before going back in and throwing himself upon the sofa. Slowly the headache and nausea eased, as he knew from experience it would. The question now was should he carry on? The wine shop at the nearby Savitri cinema would open in a while, and he could go and get another bottle and spend another day at home listening to Dire Straits. But he had carried on this way too long; it was time to go and re-join the outside world. He would take a shower, shave, have some breakfast, then go to the agency. Arjun closed his eyes, and once again saw the image he had been trying hard to forget these past few days: in the gathering darkness, flames rising up from the pyre with his father's body on it. He opened his eyes. On the table before him was the notebook. Arjun picked it up and went through his notes. His eyes stopped at the word he had written in capitals: CHINA?

8

The morning after he had taken care of Tanwar, Arjun had woken with a hangover to find several missed calls on his phone from his mother during the early hours. He knew what had happened even before he called her back. Driving to the hospital through the still empty streets of south Delhi, his hands shook on the wheel as Tanwar's smashed bloody face came back to him. His mother had asked the nurses to wait till he had arrived before taking away the body, and it seemed to Arjun that Madan Arora was still sleeping, just like when he had last seen him. He told his mother that he had forgotten to get the mousambi juice, and she had looked at him strangely.

By the time the paperwork was done and the ambulance with the body reached Nigambodh Ghat it was late afternoon. Arjun had driven with his mother to the cremation ground; she had insisted upon the Ghat as it was beside the Yamuna. He wanted to tell her that the river was as good as a drain now, but held his tongue. He had already told her that he wasn't shaving his head and that had upset her a little. During the long drive to the Ghat along the Outer Ring Road, past ITO and the Red Fort, Gita Arora spoke little, just about what would need to be done for the *shradh* ceremony. She said she would cook food and distribute it at a nearby children's shelter before the day, but Arjun prevailed on her to order the food from Juneja Sweets, a neighbourhood eatery. The sight of Tanwar's face kept coming back to him as he drove, and he kept telling himself it was superstitious to link what he had done with his father's fate. But hadn't he been okay when Arjun had left him the previous afternoon? Faced with death, the mind faltered.

Maybe Bunty Chawla felt something like that too, because to Arjun it seemed he was holding back at the crematorium. Was he thinking about the pistol and silencer he had arranged for Arjun? His ex-wife Sonali had turned up, with their daughter Rhea, and a handful of relatives from his father's side most of whom Arjun had last seen years ago. The small group of mourners stood and watched as the logs were stacked and ghee poured over them (both items bought by Arjun from a *dalal* along with marigold flowers), and Arora senior's body, wrapped in a white sheet, was arranged on the pyre, with more logs arranged above the body. And then things moved quickly: the priest reading a prayer, his mother scattering flowers on the pyre, Arjun circling it with a burning torch and then lighting the pyre.

He would have liked more time to reflect on his father's life before the pyre had been lit, and more quiet too—there were several other pyres each with its own knot of mourners—but in the end it was like life itself: there was never enough time. Arjun watched the fire spread and take hold and consume the logs and the body. He saw a child wandering the streets of Calcutta with his brother and friends in a newly independent India, and now more than six decades later this was the final end to that journey. Not for the first time, he thought how life and man were the greatest mystery of all.

People started leaving in ones and twos, and Bunty left as well after giving Arjun an awkward hug, so that by the time one of the pandit's assistants brought a stave down to crack open the skull, there was only Arjun and his mother and Sonali and Rhea left. There was a smell of charred flesh and smoke in the air. He watched the flames dance in the darkness, the reflections of several pyres flickering on the dark waters of the Yamuna, the transmission tower on the other side of the river etched against the night sky, and he was aware of a soft hand being laid on his shoulder. He turned to his ex-wife.

'Thanks for coming, Sonali.'

She smiled sadly at him. 'Take care of yourself Arjun.'

He nodded. She was still pretty, but the lines on her face were clearer now.

'You better get going,' he told her. 'It's almost over here.'

'Let me know about the *shradh*. I'll call you in a day or two ... I need to speak to you about something.'

'Sure,' he said, and held her hands for a moment. They both felt something that didn't need to be spoken, a true understanding of the fragility—and hence wonder—of life.

While she went nearer to the burning pyre to speak to Gita Arora, Arjun went back to his daughter and placed his hands on her shoulders. She turned, and he could see her eyes were wet with tears.

'It's okay,' he told her. 'He's at peace now.'

'How are you feeling?'

'I'm sad ... but ... this is life,' he said, and he saw, suddenly, his own body lying on a pyre one day, being consumed by the fire, but he felt calm, and happy that a small part of him would live on in his daughter. 'It's late, you better get going with your mother.'

An hour later it was all over, the still warm ashes handed over in an earthen pot to them, and Arjun drove his mother back home. He asked her if she wanted to stay at his place, but she insisted that she wanted to get back home. All through the long drive back to Rajouri Garden she was quiet, and Arjun was too tired and drained to make any conversation. There were a couple of calls from people they knew and she asked them to come over the next day. For Arjun the events of the previous day merged into the present: life, death, fire, killing. What Sonali had said was on his mind too. What did she want to talk about? Had he been mistaken, or had he noticed a slight stiffness between Rhea and her? Gita Arora stirred to life as they came down the AIIMS flyover and crossed Sarojini Nagar. Here the Ring Road had been barricaded down the middle for the Metro rail construction project. She peered out into the sodium light-lit harshness of the night, the trees along the service lane and the ageing blocks of government quarters, seemingly looking for something.

'What is it, Ma?' Arjun asked her.

'Is this Sarojini Nagar here?'

'Yes, it is.'

She nodded and sat back. 'Everything has changed in this city.'

'True. I don't recognize half of it anymore myself.'

'Do you remember we stayed in Sarojini Nagar for a few weeks after we came back from Manipur? Till your father found a place? We stayed with a friend of his, a South Indian man he had met in Shillong. What was his name? Krishnaswami?'

'I had forgotten about that.'

His mother chuckled. 'You were out the whole day. Your father would get very angry with you. Of course he was in a bad mood most of the time then, after being shot in the knee by those animals.'

'I would wander about by myself. Once I even reached the Azadpur sabzi mandi on a Mudrika bus. I hated the city then.'

'I think you still do,' said his mother.

He was fourteen or fifteen when they had returned to Delhi, Arjun remembered. How had three decades gone by?

It was late by the time they got back to his parents' flat in Rajouri Garden, and Arjun agreed to stay the night. His mother asked if she would make some rotis for him but he told her he wasn't hungry. He went to the second bedroom at the end of the corridor which ran down from the sitting room. With his bad leg, Madan Arora had liked to spend his days here, reading newspapers or looking out at the sliver of sky visible through the rear windows. They had moved in here on rent, and then Madan Arora had, over the years, on instalments, bought the flat from the owner who lived in Patel Nagar. Gita Arora had worked as a secretary to help run the house.

Arjun closed the door, turned off the lights, and opened

one of the windows to smoke. He could have gone out looking for a drink, but had decided to stay dry out of respect for his father. They had quarrelled several times over Arjun's decision to join the army instead of trying for the civil services, in this very room at times, but what did it matter now? He felt bereft and unsure; what he wouldn't have given for just one more glimpse of his father, if only to tell him that he forgave him for everything.

He slept fitfully that night and woke up early. Making himself a cup of tea, he went to the balcony of the second-floor flat overlooking the small, dusty park. His car was parked out on the main road. A cycle stopped below and a rolled-up newspaper came flying up. He raised a hand and unrolled the rubber band. His mother opened the front door a few minutes later, wearing a cardigan over her dressing gown.

'You're up. Do you want some more tea?'

'Yes, if you're making some.'

She joined him a while later, sitting in one of the two old chairs kept outside. Arjun read the newspaper while a vegetable seller's cry came up to them, *tori le bhindi le tamatar le baingan le*, the last word dragged out almost like a plea, followed by a woman's voice asking the man how much the tomatoes were for.

'Susan should be getting home by now,' his mother said, drinking her tea.

For someone who had lost her husband, Arjun thought, she seemed to be handling it pretty well. A while later there came the sound of an engine running below, a car door being shut, voices saying bye and see you tonight, followed by footsteps coming up, and then Susan appeared, dressed casually in jeans, sneakers and a long-sleeved tee. Her fine brown hair was tied up in a ponytail. She came towards them, nodded at Arjun, and told his mother how sorry she was to have heard the news.

'It's okay,' Gita Arora said. 'He had a long life.'

Tears welled up in her eyes, and Susan laid a comforting hand on her shoulder. Arjun picked up the tea cups and went inside. His mother and Susan, who came from Shillong, got along well, and several times she had tried to match them up, brushing aside his objections of her being much younger.

'She keeps her place so clean,' she would say. 'Does all the housework herself.'

By the time he'd washed the cups and smoked a cigarette and come out again, Susan had gone upstairs. His mother put down the newspaper and looked at him.

'I'll go with Susan to the market in the evening. To buy some things.'

Arjun nodded. At least she had some company at home.

'Do you want me to stay here?' he asked her.

'No need. Just come the day before the *shradh*. You have your own work.'

'I'll come before that. I'll get you what you need.'

His mother nodded absently, then said, 'And I've been thinking. After the *shradh* I'll make a trip to Siliguri. I can take a Rajdhani train from here. Susan will do my ticket online.'

'Siliguri? For what?'

'My cousin sister Sunita is there. Your grand-aunt

Pushpa's daughter. I've been in touch with her. She asked me to come over for some time and I agreed.'

'Do you want to go?'

'Yes. It'll be good to get away for some time.'

Arjun realized, almost with a sense of shock, how in a way his father's death might have come as a relief for her. It wouldn't have been easy being stuck with a bitter, physically handicapped man for decades. He himself had gotten away as soon as he had been able to, by joining the army.

'You could come and stay with me,' he said.

She nodded, looking thoughtful. 'Maybe once I'm back. What'll you eat? Should I make some rotis?'

'Don't trouble yourself. I'll go and get some chholey bhaturey for us from Juneja Sweets. Need to see whether my car is all right too.'

'Okay. Tell Juneja I'll be coming there soon, to order food for those children.'

He drove home after breakfast. All the way back to CR Park he thought of her decision to go to Siliguri. If she had asked him to come along, he would have refused, but the fact that she hadn't asked him rankled a little. The truth was she knew him as well as she had known his father. And she was stronger than either of them. What was that he had remembered her saying from the Gita when he had been young, about death? 'The spirit is not destroyed when the body is destroyed.' Or something like that.

9

After Mrs Vats had left him, it was early afternoon by the time Arjun drove the short distance from his flat to Kalkaji and pulled up in his Scorpio near the detective agency. He rolled down the window, lit a cigarette and sat in his car for a while. The trees were green but the summer heat still lingered. Another year in Delhi. He felt trapped here, with no way out. Who was it that had said the fate of modern man, as he awaited death, was simply finding ways to distract himself?

He got down and walked to the building and up the steps to the darkened glass exterior that had the words 'Nexus Security' stencilled on them. Of late every time he saw it, he found himself wishing he had thought of another name when the signboard painter had shown up, instead of having picked one at random from the display case of the mobile phone outlet below them. Anyway, it was too late now. Next door was the footwear shop and the Chinese restaurant below it, Kolkata Hot Pot. Mobile phones, shoes, chow mein, and his detective agency, he thought as he took the last drags on his cigarette: like his father, he too had travelled a long way in life.

Arjun pulled the door open and entered; Liza Thomas

looked up from her typing and so did Chandu, who was arranging papers in some files opened on the glass-top table before the sofa. The television set fixed above in one corner was tuned to a Hindi news channel.

'Arjun ji, how are you?' he asked as he stood up.

Liza got up too. She was wearing a sari and looked tired. The inner glass door opened and Ujjwal Negi came out, followed by the new girl, Shyamali Kundu. There was something expectant in their looks, a desire to know how he was coping with his father's death.

'I'm okay,' he said, looking at them. 'It's good to see you people.'

He meant it. He was back at the business he had built by working at something he was good at, among people who had assisted him along the way.

'Liza, are you okay?' he asked. 'You look tired.'

She smiled wanly. 'There's so much work.'

'I appreciate you handling it. All of you in fact.'

'It's good you've come,' Liza said. 'The freelancers have to be paid. You need to sign the invoices.'

'How many do we have now?'

'There are eight of them in total. Four more we took during the last six months. Ujjwal arranged for them.'

'Four more? Good, good. Show me the papers.'

He sat down on the sofa while Liza went to the filing cabinet near her desk and opened a drawer. They had earlier had four freelancers for routine work like trailing suspects and surveillance, but Arjun's absence while in hospital and during recovery along with more clients had seen an addition in freelancers, all of them vetted by Ujjwal Negi who was still sticking on at the agency. Arjun had suggested hiring another full-time investigator, and Negi had come up with the girl Shyamali Kundu through his magazine contacts. She was a Bengali girl from CR Park, and had wanted to leave her earlier detective agency in Rajendra Place where she had started out as a trainee, saying that it was too far. Arjun had taken her on as a junior investigator, and Liza had informed him after she had joined that apart from the distance there was also the issue of sexual harassment by the owner of her earlier agency. He asked her now how she was finding the work.

'It's okay sir, it's nice here,' she said, looking at Liza.

'Good,' he said, and turned to Ujjwal. 'What are you two working on now?'

'Arjun ji, she's working on two pre-mat cases. Both in south Delhi. I'm working on the case of the missing wife.'

'Missing wife?'

'I had told you on the phone. Married woman gone missing from GK 1. Seems to have run off. Husband's family don't want the police involved.'

'Any idea where she might have gone?'

'Rajasthan possibly. Computer Baba is helping with the phone traces. I might have to go to Jaipur some time.'

'All right. Only if necessary, okay? Chandu, can you get us some tea?'

The gangly office helper nodded, picked up the thermos flask from the small pantry area in one corner, and left for the tea shop in nearby Market No.1. Ujjwal and Shyamali were still standing there, and Arjun told them to return to work. He picked up the remote and turned up the volume on the Hindi news channel: political defections in a southern state, following the BJP's landslide win in the general elections earlier in the year.

Liza came up to him with the invoices and as he signed them one by one, she still stood there. He handed the invoices back to her and asked her what it was. She indicated the television with her eyes.

'Chandu keeps putting it on to the Hindi news channel.'

'So? News is news, isn't it?'

'He wasn't like this before. Nowadays he makes it a point to change to a Hindi news channel. I'm tired of asking him to change to an English news channel.'

So, the divisions elsewhere in the country had apparently reached his office as well. It was inevitable, he supposed. He sighed, and told her he would speak to the boy.

'Oh and Liza, that woman, Mrs Vats. When did she come here?'

'Yesterday. She said she would only speak to you. Then she came today as well. So I sent her to your place. I hope that was okay?'

'Yes, it's fine.'

'What did she want to see you about?'

'Her husband was killed. In Kolkata. She wants me to clear his name. For insurance.'

'Will you go there?'

Arjun stretched out on the sofa and yawned. 'Let's see.'

Chandu returned with the flask of tea, and poured out four cups in the pantry area and handed them out. Arjun took a sip of his tea: oversweet as usual. That small unchanged fact somehow comforted him. He drank his tea and stood up to leave. From his wallet he took out some money and gave it to Chandu.

'Get some chow and chilli chicken from Kolkata Hot Pot for yourselves,' he told Liza.

'We already had lunch, sir,' she told him.

'Get it tomorrow then. Okay?' he said to Chandu, who nodded.

'And Chandu.'

'Ji, Arjun ji?'

'How's your spoken English? Not too good, is it?'

'I can read it and do sums, but speaking...'

'I know, you need to improve. So that you can talk to more people. Which is why,' Arjun picked up the television remote and switched to an English news channel, 'you should watch more English news. And if you can't understand any words, ask Liza madam here.'

Liza shot him a furious look, while Chandu appeared too confused to speak.

'All right,' he told them. 'Carry on with your work. I'll be back tomorrow.'

He allowed himself a smile only once he was inside his car.

The evening found him sitting out on his balcony with a bottle of Blender's Pride for company. He smoked and threw the butts in the flowerpots with their long-dead plants and flowers. Down below in the park they were continuing with the work on the puja pandal. For a couple of days there would be crowds and traffic in this normally quiet corner of CR Park. If only he could leave, go somewhere. But something had turned in him, he realized, since his father's death. His solitary nature had turned further inward, and he only felt a quiet, dispassionate sense of alarm about it. As if it were something happening to another person. Arjun poured himself one more whiskey and went to the kitchen for water, then came back and lit a cigarette.

The doorbell rang. Who could it be? He felt a stab of irritation at having to put out his cigarette and get up from his chair again. Through the peephole in the front door he saw two men standing outside, one of them vaguely familiar: a short overweight man with a bald head wearing a dark blue tracksuit. Behind him was a younger man, shabbily dressed in dirty jeans and a t-shirt, and picking his nose. Arjun opened the door halfway.

'Arjun ji!' the bald man exclaimed. 'How are you? Recognize me? Just looking at your face I can realise you haven't! I'm Prince Kapoor. Now you recognize me?'

'How are you Prince ji?' Arjun said. 'After a long time.'

'I'm fine by the mercy of the One above. It's you we don't have the pleasure of seeing.'

Arjun opened the door and called them in, and asked them to sit and brought them water. He cursed himself for not recognizing the other detective right away, or he wouldn't have opened the door. Prince Kapoor ran Kapoor Associates, a shady detective agency (and property broker as well) in Connaught Circus, and had a reputation as a blackmailer. Something told him that the visit was not a normal one. Sure enough, after Kapoor had talked about the upcoming Delhi Detective Association meet and got Arjun's promise to contribute, he steered the conversation in another direction.

'You must have heard what happened to poor Prem Tanwar. No? He was shot.'

'You mean he's dead?' Arjun acted surprised. 'When did it happen?'

'Five days ago. It was in the papers. You didn't see?'

Arjun shook his head.

'Outside the property dealer Devinder Jaiswal's office in Bhikaji Cama. Strange you didn't know. I thought you two were friendly.'

'Not as friendly as you were with him, Kapoor ji. I hadn't met him for a long time.'

'He used to mention you frequently,' Kapoor said, and kept looking at Arjun, his stomach rising and falling under his track jacket. Then he looked around. 'Staying alone nowadays?'

'Yes,' Arjun said, his face hardening. 'Who killed him, have they found out?'

'They're looking into the case. Must be someone known to him.'

'He did have enemies.'

Kapoor nodded. 'Anyway, his *shradh* is on the 28th. At his residence. Hauz Khas police lines. Come by and pay your respects to his family. Okay?' Without waiting for an answer he turned to his silent henchman. 'Get up, we're going.'

Arjun saw them to the door. It was with an effort of will that he didn't bang the door on them. Coming out to the balcony he took a large gulp of his drink and re-lit his cigarette with shaking hands. They had come looking for him at his house, the bastards. Kapoor had known Tanwar,

Kapoor knew several cops, as well as journalists, with the help of whom he carried out his sleazy blackmailing jobs. Did someone suspect something, and want Arjun to know? He looked at the lights of the buildings across the park and realized he needed to get away from Delhi for a while.

10

The Vats family residence in Defence Colony was a modest white-and-red painted two-storey brick structure. All around this remnant of the old Defence Colony, when it had been on the outskirts of the city, were refurbished houses and apartment blocks clad in marble and glass, expensive cars parked outside them on the narrow streets. It was roughly equidistant from the Colony's Sukun Park, the Colony Club and the market. Driving around looking for the address, Arjun had passed another old house, that of Professor Prakash Saxena, which he had visited two years ago in connection with a case involving a missing Bollywood actress from the 1960s. Arjun had never regarded Delhi as home, but the city was now full of reminders from his past, both private and professional.

A row of dusty Ashok trees rose up from behind the front wall, and as Arjun opened the gate and stepped in, he saw there was a small patch of equally dusty lawn between the trees and the house. There were two cars straight down from the gate on the driveway beside the house: a small car and a sedan. The movement of a curtain in an upper window caught his eye, and he glanced up to see an elderly man in a red dressing gown looking down at him. He went up to the front door and rang the bell. In one corner of the lawn was a football and a broken children's cycle. Pinky opened the door for him. She was better groomed today but wearing a plain green and white salwar kameez, house wear obviously.

'Thank you for accepting the case,' she said. 'Please, come in.'

There was a small hallway where he had to take off his shoes; two doors led off to the rest of the house, besides a carpeted staircase. He followed her into a darkened sitting room; the second set of gauze curtains across the windows looking out to the dusty lawn hadn't been parted. On a table beside a glass-fronted bookcase by the windows was an enlarged photo of a face, framed and garlanded, a lighted diya before it. Rohit Vats.

'Let me get you some tea,' Pinky said. 'Please, sit.'

She disappeared behind a curtain at the far end of the room. Arjun went across to the photo. The hair was starting to thin at front otherwise the fair skin and sharp nose suggested someone far younger. Rohit Vats, Prem Tanwar, Madan Arora, he thought absently as he touched the marigold garland: all gone from this earth. The flowers had started to wilt, the flame flickered.

'*Decessit vita patris*,' said a hoarse voice behind him. 'To die before one's father.'

He turned to see the elderly man in the red dressing gown, a polished wooden cane in one hand. There was something crazed-looking about him with his staring eyes, sallow skin and unkempt white hair.

'Latin?' Arjun ventured.

The old man nodded. 'Something which goes against nature.'

That said, to lose one's father was no solace, Arjun thought.

'Pinky told me you were in the army,' Vats senior said, coming forward. 'Regiment?'

'Rajput.'

He nodded, and said, 'I was in the army too. A long time ago.'

'Your daughter-in-law told me. I believe you fought during '62?'

'Fought? Hah. The bastards sent us there to die!'

'Which regiment were you in, sir?'

'Garhwal Rifles. The bloody Chinese overran us in Tawang and Bomdila. Thanks to Nehru and his jokers Menon and Kaul. No wonder he kicked the bucket in '64. Died of a broken heart. Strong leaders are what we need, look at what's happened in the Lok Sabha elections.'

Arjun smiled politely. It seemed he would have to hear a lot more about the elections. Pinky returned with a tray with three cups of tea and salted biscuits. She put the tray down on the centre table and handed Arjun and her father-in-law a cup each and took one for herself. They sat down facing each other while Mr Vats moved toward the windows with his cup.

'Where do you plan to start?' she asked Arjun.

'Well, I need to get a sense of him. So, talk to his friends. Visit his office. Have a look at his room here. A workspace if he had one.'

Mr Vats said from the windows, 'Kunal. Kunal was his friend. You should talk to him.'

Pinky shot her father-in-law a look, and suddenly Arjun knew who had driven her to his place the previous day.

'I'll need his number and his address. Also the contact of his boss at work. And, anyone else you might think relevant,' Arjun said, looking at Pinky, and she nodded.

'Where are your children?'

'At home. With my parents.'

'You can bring them back after a few days,' Mr Vats said, looking out at the lawn.

'Who stays here?' Arjun asked Pinky.

'At the moment? Just Daddy, and Raju our old worker. Neha was here but she went back to Pune two days ago. Rohit's sister. I came today to settle the place a bit—we had the *shradh* some days ago—and to pick up some clothes.'

'There's a study-cum-library above,' Mr Vats said, turning around. 'Rohit used it as well. His home computer is there. Do you want to have a look?'

'Sure,' Arjun said.

He followed Pinky out to the hallway and up the staircase to a carpeted corridor along which an open door led to the study. As they went up Arjun asked her where she worked.

'It's a publishing company in Panchsheel community centre. Beside Shahpur Jat. I do design work for them.'

There were several books she had worked on, illustrated reference books, arranged on a shelf in one of the bookcases in the room, which Arjun realized was where Mr Vats had been standing and looking down from. Here too the gauze curtains hadn't been pulled aside, giving the room a library-like atmosphere of gloom.

'Could you look around on your own?' she asked him, as she switched on the ceiling fan. 'I'll be in the kitchen downstairs. Nothing is locked.'

He looked around after she had left. There were four bookcases against the walls on either side of the windows, two on one side with glass shelf-covers. Below the closed windows were two cane chairs, and a work table with a laptop and a printer, a stack of files and a textbook of medical pharmacology on it. Behind him on the wall was a large WWF calendar with an image of a snow leopard for that month, and three framed photos: Rohit, Pinky and the two children, on the lawn before the house; Mr Vats in an army jacket with his late wife beside him, coming up to his shoulders, in a black-and-white photo somewhere in the mountains; Mr Vats and his wife and a teenage Rohit and a young woman, possibly the sister, their heads covered with handkerchiefs and behind them the waters of the Harmandir Sahib at the Golden Temple in Amritsar, in a faded colour photograph. Maybe Mr Vats had been up here for the same reason Pinky hadn't wanted to stay long: Arjun could feel the weight of memories within the room.

He sat down at the desk and pulled the files toward him. On their covers were scrawled with black felt-tip pen things like 'supply schedules' and 'API invoices' and inside them were office print-outs from Pure Life: inventory lists, orders, distributor e-mails. Arjun went through them. Several of them mentioned a 'Zhejiang Huasheng Medicine Co. Ltd.' in Shanghai, and there were lists from what appeared to be a Pure Life plant in Sikkim. There were several references to API in the print-outs and he made a mental note to look it up. He pushed the files away and sat back in the chair, looking at the books around him. There were encyclopaedia volumes, history books and old thrillers from the likes of Fredrick Forsyth, and a shelf of newer books with a few Indian names, including authors of romance and campus novels. Among the history books, he noticed, were thick volumes on Tibet, the 1962 war, and China.

Arjun went to the bookcases and pulled out a couple of the books, including Neville Maxwell's *India's China War*, which he had last seen while at the NDA. At one end of the line of newer books behind glass were what seemed like unmarked spines: when he lifted the glass-cover he found they were a couple of old photo albums, the colour faded from their plastic flexi covers. They seemed to belong to Rohit Vats, and were all from different stages of his life: birthdays parties as a schoolchild, hanging out as a teenager with friends, then several photos in London, mostly alone and with another Indian boy. Each see-through plastic page held four photos in its two sleeves, with two photos inserted back-to-back, and as he turned a page with Rohit in jeans and an overcoat at Trafalgar Square, he stopped.

The two photos in the lower sleeve seemed thicker for some reason, and as Arjun pulled these two photos out, he found out why: hidden in-between was another photo. It appeared to have been taken on the Embankment, with the Thames in the background. There was Rohit and the same Indian boy, and between them a shorter Oriental-looking girl. All three were smiling. The girl seemed to Arjun very much a Chinese. He stood looking at the photo, then quickly slipped it into his shirt pocket. Next he went back to the table and turned on the laptop. He spent a while exploring folders and documents, but it became clear that Rohit was someone who liked keeping things clutter-free. It was only when he opened the internet browser and went through the history that he felt a quickening of interest akin to coming upon the photo: among the Pure Life website and Facebook and Rohit's email were pages on Hong Kong and Thailand, and several pages on wildlife trafficking: things like rhino horns, tiger bones and pangolin scales. Why had Rohit been interested in them?

Arjun took a few screenshots of the browser history and sent them from one mail account of his to another. Then he turned off the computer and returned downstairs.

11

The dining room and attached kitchen was behind the sitting room, and the sunmica-topped dining table was like a reminder of a simpler past. Just outside the windows at the back was the high rear wall. Pinky cut vegetables and tended to the dal on the stove while Arjun sat at the table and the helper Raju stood before him. A stout elderly Kumaoni wearing a topi, he would probably have landed up in Mr Vats' household long ago through some army connection, but Arjun didn't go into that. He asked him how Rohit had been lately.

'What can I say?' Raju said slowly. 'It was difficult to understand Rohit babuji since he was small. Didn't talk much.'

'Was he unhappy? Was anything troubling him?'

Pinky looked at their helper as she stirred the vegetables in a kadhai. Raju scratched his head, thinking.

'There wasn't any tension,' he said, using the English word, 'He was as he always was. Only...'

'What?'

'He seemed a different person after he had returned from China.'

'Different how?'

'Absent minded. Like he was thinking of something.'

'Did he tell you anything? About what might have happened?'

Raju shook his head.

'He went to Kolkata. Did you know about that?'

'No. He had said he was going to Mumbai.'

'How did he seem? The morning he left. Did you see him?'

'Yes. I made breakfast before he left. He seemed to be in a hurry to leave. Usually he wasn't like that. He would have his tea and read the newspapers and then leave. But that day he was in a rush ... as if he had some important work.'

Arjun nodded. Just impressions; still, they could be useful later. One more thing.

'Did Rohit eat meat?'

'Yes sir, babuji used to have non-veg. Everyone in the house has it.'

'Are you done?' Pinky asked him. 'I need to send him to the market.'

'Yes, you can send him,' Arjun said.

After Raju had left, Arjun jotted down a few points in his notebook. Pinky had washed a couple of utensils and was wiping the kitchen counter down.

'I've cooked for them for the next two days,' she said.

'When will you be back from your parents' place?' Arjun asked.

'Let's see,' she said. 'But I'll bring the kids over. To meet Daddy.'

'Do you remember anything he might have mentioned? After he got back.'

Pinky shook her head. She stood there with the damp washcloth in her hand, a grave look upon her face. A grieving family, an empty house, and here he was, come to poke his nose into it: Arjun felt a sudden distaste for what he had to do. He put the pen back in his shirt pocket, touching the photo with his fingers as he did so.

'Was Rohit studying in London earlier?' he asked. 'I saw some photos.'

'Yes. He did his MBA and was working there for two years before he came back. This was before we were married.'

'Did he have any friends in China?'

'Not that I knew of, no. There was a Chinese guy he knew, but he was from the company that Rohit's company was working with,' Pinky explained.

'Zhejiang Huasheng? The name of the company?'

'Yes. How did you ...? Oh, yes, it would have been in his papers.'

'His name? The Chinese guy.'

She shook her head. 'I can't recall it. Mr Sahoo will be able to tell you. Rohit's boss.'

'Ok. You need to send me his contact, and Kunal's contact as well.'

'Sure.'

'I also want to look at the stuff from Kolkata. Photos, the FIR. Whatever you have.'

Pinky took a deep breath and nodded. 'I have them on my phone.'

'I'll also need to check his social media. So, accounts and passwords. If that's ok.'

'I'll send them. No problems. Anyway, he wasn't much of a social media user.'

'Well, that's it for now. I'll get in touch if I need anything else.'

He got up, and then remembered something.

'Do you have a photo of Kunal you could show me?' he asked.

Pinky went through her phone and showed him a photo: Kunal and Rohit standing together with drinks in their hands at a party, smiling. Arjun enlarged the image slightly. There was no doubt about it: Kunal was the one in the photo with Rohit and the Chinese-looking girl, and also the person who had driven Pinky to CR Park.

'When are you going to talk to him?' Pinky asked.

'Oh, as soon as I can,' Arjun said.

He put on his shoes in the hallway and when he stepped out saw Mr Vats standing at the gate.

'If you don't mind, I won't come out,' Pinky told him at the front door. 'There's a lot of laundry to be done. Keep me posted with what happens.'

'I will,' Arjun said.

He walked down the driveway to where Mr Vats stood. The ex-army man was looking towards a block of flats coming up some distance away on the other side of the street.

'That was Colonel Mathur's house,' Mr Vats said. 'Son lives in America now and sold the place to a builder. Bloody dust from the construction is burying us alive.'

Arjun nodded and looked at the new building, then turned to Mr Vats.

'If you don't mind me asking. Your daughter-in-law told me you were a POW in '62?'

'Why should I mind? Yes, we were captured by the Chinese. They kept us in a camp south of Lhasa for a couple of months that winter. Don't ask me anything about it, I've forgotten everything except that it was bloody freezing.'

'I heard they tried to convince the POWs about the superiority of their system.'

'Yes, they tried to brainwash us. Nothing happened of course.'

'How did you feel about your son going to China?'

Mr Vats frowned at him. 'What happened to me was a long time ago. They're not even Communists anymore over there. Maybe they never were. It's all about the Emperor with them, isn't it? You want to ask me if Rohit's death had anything to do with my time in China? I don't think so, Mr Arora. I think you need to get to Kolkata.'

The old man was breathing deeply now, a bit worn out from the talking he had done.

'I will,' Arjun said to him. 'And you should go inside, sir. The dust.'

Half-an-hour later he was at Nexus Security. The television was tuned to an English news channel with the volume turned low. Negi was briefing two of their freelancers on a corporate surveillance job. To one of them he handed a small magnetic GPS tracker which could be stuck onto a car or truck. Arjun waited till he had finished and the men had left.

'How are they?' Arjun asked Liza. 'Their work.'

'Good,' she replied. 'Detailed and systematic. Ujjwal had arranged for them.'

Arjun nodded. 'Listen, there's a new case. The woman who had come to the office.'

'You're taking it?' Negi asked.

'Yes. I met her a while ago. Call Shyamali, she should know about it too. Chandu, you listen too.'

They sat down on the comfortably worn sofas and Arjun told them everything about the case so far. Then he sat back and asked them if they had any questions or observations.

'When are you going to Kolkata?' Liza asked.

'After I've spoken to Rohit's friend and his boss.'

'You said Pure Life has a plant in Sikkim,' Negi said. 'Was Rohit headed there?'

'Maybe I'll find out in Kolkata.'

'And China is next door to Sikkim,' Negi went on. 'The Nathu La pass.'

'Yes, I know about Nathu La, but let's not get ahead of ourselves here,' Arjun said. 'Shyamali, there's someone I want you to look up.'

'Yes sir?'

'Ranjana Ganguly. She was a colleague of Rohit Vats. Might have been having an affair with him. Find out about her, and her husband Subir. He's some big shot at the Railways Ministry.'

'Sure sir,' the newest member of the team said, noting the names down in a pad.

'What if he was just unlucky?' Chandu thought aloud. 'A robbery.'

'But why tell his wife he was headed to Mumbai?' Liza replied.

'Maybe he was meeting Ranjana Ganguly in Kolkata?' Shyamali ventured.

'Could be,' Arjun said. 'Which is why you need to look her up. I'll have a word with our fellow in Nehru Place about the phone records.'

He looked around at them. 'Okay, meeting over. Let's get to work.'

It was early afternoon by the time he got home, and he had whatever leftovers were in the fridge for lunch, after which he sat on the sofa and took out the photo from his shirt pocket. Two friends and a girlfriend, all in their early twenties, their lives stretching ahead of them. It reminded him of himself, Sonali, and Bunty at Delhi University, endless days. He lit a cigarette, and as if on cue his ex-wife called him on the landline.

'How are you, Arjun?'

'I'm fine, Sonali. Holding together.'

There was a pause, as if she was unsure of how to proceed.

'Ah ... well, good to hear that. Are you going to the agency?'

'Yes. I have a new case too.'

'That's great. You remember I said I wanted to talk about something?'

'Yes. I've been waiting for your call.'

'Well, it's about Rhea.'

'I guessed.'

'Has she told you anything?' Sonali enquired sharply.

'No. What's happened?'

'Nothing's *happened*, just that her new boyfriend ... he's a Kashmiri.'

'New? What about Armaan?'

'It's this boy now. Bashrat.'

'So what's happened?'

'Will you stop saying that!' She lowered her voice. 'I told you, he's a *Kashmiri*.'

Then he understood, and controlled an urge to laugh out loud. Sonali Kapoor, he wanted to ask her, do you remember what your parents had said about me?

Instead he asked, 'Okay, what does he do?'

'He's studying. Masters, I think. I want you to check him out, Arjun.'

He felt a perverse desire to tell her to ask her present husband, Rohit Khanna, but held his tongue again.

'Sonali, not all Kashmiris are terrorists.'

'I know. But his father is some politician over there. That's what I'm worried about, do you understand?'

'Hmm. All right, I'll talk to her and look up his father.'

'Try and meet him, Arjun. Find out more about his father. You know how things are nowadays, ever since the elections. I just don't want Rhea to get hurt in any way.'

'Okay, I'll talk to Rhea about it, all right?'

'Thanks Arjun.'

He tossed the phone onto the coffee table. It was almost like being put on another case. And Sonali knew that bringing up Rhea's safety was her trump card. Another reason for him to want to get out of Delhi.

12

Manu Kumar aka Computer Baba had once provided the technical inputs for a certain woman's honey-trapping activities; Arjun had become aware of him while helping a businessman who was being extorted by the woman, but hadn't informed the police about him. Now for several years, Baba had been assisting in Nexus Security's investigations, mainly in obtaining CDRs or call detail records. After finding a parking space with much difficulty under the shadows of the grim socialist-style towers of Nehru Place, Arjun made his way through the crowded marketplace that had come up in the canyons between the buildings and went up a dingy staircase and then along an outer corridor lined with computer hardware suppliers. Baba's shop was right at the end, the small space cluttered with cartons of all manner of computer supplies, the walls plastered with hardware advertisements and prints of gods and goddesses, and a low false ceiling above which two employees of Baba repaired laptops and from where now came the strains of a Kishore Kumar number: *Aane waala kal*. Baba himself sat at his desk eating grapes out of a stainless-steel container. He yelled at the two workers to turn the volume down.

'Arjun ji! How are you? Sit, have some grapes.'

He pulled a stool out of the mess, took a handful of grapes, and sat down.

'Looking different Baba, what happened to you?'

Gone was the greasy, shifty long-haired Baba with grimy fingernails and a dark stubble on his gaunt cheeks; now he was wearing a clean white shirt, clean shaven, his hair cropped short, and looking decidedly healthier. Another change was the broad red tika on his forehead.

'What was there to happen, Arjun ji. Marriage, and then a child. Doctor said I have high BP, so now I take a morning walk and eat fruits.'

'And going to the temple too?'

'Yes, I go nowadays. Makes me feel good. I've given up smoking. Just an occasional drink.' He glanced up and leaned over the table and said in a low voice, 'No more porn DVDs.'

'Do you remember how we met?' Arjun asked him. 'That woman from Lajpat Nagar?'

Baba stuck his tongue out and bit it, and crossed himself hurriedly. '*Chi chi*. I was a sinner then. But you saved me Arjun ji. If you had handed me over to the police...' he shuddered. 'But tell me, how are you now? I went to your office once. Your secretary told me you were in hospital. Are you back at work?'

'I'm fine now. And I'm back at work. Which is why I'm here. Take this number down. A person from Delhi, was murdered in Kolkata some time back. I want his CDRs and message details going back a month from the time the phone went off.'

'Kolkata? West Bengal? It'll take a few days.'

'No problem. Just get it done.'

'Okay, Arjun ji. So nice to see you again.'

'Same here, Baba. See you soon.'

Arjun stepped out to the corridor, then turned back. 'How old is your child? Is it a boy or girl?'

Baba beamed at Arjun. 'It's a boy. He's six months now.'

'Good. I'll send something for him one of these days.'

He walked off with Baba's voice thanking him trailing off behind him.

Rohit Vats' friend Kunal Mendiratta lived in Noida, where he also worked at a property firm, but he told Arjun they could meet in New Friends Colony as he was coming to Delhi for some work. It had been a while since Arjun had been to NFC; nearby was Jamia and Batla House and then the black waters of the Yamuna. He drove there from Nehru Place and reached early, so he walked around the market for a while. The smell of food was everywhere—chaat and tandoori chicken and kebabs—as were plump middle-class people, going into restaurants or clothes shops, while a gang of urchin kids roamed around begging. There was a smaller one trailing them who looked as though he had suffered a beating at the hands of the older ones, and Arjun handed him 20 rupees which he took and scurried off. Just children, they were living a dog-like life. While the stray dogs in the markets were dirty and lazy and fat from eating scraps: what sort of offspring would they beget? Outside a liquor shop an oversized fellow was talking business with a couple of tall and well-built youth, toughs of some sort they seemed to Arjun.

They were meeting in an old restro-pub in the community centre market, so Arjun headed there and ordered himself a draught beer. The place was almost deserted at this hour. He went through a newspaper he had bought. His eye was caught by an item about a nineteen-year-old gang member from Haryana who shot his grandfather and then two more people within a week. What sort of human beings were being produced in the National Capital Region, he wondered. Just like the misshapen strays he had seen. Who knew if the kid he had given money to would one day turn into a gang member as well?

'Sorry if I'm late. Hope you didn't wait for long.'

Arjun looked up from the paper and saw the youth from the photo, older though and with several extra kilos on his frame.

'Not at all. I got here early.'

Kunal put his laptop bag on a chair and pulled out one for himself. Arjun asked for another beer after the other man said he wouldn't mind one.

'You said you had some work. I hope the beer...'

'Oh no problems. Just something routine. And I love beer.'

Arjun wondered if he was going to meet Pinky.

'Do you come this side often? *Jamna paar*. Pinky told me your office is in Noida.'

He thought he saw a flicker of annoyance pass over Kunal's face.

'I need to keep coming this side on work. Clients, properties.'

'Of course. Anyway, cheers.' They drank, then Arjun asked, 'Did you pick up a taste for it in London? Beer.'

'Oh, yes.' Kunal patted his stomach. 'It shows too. Ha ha.'

'You were there with Rohit, right?'

'Mm-hm. We were both doing our MBA. Marketing. From Goldsmiths College. Stayed together as well.'

'Must have been ... interesting.'

'Yes, being away from home on our own. London town. Good times! But then after a point you want to get back to your own country. *Hai na*?'

'And you were working there? After your MBA? Both of you?'

'Yes. We worked for a year, both of us. Then we came back. We got jobs after we got back and didn't change them.'

'How did Rohit land up in pharmaceuticals?'

'A friend of his father, some colonel, retired fellow, he was on the board of directors and recommended Rohit. That's how he got his job.'

'What about you? Any recommendations?'

'Me? No, I went for interviews. Till I finally got this job.'

They sat in silence for a while drinking their beer before Arjun asked the next question.

'So what do you think happened to him?'

Rohit pursed his lips and shook his head. 'I really don't know.'

'Did you know he had gone to Kolkata?'

'No, he never told me. I called him twice while he was away, both times the phone rang and he picked up straight away.'

'What did you talk about?'

'Just, usual stuff. Where we would go out after he got back from Mumbai.'

'After he returned from China, did you guys go out?'

'No. Something was troubling him.'

'Did he tell you what it was?'

Kunal shook his head. Arjun took a sip of his beer, then took out the photo and placed it on the table between them. A few more customers had come in by then, and the music had been turned on, but not too loud.

'I found this in one of Rohit's albums. Appeared to be hidden away. Who's she?'

'My God!' Kunal exclaimed softly, picking it up. 'He kept this. He told me he had got rid of her photos.'

'Why? And who is she?'

'Well because Pinky might not have liked it. She was a Chinese girl Rohit was friendly with in London. Vivien.'

'A girlfriend?'

Kunal kept looking at the photo before raising his eyes and replying. 'Yes. But then one day she disappeared...'

'What do you mean?'

'Rohit hadn't met her for some time, she wasn't answering his messages and calls, so he went to her apartment block one day. There was a Chinese guy there who tried to attack Rohit. Tall, with a scar on his face. She asked Rohit to leave, saying she would explain later.'

'Where was she staying?'

'Near Commercial Road. East London, not a very nice place.'

'With whom was she staying?'

'With an elderly Chinese woman whose husband had passed away. Anyway, the next time Rohit tried her number it was switched off, so he went to the apartment again. The old lady didn't speak any English, but the family in the next flat told Rohit that she and the man had left the UK.'

'And he never heard from her again?'

'No. He sent her several e-mails, no answer.'

'But he obviously remembered her, if he had kept the photo. Did he go looking for her this time, while he was in China?'

Kunal shrugged. 'He had gone on a work trip.'

'He could have. Did he say anything to you?'

Kunal shook his head. 'No.'

'Where was she from? Which place in China?'

'I don't know. She was in Hong Kong for some time I think.'

'You didn't meet him after he got back from China, how did you know he was troubled? Did Pinky tell you?'

Kunal held his eyes for a moment before nodding. 'Yes.'

'What do you think it could have been? Did she tell you?'

'I thought it was work pressure, isn't that the case usually?'

'You didn't think it could have been because of the Chinese girl?'

'I had forgotten about her. Till you showed me the photo.'

'How long before you two had left London did it happen? The girl leaving.'

'Oh, about a year, I think. Mr Arora, don't mind me asking, but is this your line of investigation?'

'No, just routine enquiry. I'll be going to Kolkata soon. Did he know anyone there?'

'Kolkata? Not that I know of.'

'Do you remember him ever telling you anything about Sikkim?'

'Sikkim? No, I don't think so. What's in Sikkim?'

'Pure Life has a factory there.'

'Ok. He may have mentioned it once, I'm not sure.'

Arjun drained his glass and considered asking for a repeat but thought the better of it. He still had to do his physiotherapy for the day once he got home.

'That's it, for now,' he said to Kunal. 'I'll get in touch if I need to ask you anything.'

'Sure. I hope you find out what happened in Kolkata. He was a good friend.'

Arjun considered him for a moment. 'One last question. What did he feel about China?'

'What do you mean?'

'What did Rohit think of China, as a country? His father was a prisoner-of-war in Tibet after the '62 war, I think you know that. Then the incident with this girl. Do you remember anything he ever said about the place?'

'About China?' Kunal pursed his lips again. 'He used to say it was a strange place. Which is what the rest of us feel too, don't we? Now if you'll excuse me...'

'Sure,' Arjun said, and shook his hand. 'Thanks for your time.'

After Mendiratta had left, Arjun sat there looking at the photo. Vivien: did she have another Chinese name? And what did *he* think of China? A vast uniformity came to mind, like the USSR when the Iron Curtain still existed. They had touched upon it in their studies just after he had joined the army, which he had long left. The Middle Kingdom, or *zhongguo*. He raised a hand and signalled to the waiter for a repeat.

13

Instead of his physiotherapy, he came home after having drunk four mugs of beer, and took a short nap on the sofa. He woke, showered, and set out again in his car, this time towards west Delhi. He put on Led Zeppelin from a pen drive as he headed north-west across the city toward the Karampura industrial area, which lay between Patel Nagar and Punjabi Bagh.

He was on his way to the head office of Pure Life on Najafgarh Road. By the time he was going through the ridge forest beside Pusa darkness was settling among the keekar trees. Najafgarh: the name reminded him of Najaf, where he had initially been sent with the American security contractors before they had headed north to Ramadi, where Arjun had been lucky to have been saved from being beheaded. And just a few months earlier Ramadi had fallen to the IS; the same old game, with different players.

To stop being reminded of those horrors from his time as a mercenary, he called his mother over the hands free, and told her he would be there in the morning to help with arrangements for the *shradh*. She told him she was lucky Susan was there to help, and what she wanted Arjun to get—fruits, a few twenty-litre water containers, some cotton *gamchas* from the CR Park market no.3—when he came. He told her he wouldn't forget, and hung up, feeling slightly guilty thinking about his plan for the day of the *shradh*. He would stay the night, be there in the morning as the pandits came and started the prayers and the first visitors arrived, then he would go out telling his mother he had some urgent work, pay a visit to the agency, and return in the evening by when the guests and handful of relatives would have left. It was something his father would have understood: Madan Arora had always disliked gatherings of any sort and distrusted displays of sentimentality, maybe as a result of the Partition days he had lived through as a child.

The Pure Life office was in a commercial building towards the upper end of Najafgarh Road, not far from the Zakhira transport market. Arjun entered a side road and parked near a Mother Diary outlet and got down. The area had the anonymous commercial character common to places outside the main city, and he could pick up the stench from the nearby Najafgarh nala, a seasonal river which turned into a blackened sewer in Delhi before emptying into the Yamuna above Delhi University. As he walked up to the building ahead he could see some distance beyond it, towards the nala, the towers of a residential project, while to his right was a large new development project and a DDA park beyond it. Delhi kept mutating, changing.

Pure Life occupied two floors of the building, and Arjun took the lift up to the higher floor where he was asked to make an entry in a register at the reception by the night guard before being asked to wait. He sat down on one of the sofas in a corner while the guard made a call. Framed advertisements on the walls and flex-printed standees showed some of Pure Life's products, and on the table before Arjun were the company's pamphlets and brochures. The guard told him he could go in, so Arjun went through a brightly-lit working area where there were a few people still at their laptops and into a glass-partitioned room. An elderly man in a dark-blue full-sleeved shirt wearing glasses beckoned him to come in from behind his desk.

Arjun opened the door and went in. The small space was chilly from an air conditioner.

'Mr Arora, good you came,' the man said. 'I was about to leave in a while.'

'I came driving, otherwise I would have been here earlier,' Arjun said, and added, 'Thank you for seeing me Mr Sahoo.'

'Please, sit. You should have taken the Metro. Green Line.'

'I prefer driving,' Arjun said. 'Gives me time to think.'

Sahoo nodded. He was dark complexioned, with unnaturally jet-black hair, and gave the impression of a certain competence arrived at by virtue of long experience, reminding Arjun of another Oriya from when he had been in the army, a supply officer who had run a thriving black-market racket in Guwahati.

'I wanted to ask you a few questions about Rohit,' Arjun said.

'Mrs Vats had told me,' Sahoo said. 'You are investigating his death?'

Arjun opened his notebook and took out a pen. 'Yes, I am.'

'One thing, I've asked our accounts people to follow up with the provident fund office regarding his dues.'

Arjun nodded. 'Mrs Vats was more concerned about the status of his insurance policy.'

'I was just informing you. Please, ask what you want to know.'

'No one knew that he had gone to Kolkata?'

'He just said he wanted to take leave for a few days. Some family issues, he said.'

'He told his wife he was going to Mumbai on a work trip. Why would he do that?'

'I don't know. He must have had some plans. What plans, I have no idea.'

'How did he seem to you when he got back from China?'

Sahoo took off his glasses and rubbed his eyes. 'He was quieter than usual. At that time, I thought maybe jet lag or something like that.'

'Did anything happen in China?'

'He sounded normal in his phone calls and e-mails when he was there. I asked Chen Song too, he was Rohit's contact over there, but he didn't notice anything unusual about Rohit.'

'Was he from the Chinese government, this Chen Song?'

'No, from our suppliers, Zhejiang Huasheng Medicine company limited.'

'So Rohit was a quiet sort of person you would say?'

'Yes. And he was a good worker.'

'I heard he got this job through the reference of someone on the board of directors?'

Sahoo nodded, putting on his glasses again. 'Colonel Tyagi. Rohit's father's friend. He's no more now.'

'How was he as a worker? I mean, were there any problems with him at any time?'

Sahoo shook his head. 'Private person. Did his work well right from the start. We'll miss him.'

'Did he have any friends among his colleagues here?'

'Friends? Well, he was a private person, like I said. Kept to himself.'

'What about Ranjana Ganguly?'

Sahoo gave Arjun a thin humourless smile. 'You've done your homework before coming here.'

Arjun shrugged. 'I have to do my homework. Mrs Vats told me about her.'

'Mrs Vats didn't like her, in my opinion. They were friendly, yes. But I don't think there was anything more to it. Just colleagues.'

'And even she didn't know about Rohit going to Kolkata?'

'No. I asked her later. She said he never told her.'

'Is she here now? Can I talk to her?'

'She's already left for the day. Tomorrow she's going to Mumbai on work.'

'I see. Give me her number please, I'd like to talk to her too.'

While Sahoo took out his phone and searched for the number, Arjun looked around. One side of the room had shelves full of thick medical and pharmacological books, the other side had two filing cabinets, while behind Sahoo were framed advertisements, some of which he had seen at the reception. He took down the number as Sahoo read it out to him.

'What is Azitochryme?' he asked, pointing to one of the advertisements behind Sahoo.

'It's an antibiotic. One of our best-selling medicines.'

'Why did Rohit go to China? Do you sell medicines there?'

'It seems like you haven't done your homework regarding that.'

'What do you mean?'

Sahoo leaned back in his chair, which creaked loudly with his weight. 'We can't sell medicines in China, Mr Arora. Not yet. They don't allow it. We import our requirements from them. Rohit was one of our smarter employees, so I decided to send him to China. It was a routine visit, liaising with our suppliers. Also submitting applications to the Chinese government for permissions to sell our drugs there.'

'What does Pure Life import from China? Is it something called API?'

'API stands for active pharmaceutical ingredient. The active component in any tablet, oral suspension, injection, any kind of medicine. The Chinese are the cheapest bulk suppliers of APIs. We buy several APIs from them, and then use them in our formulations. Which means making the medicine,' Sahoo explained. 'Antibiotics, steroids, vitamins, all need APIs. Along with the API we need to add excipients or fillers for stabilizing and bulking.'

'So the API is just part of the actual medicine?' Arjun asked.

'Exactly. For example, in Azitochryme the API is actually Azithromycine.'

'How do you get your APIs into India?'

'By flight. By cargo ship. To Delhi and Kolkata. They come in plastic drums. From there they go to our factories in Himachal and Sikkim.'

'Did Rohit ever go to your Sikkim factory? Did he ever ask to be sent there?'

'Sikkim? Not that I can remember, no.'

'These APIs. Can't India manufacture them?'

'We used to, till the 1980s. Then the Chinese got into the game. Their costs of production were the lowest so they captured markets around the world.'

'I see. Mr Sahoo, did Rohit ever talk about his father being held as a prisoner of war by the Chinese in 1962?'

'No, he didn't,' Sahoo said, frowning. 'I didn't know that he was a POW.'

Arjun nodded, taking down his notes. 'This trip to China. Did he ask to be sent? Knowing that Pure Life's business had links with China. Please think carefully.'

Sahoo scratched his nose. 'Did he ask ... no, I don't think so. I gave him a few hints that I was thinking of sending him, that's all. He seemed interested.'

'Did he ever mention any friends or contacts he might have had in China? To you or to any of his colleagues?'

'Chen Song was his main contact there. Apart from work Rohit did some sightseeing in Shanghai, that was all.'

'Did he mention anything about going back to China? When he came back?'

Sahoo nodded. 'Yes, he had asked to be sent again.'

Arjun noted that down.

'What did he think of China? Did he have any views about the country, the people?'

Sahoo gave him a thin smile. 'Mr Arora, you are asking so much about China, but he was killed in Kolkata, isn't it? Are you trying to find some Communist connection here?'

'Nothing like that. I'll be going to Kolkata soon to find out more. But I need to look at all possibilities, all angles. That's why I asked what he thought about China.'

Sahoo nodded. 'Okay. Well, he was impressed, like all of us who go there. Here we are last sixty-seventy years since British left us fighting over mandir masjid, this political party that political party, all useless, waste of time! See what they have done, how many millions lifted out of poverty, their factories supplying the whole world. He said we could learn from them, that's what he said, yes.'

'Ok. So he was sympathetic towards them? Towards the country?'

'Yes, as a businessman,' Sahoo said quickly. He leaned forward on his desk and picked up a glass paperweight in both hands. 'What happened to his father was a long time ago. See, Mr Arora, you asked about APIs. India used to...'

'Manufacture them before,' Arjun completed. 'You told me.'

'Till the 1980s. At that time China was at India's level. People forget that nowadays. But they decided that things had to improve. Bye bye Mao, hello USA.' Sahoo raised a palm up in a 45-degree angle, mimicking a plane taking off. 'Factories started coming up everywhere. But unlike India, the state was behind businesses. They started bulk manufacturing APIs, both fermentation-based and synthetic. No worries about pollution control or market regulations. Just produce as much as you can, with the state helping in every way. Whereas in India, half our time was spent with babus arranging for this permit and that permit. From pollution control board to sales tax department, everyone was out to screw us! Now we have factories in special zones in Himachal and Sikkim, but China has left us far behind. Which is why even our NSA said recently that we are over-reliant on Chinese APIs. So that is *my* view.'

'You seem to know a lot about China,' Arjun observed.

'Well I went there a few times when Pure Life was started. I kept my eyes open.' Sahoo now lifted his hand and looked at his wristwatch 'Mr Arora, I think we've discussed enough for today. I have a dinner to attend, so...'

'Sure, I'll call you if there's anything else,' Arjun said, closing his notebook. 'Just one last thing. Does Pure Life use animal parts in any of its medicines? Rhino horns, tiger bones, that sort of thing.'

'Animal parts?' Sahoo asked with a frown, as he switched off the air conditioner with its remote. 'No, we don't.'

'What about Zhejiang Huasheng Medicine company?'

'No, I don't think so. As far as I know.'

'Or do you use animals for testing? New drugs, things like that?'

'No, our development division doesn't do animal testing,' Sahoo said, a trace of exasperation in his voice. 'What is this about?'

'Rohit had been going through websites on animal trafficking on his home computer. Also places like Thailand and Hong Kong. Why would he be interested in that?'

'Who knows? Maybe he ate tiger meat in China and wanted to find out more about it.'

Sahoo stood up and reached for his briefcase behind his chair, and Arjun stood up to leave as well.

'Thank you for your time. Could I have a look at Rohit's workstation?'

'Come, I'll show you.'

'What about his office laptop? Is it still here?'

'No, he had taken it with him. It must be with the police in Kolkata.'

There was an aisle towards one side of the outer room which separated the general working area on the left from the managers' area to the right. The workstations on the right were roomier, and Mr Sahoo showed him Rohit's. There wasn't much there, apart from some folders, bound project reports, product brochures, and, pinned to the felt-covered half-partitions, schedules and hand-written notes. A family photo of Rohit, Pinky and the two children with Diwali lights around them was the only personal touch.

'Mr Arora, I have to go,' Sahoo said. 'You can...'

'Yes, I just want to go through his things if that's ok.'

'Take your time. The guard will show you out.'

'Which was Mrs Ganguly's desk, could you show me please?'

Sahoo pointed it out to Arjun, then turned and walked away. Ranjana Ganguly's workstation was similar to Rohit's, a little untidy if anything, and with several personal touches: a small potted cactus, a pile of restaurant menus, pinned postcards of holiday locations, a pair of tiny speakers. But no family photo. Her desk, Arjun saw, was in line of sight of Rohit's desk. He went back and sat down in Rohit's chair. On the other side of the aisle, a lone male employee typed away.

How could a person spend his life chained to one job, one company, one desk? But that was just his personal opinion. Arjun went through the folders and reports, opened the drawers. Nothing that struck him as being meaningful—yet. There would have been boredom. Ranjana, within eyesight, might have been a distraction from work and family. He remembered what Kunal Mendiratta had said earlier in the day: *good times in London town*. Had Rohit remembered Vivien as he sat and worked out his visits to drug wholesalers? After Sahoo had told him he would be going to China?

It was night by the time he got back to his car, where he saw three local toughs lounging on it and smoking. A curt word from him and one good look at Arjun saw them hastily move away. That was Delhi, you always had to be ready to fight. On his way back home he called Liza, and told her to book him a return ticket for Kolkata two days after the *shradh* (with the return open), and to remind Shyamali to look into Ranjana Ganguly.

14

Arjun strained to make out the words crackling on the PA system as he stood with his mother on one of the platforms of New Delhi railway station. Before them was a Rajdhani train, dusty on the outside, the people inside half-visible through the blue-tinted plastic windows. Gita Arora's luggage—a single suitcase and a cloth bag—had already been stowed under her lower berth. All about them was the hubbub of the platform, people hurrying with bags and children.

'It's about to leave, you better get inside,' he said to her.

'Okay. Take care of yourself. Do your physiotherapy. Don't drink too much.'

'Yes, yes. You take care of yourself too. Don't forget your medicines.'

His mother started rummaging in her handbag. 'There was something I forgot to show you. I found it inside a book while cleaning the house yesterday. Here it is.'

She handed him a small square photograph, the black and white faded to a sepia tint, and it showed his parents, much younger, standing stiffly as they looked at the camera. Behind them were hills, and his mother wore a salwar suit and a cardigan while his father, unsmiling, was in an overcoat. Arjun turned the photo around, and saw, scrawled in his father's hand, 'Kalimpong. October 1968.'

'I was carrying your brother then. He didn't survive.'

He remembered his last conversation with his father.

'Papa told me. You were going to call him, Arjun?'

She nodded, patted his cheek, and made for the coach entrance. A horn sounded.

'The photo?'

'Keep it with you.'

She clambered in, and he waited till he could see her inside her compartment, where she had a family from Darjeeling for company. He waved at her, and she waved back and said something he couldn't hear, but he still nodded. The train started moving. Arjun stood there watching it pulling out till it had disappeared from view. He looked at the photo again, then put it into his wallet and started walking toward the steps leading to the overbridge. Amid the crowds, he felt within him a deep desolation.

He had left his car in the Ajmeri Gate parking lot, behind the station, and as he made his way through people, cars and push carts looking for his vehicle a sticky warm rain started falling from an orange-hued sky. When he had located the car and got in, he let down the windows and lit a cigarette. His mother was on her way to Siliguri, and he would be on a flight to Kolkata within twenty-four hours, both of them headed eastward, just like Madan Arora decades ago. His father's *shradh* had gone off smoothly, and he had managed to get away to the agency during the day. Rhea had come, but not Sonali, and Arjun had told his daughter he would call her regarding some social media accounts related to a case. About Bashrat he hadn't said anything, yet.

Arjun flicked the cigarette butt out, put the windows up, turned on the AC and made a call from his mobile phone. The voice at the other end was husky and inviting as ever.

'Hello stranger.'

'How are you?'

'How come you remembered me?' Poppy Barua asked.

'I ...' he took a deep breath and exhaled, 'my father passed away.'

'Arjun, I'm so sorry. When?'

'A few days ago. He was already in hospital. Respiratory infection. Old age too. The *shradh* was yesterday.'

'I'm so sorry. Anything I can do...'

'Where are you now? In office?'

'No. I've taken the day off. Getting the flat painted.'

'Oh...'

'Where are you?'

He told her.

'What about tomorrow?'

'I'm going to Kolkata tomorrow. A case. A Delhi boy was murdered there. Listen, could you try and find out about him from your reporters?'

'Sure. Wait, Rohit something wasn't it?'

Arjun smiled. Her memory was as good as ever. 'Yes. Rohit Vats. He worked for a medicine company which imported from China. In fact, he had been to China just before that.'

'I'll look into it. Maybe we could meet after you're back from Kolkata?'

'Sure. That'll be nice.'

'Talk to you later then. Take care.'

He hung up, and for a while watched the raindrops pattering on the dusty bonnet of his car, before starting it and turning right from the entrance headed toward Minto Road and CP—Connaught Place. Like most true Delhiites he could never think of it as Rajiv Chowk.

The traffic along the Outer Ring Road on the way to the airport was terrible the next morning, and Arjun only narrowly made boarding, which then saw him sitting in an aisle seat instead of his preferred window seat. It was stuffy inside the plane, and Arjun tried to read the inflight magazine for a while. Somewhere behind him a baby bawled. He took out the London photo once again and studied it placing it in between the pages of the magazine. Rohit Vats. Someone with his own mind, that was what Arjun felt. They had discussed the case in the agency, and Arjun had told them he had three vague lines emerging: spying, corporate espionage, or a love affair.

Looking at the photo now, he couldn't say why he had a premonition that he would be headed further east than Kolkata. What were the things hidden in the photo? Like the photo his mother had given him: no one would know, by just looking at it, about the other Arjun who hadn't survived. He saw a food cart with overpriced snacks being pushed up the aisle, and he put away the photo and the magazine, reclined his seat and closed his eyes.

It was early evening by the time he collected his suitcase off the conveyor belt and came out of the airport building.

The airport had improved, no longer were there the swarms of mosquitoes he remembered from long ago, but the weather outside was muggy as ever. Arjun got a pre-paid white taxi for Gariahat—that was where Rohit Vats had stayed, according to the Kolkata Police material Kadambari Vats had messaged him on his phone, and he had done a booking at the same guest house.

They came out of the airport: Dum Dum had turned into a crowded jumble of buildings and hotels. Arjun rolled down a window to smoke, and could soon feel his throat itching from the smog-laden air. They passed by yellow Ambassador taxis and maroon city buses packed with people. The lanky young Bengali taxi driver liked to talk, and told Arjun that when they had been in school it would start getting a little cold by now, with pujo approaching, whereas nowadays it was cold only by January.

'The whole world is heating up,' Arjun replied, much to the other's appreciation.

'You've come from Delhi, sir?' he asked, looking up at the rear-view mirror, and Arjun nodded.

There was a round sticker on the windshield showing a stocky man with his hands joined together. Arjun asked who he was. '*Didi ka khas admi hai*,' came the answer: 'a special person of the CM'. It seemed he was the cab guild boss. The taxi driver went on talking, coming to the topic of Marwari businessmen for some reason. They didn't do any work, he said, they only bought things and cornered the market, and their children all had *ghamand*. 'I've heard that's the case in Delhi as well?' he asked.

The old leftist spirit was still around, Arjun observed. He

could smell the canal at Bidhannagar, and rolled the window up. They crossed Tangra and Science City on the flyover, then came down and turned right towards Beck Bagan and Ballygunge. After the crowded commercial environs of Ballygunge and Gariahat, Hindustan Park, where the guest house was located, had a middle-class genteelness to it with its crumbling old buildings and roadside food vendors, a few new apartments and cafes scattered among them.

The Darjeeling Guest House was in a quiet street off Purna Das Road. Arjun got down with his suitcase and paid the taxi driver Prasenjit, whose phone number he had taken down. It was an old-fashioned white and green coloured building with an awning-covered side entrance. He went to the entrance at the back, outside which on a wooden stool sat an elderly guard in a faded uniform. Inside, he could see a small reception counter under a flight of stairs, and a young man leaning on the counter with his attention fixed on his phone, held sideways. The guard stood and gave a shaky salute; Arjun nodded and stepped in, and the youth looked up from his phone. He was unshaven and wore thick glasses.

'Arjun Arora. I have a booking.'

'Mr Arora. Certainly. I am Tapan. Please make your entry here.'

He spun around a hard-bound register for Arjun, and asked him for an ID, of which he took a photo with his phone. When Arjun was done, he raised the counter flap and stepped out, calling out to the guard in English: 'Dadu, please take the gentleman's suitcase.'

They went up the dim-lit stairs with Tapan ahead of Arjun and the guard behind him.

'I had asked for the room where Rohit Vats was staying,' Arjun said.

'Yes, certainly, it has been kept for you.'

They went up a second flight of stairs. It seemed to be an old house, refurbished as a guest house, and the name hinted at the eternal romance between Bengalis and the hill town.

'How many rooms do you have here?' Arjun asked him.

'Eight in total. Three on first floor, three on second floor, two on third floor.'

'And the ground floor?'

'Owners have kept it,' Tapan said, and added, 'I am related to them.'

On the second floor Tapan made for one of the doors. He unlocked it and held it open, breathing heavily after the climb, and Arjun walked in. The modest room was spotlessly clean; there was a double bed (with a brown and maroon block-print bedcover) and an almirah, a television, chairs and a table. He walked out to the narrow balcony and looked at the street below before coming back in. The guard put down his suitcase, saluted once more and shuffled out of the room.

'It's all been cleaned, hasn't it.'

'Yes we cleaned. After the police had finished their work.'

'They took all his things, I suppose?'

'Yes they took his suitcase and whatever else was here. Mr Arora, you are...'

'Oh, sorry. Like I mentioned earlier over the phone, I'm a family friend of Rohit Vats. They asked me to come and talk to the police here.'

'Ok I see. His wife and her father were staying here when they came for his cremation.'

Arjun nodded. Pinky hadn't mentioned that to him.

'In this room?' he asked.

'No, this one wasn't available then. They were on the first floor.'

'The suitcase, and what else did the police take?'

'His laptop. Toiletries. Everything.'

'There's nothing at all they left behind?'

Tapan shook his head, then seemed to remember something. 'Actually...'

'What?'

'Oh, just a printout. We found it later. When the room was being cleaned.'

'Printout of?' Arjun said sharply.

'Printout of some medical things. China also.'

'Had he hidden it?'

'It was in-between some newspapers on the table. I don't think it was hidden, just covered by that day's newspapers. The police didn't even see it. I found it while going through the newspapers.'

'Did you tell them about it?'

Tapan shrugged. 'It's just a printout so I didn't bother. But there was something written on it.'

'Could I see it please?'

'Sure. I'll send it up. You want to have some tea or coffee?'

Arjun washed up after Tapan had left. The bathroom was small but clean. He put on the air conditioner and sat down on the edge of the bed. Now that he was in Kolkata, the enormity of the task before him became clearer. What could he possibly find out? He lay back on the bed and closed his eyes. This was what detective work was. Going here and there, chasing ghosts, chasing something within himself. He had become an itinerant like his father had been.

'Dada, your tea,' a voice said in Bengali, and Arjun sat up.

It was a young boy in shorts holding a tray with tea and Marie biscuits, and the printout. Arjun sat in one of the chairs and went through the printout while he drank his tea. It was an article from a British medical website, four A4-size pages stapled together, and was about viruses jumping from animals to humans, with special mention of the SARS outbreak of 2003, and viruses from bats reaching humans through animals like pangolins in the 'wet markets' of China and SE Asian countries like Vietnam and Thailand. He understood the gist of the article, but wondered why Rohit would have been interested in it.

On the reverse of the last page scrawled with a ball pen were a number and what was possibly a name. The number had eight digits and seemed to be a landline phone number, while the name, underlined twice, was 'LEONG'. He took photos of the document with his phone, then sat looking at the last page for a while before going out to the balcony and lighting a cigarette. The quiet street, the orange glow of the streetlights on the damp leaves of the trees, the old building: he somehow felt at home.

15

After his tea, Arjun went out for a walk. He struck out in a northerly direction, going past a building site, a North Indian dhaba at a corner of a crossing with a tandoor out front, and a string of tea stalls till he came to Rashbehari Avenue. There was a line of saree shops with nighties hung out front—it struck him that he had never seen those in North India—and food stalls lining the pavement; he stopped at a phuchkawala and had his fill of the crunchy, spicy and sour snack. He passed old buildings, a 'lodge' and then a 'cabin', which was a small eatery, till he came to the wine store Tapan had told him about. He bought a bottle of Blender's Pride, and on his way back got two large rolls from the dhaba for his dinner. The guest house served Bengali food, but Arjun wanted to try the Kolkata rolls first. He recalled there had been a small roll shop on Park Street—and that brought back more old memories.

Back in his room he turned on the air conditioner and poured himself a drink, then called his daughter and told her he would be sending her the social media details of Rohit Vats that he wanted her to go through.

'When do you want it by?' Rhea asked him.

'Your report? The earlier the better.'

He then told her about the printout, as well as the number and the name on the back. She advised him to do an internet search on the number.

'Leong ... what if it's the name of someone in China?' she asked him.

'We'll have a few million suspects then,' Arjun said, yawning. 'Sorry, I'm tired, and this case is confusing to say the least. A part of me wonders what I'm doing here.'

'You *always* say that. Where do you think this printout was taken?'

'Maybe at his home or in the office,' Arjun said, recalling the printer in the study at the Vats residence. 'It still had that new paper feel to it.'

'He was looking into something he found out in China?'

'Could be,' Arjun said. 'Medicines are big business, don't forget.'

'Anyway, I'll go through his accounts and let you know if I find anything.'

'Okay. Oh and Rhea ...'

'Yes?'

'You have a new boyfriend I heard?'

'Who told you?' she asked sharply.

'I'm your father, I know,' he said.

'Mom must have told you, didn't she?' Rhea made a sound which she did when she was annoyed. 'I can take care of myself.'

'I know. Just that if there are ever any ... problems, you can let me know, okay?'

'Okay,' she said sullenly, then reminded him. 'Don't forget your physio exercises.'

'I won't. Good night, Rhea.'

He put the phone down. Their thought processes were remarkably similar. Arjun allowed himself a proud parental smile before turning on his laptop and doing a search on the number. No luck. He tried adding the Kolkata code which was 033 and typed in 'Kolkata' as well, but still no luck. No exact matches.

He took a sip of his drink and sat back in the chair. There was the temptation to try dialling the number, but only after he had more information. Might Rohit have called that number, and then ended up dead? He spent the next half hour looking up the internet for wildlife trafficking in India. A lot of it was connected to the North East, from where body parts of pangolins, tigers, geckos and rhinos were taken out of India, through the Myanmar border and also through Kolkata, ending up in South East Asia and China. Then he went back to the articles Rohit had been looking up on his laptop, opening the links one by one. In one, an official from the Kolkata Customs had been quoted, an Anil Sinha. Arjun switched off the laptop, poured himself a last drink and unwrapped the foil from one of the rolls.

He slept well and woke up early. The real mugginess of the day hadn't started, and he went through the physiotherapy exercises that had been shown to him at the hospital. The doctor there had told him that it was his physical condition that had allowed him to recover so quickly once he had woken up from his coma. No long-lasting damage, touch wood.

Arjun had forgotten to pack his razor, so after a cup of tea and a bath he went out looking for one. The two small grocery shops in the vicinity didn't have the multi-blade cartridge he used, so he ended up walking ahead to a little saloon across the road from a collection of vegetable and fruit vendors, their stalls set up against an old abandoned-looking building. The Bihari barber had just finished cleaning the shop and the outside and Arjun was his first customer. He sat folded up in one of the three chairs in the tiny shop as the barber lathered and shaved him, while on an old transistor radio (with a leather cover) a male and a female announcer were taking turns reading out all the great events from that particular day in history.

He felt himself a child again, listening to Kishore Kumar on a similar radio while getting his hair cut in a saloon in some small town in the North East, Diphu or Tura or Pasighat, while his father sat on a bench reading his newspaper. The barber charged him 30 rupees for the shave, less than half of what he would pay in his regular saloon in CR Park's Market No. 3. Walking back by a different route, he had hot puri and ghugni being made at one of the pavement food stalls that had just opened; in other stalls under tarpaulin sheets family members were cutting vegetables and frying fish, preparations for their lunchtime customers.

Back at the guest house, he called Prasenjit the taxi driver and then got dressed. Fifteen minutes later he was in the taxi headed toward Garfa police station. In his hand was the folded printout. They went south from Gariahat through the morning traffic and took a left before Jadavpur

University. The road narrowed, with gaudily-coloured buildings appearing, then narrowed further with residential buildings packed together and a wide, low canal running on the left. They passed two crossings over the canal and at the third crossing turned right past a pond and drove around what seemed to Arjun like a jumble of small roads and rundown apartments till they reached the thana.

The police station was a small, single-storied building with a sentry box outside and two wireless antennas above it. There was a modest little park to its left, and outside the station stood two police vehicles and a police van. He told the driver to stop the car beside the park and wait for him. Near the van stood two constables, while before the entrance stood a couple of members of the general public, including a stocky man with a moustache and a nervous-looking elderly woman. *What a name, Garfa!* he remembered Kadambari Vats saying to him at his flat.

Inside, in a small space more like a partially walled-up veranda, was the desk of the sheristadar or record keeper, where a big bald constable and a younger female constable in a track jacket, short and plump, were listening to a lady explaining something about starting a maid agency from home and needing a no-objection certificate but there were problems with her brother who owned the building and who was running a cable TV business.

A middle-aged lady constable in a salwar uniform asked Arjun what he wanted, to which he replied that he was here to meet SI Shankar Munda. She pointed to a row of metal seats and asked him to wait, then walked off past the desk of the sheristadar. The stocky moustached man walked in, his belly straining against his striped sports shirt. He stood beside the lady now explaining a property dispute between her and her brother. Possibly the husband, Arjun thought, observing this small human drama unfolding before him. A tall, dark-complexioned man in a white uniform and black boots came walking along the corridor with a slight swagger. He paused by the desk to listen, then fired off a series of instructions to the constable, even as the lady protested; he seemed to be familiar with the whole thing.

The man in the white uniform came up to Arjun. 'Mr Arora?'

'Yes. SI Munda?'

The man nodded. 'Please, come.'

He turned and walked back along the corridor. Arjun followed him. A great babble had broken out by now at the desk. The corridor was enclosed, lit by a tube light, with file cabinets at the end, and Arjun passed the systems room, the male lock-up (empty, with thick bars), and the *maalkhana* or evidence room before entering the IOs' or investigating officers' room.

It was a cluttered space with several tables covered with paperwork, only one of which beside the door was occupied. SI Munda went and sat behind his desk at the far end. There was an AC fixed on the side wall but only the single ceiling fan was running, and on the grimy walls were several LIC calendars 'with compliments of Abhijit Saha' besides a plainer one from 'Dey's Keo Karpin Oil'. Arjun sat down in a metal chair opposite the SI, who himself sat with his forearms on the desk and his large fingers intertwined. Early middle age, Arjun estimated, seemed polite. There were two stars on his shoulders above the 'KP'.

'Of what service can I be, Mr Arora?' he asked.

'I'm a detective. I was in the army before this,' he added. 'Rohit Vats' wife approached me. There's a problem with the insurance policy her husband had, you must be aware?'

'Yes, I am aware of that. Madam told me. I spoke to the insurance agent and his boss. They found out from the victim's office in Delhi that he had told them he was going to Mumbai. That makes his death suspicious. That's why they are holding back on the insurance claim.'

'What progress on the case?'

The sub-inspector moved his head, stretching his neck muscles, before sitting upright.

'Moving slowly. We don't have any leads.'

Arjun produced the printout and handed it to the SI.

'Your men missed this,' he said. 'It was in Rohit's room.'

SI Munda looked at the printout, then up at Arjun, then went through the printout.

'I heard he had gone to China before coming here,' SI Munda said, almost to himself, and then to Arjun, 'Who is Leong? And what is this number?'

'Could you trace it? Might be a Kolkata number.'

Before the other man could reply, someone came bustling into the room and stood beside Arjun and launched into a harangue at the sub-inspector. It was the moustachioed man in the striped sports shirt, and Arjun could follow something about local-level committees. The SI kept his cool, and placated the man by telling him that he would come by soon to look into the matter, following which he left the room.

'You see?' SI Munda said to Arjun. 'How to do a murder investigation with all this nonsense.'

'Local politics?' Arjun said, and the other man nodded, and then looked quizzical.

'You understand Bengali?' he asked, in Bengali.

'Yes, but I can't speak it well,' Arjun replied, also in Bengali. 'I grew up in the North East.'

'Cherrapunji, Kaziranga,' the SI said with a smile.

He called the other man in the room, handed him the printout, and told him to go to the systems room and check if the number was from Kolkata.

'Can you tell me what happened on 11th September? That's the date isn't it?'

'Correct, September 11, the day the body was found. One elderly gentleman was going for morning walk, he saw the body. His nephew is at Jadavpur police station, so he informed him. They called me, so I took two constables and went to the area. It is called Canal Road. The canal goes through the area, and the body was at the side, as if someone had thrown it down from the road. Wallet and phone were missing, no other identification. We sent out an alert with a face photo. Autopsy was done, report said death caused by manual strangulation, no water found in the lungs. Then few days later we got a call from headquarters at Lalbazar asking us to check a missing-person report and photo sent from Delhi. Same person. And then I informed madam.'

'And then she came here with her father.'

'We arranged for the cremation. Morgue ambulance took the body from Katapukur morgue to Kalighat where it was cremated. Madam collected the ashes.'

'How did she seem to you?'

'How else? Sad.'

'I want to try and help you. To find out what happened. So that Mrs Vats can claim the policy. Are you okay with that?'

SI Munda nodded, and leaned back in his chair. 'But keep me informed please. Nothing illegal. You've been in Kolkata before?'

'Yes, I know the city. I was at Fort William years ago.'

The SI nodded, looking thoughtful. Then his face broke out in a smile. 'Tea!'

A vendor carrying a large kettle came to the table and poured out steaming mud-coloured liquid into two small paper cups. SI Munda took a noisy sip, and Arjun followed him. It was overcooked and too sweet. He put the cup down and asked, 'The victim's possessions?'

'The suitcase? In the *maalkhana*. Let Roy come back from the systems room and I'll ask him to get it. Are you married, Mr Arora?'

He was saved from having to answer by Roy rushing back into the room.

'Yes, it's a Kolkata number,' he said to SI Munda, handing back the printout. 'Kolkata Customs. The office number of Mr Anil Sinha.'

It took Arjun a moment to remember where he had come across the name. But he didn't say anything. The SI asked Roy to go get the suitcase from the evidence room.

'What business did he have with Customs?' SI Munda wondered.

'I think better not call the number right now,' Arjun said. 'Find out more.'

'True,' the SI said, slowly nodding his head. He drank

some more tea, then said, 'I will show you the place where the body was found. It might help you.'

By the time they finished their tea Roy was back with a purple plastic-shell suitcase, carrying it with gloved hands. He placed it on the desk and handed each of them a pair of rubber gloves. SI Munda put them on and sprung the locks on the front. Arjun stood up to look as the sub-inspector folded back the upper half. Inside were a few clothes and a toilet bag.

'This is all,' SI Munda said.

Arjun went through the clothes then looked inside the toilet bag: toothbrush, lotion, shampoo sachets, razor, deodorant, coins. Something in the zippered flap on the inside of the suitcase cover caught his eye. He opened the zip and took it out. It was a brown wallet, not brand new but seemingly unused, with a raised diamond pattern on the leather.

'And this?' Arjun asked.

'It was where you found it. Strange pattern. Maybe from China?'

Arjun placed the wallet on the desk and took a few photos of it with his phone, before Roy carried the suitcase back to the evidence room, along with the gloves. SI Munda finished his tea and got to his feet. On their way out, Arjun noticed the small nervous woman walking away from the desk, with the large constable telling her that this was her son's last chance. Outside, the sub-inspector stopped to talk to the pair of constables. Arjun went across to the taxi to tell Prasenjit to wait for a while longer. He stood in the shade of a tree on the park boundary and wiped his face and forearms with a handkerchief, then lit a cigarette.

The woman was nearby, talking on the phone. A thin woman, her face lined and worried, she was trembling as she spoke. She was telling her son to come home from where he was, nothing would happen, and to call his father and tell him he was ok, she couldn't look after his son. Near her Arjun noticed a small lanky boy in loose jeans and sandals. What would the boy grow up to be? He thought of his father's story about their street gang and the boy who had drowned in the Hooghly.

'Arora ji! Come.'

He hadn't noticed SI Munda standing near him. They got into a white Sumo and the sub-inspector drove the short distance to the crime scene by the canal. Arjun was glad they hadn't walked; he would have been drenched in sweat. Not that it was comfortable once they got down from the vehicle. The sun was high, so was the humidity, and the black waters of the canal stank. SI Munda pointed out the spot to Arjun: plastic bottles and packets entangled among weeds growing out of a muddy patch.

On the other side was a road and trees and buildings; on their side the road was narrow, and behind them were shrubs and coconut trees and makeshift huts of tin, bamboo and plastic sheets. The sub-inspector watched as he looked around, and said, 'No CCTV.'

Arjun nodded. 'No one saw anything?'

'We questioned everyone. That jhopri there, those buildings over there across the canal. No one saw anything. They all said they were asleep.'

Arjun took out his phone and took a few photos: the canal, the surroundings. SI Munda lounged against the bonnet, every inch the tough local cop, and passers-by going past looked at them curiously.

'So a car drives past. Rohit has been strangled. They throw his body out here.'

'Correct. If they came this way, it means they know the city. Could be locals.'

Something stirred in his mind: the wallet. But he couldn't focus on it.

'Light me a cigarette please,' the sub-inspector said, and Arjun lit one for himself too.

'Do you know why I'm helping you?' he asked Arjun, taking a drag. 'I could be non-cooperative too. A Delhi resident, doesn't have anything to do with us.'

'Then why?'

'I noticed you were listening to that woman talking on the phone. Curious about human beings. You need that to be a good policeman. Or a good detective. Do you want to know her story? Her husband is bedridden. Her son is a history sheeter. Used by both political parties. Intimidation, stabbing, that kind of thing. His wife ran away leaving the son behind. Some people came looking for him one day, he had a quarrel, stabbed one of them and fled. Now they're after his blood. I've protected him so far, but one day he's going to end up dead. And in a few years the son will start getting into trouble. I have a son of the same age. He has a stable life, goes to school. And this boy?' SI Munda sighed. 'It is in these kinds of things that my life is getting spent. But this case ...' He made a gesture, his hands coming up and going out. 'It's about something bigger. I'll give you whatever help I can. If you help me.'

'Sure,' Arjun said. 'What's your email ID?'

They drove back to the police station. A new lot of petitioners were hanging around outside now. As they got down Arjun remembered something. 'Sub-inspector.'

'Yes?'

'There would have been a laptop? In the victim's room?'

'Yes. Password protected. We sent it to the cyber crime unit, should be back soon.'

'Okay. I'll mail you a photo and some links. When the laptop is back you could check if there are any connections. Anil Sinha from Kolkata Customs, his name appears when you open one of the links.'

'All right. Whose photo by the way?'

'I'll mention it in the mail,' Arjun said.

SI Munda smiled and nodded, then turned and walked into his police station.

16

On the way back to the guest house Prasenjit asked Arjun why he had come to the police station.

'It has to do with a police case. Someone from Delhi.'

Prasenjit looked at Arjun in the rear mirror, as though he wanted to say something, but kept quiet. Arjun got down before the guest house, and bought a couple of bottles of cold mineral water and some bananas from near the puri shop where he had stopped for breakfast in the morning. Back in his room he drank a bottle of water before taking a shower and changing into boxers and a t-shirt. The heat and humidity of the east: he had forgotten exactly how sapping it could be.

He had lunch in his room—the boy brought it up from the kitchen—rice, fish curry, crunchy potato fries. Then he sat watching the news on television and dozing off. His daughter called him.

'Hi, Rhea,' he said, sitting up in the chair and rubbing his face.

'Hi Dad. I went through his accounts. Nothing much. He wasn't much of an online person it seems.'

'About his trip to China? Kolkata?'

'Just a few touristy pictures of Shanghai, that's all.'

'Any pictures of a Chinese girl?'

'No. Who is she?'

'Just a hunch. I'll tell you later.'

'Ok.' A pause. 'How was your day?'

He told her about his visit to the thana and meeting Shankar Munda.

'That sounds promising.'

'Maybe. Oh there was one thing.'

'What?'

'A wallet with a peculiar pattern. In his suitcase.'

'Could I have a look?'

'I'll send you photos I took of it.'

'Ok Dad. Talk later then.'

Arjun sent her the photos of the wallet straightaway, then lit another cigarette. The social media accounts had been a long shot anyway. He thought about Shankar Munda. His surname indicated roots in tribal central India. A middle-aged, low-ranking police official, but one who had a sense of the larger world around him. Talking to him had been a different experience compared to Arjun's usual interactions with the Delhi Police, suffused as that force generally was with overbearing north Indian machismo. Arjun turned on his laptop and sent SI Munda the links he had copied from Rohit's home laptop along with the photo, which he first sent from his phone to his laptop, and a brief note in the email about who the other two persons in the photo were. Hopefully SI Munda would come up with some information on Anil Sinha.

He had just turned off the laptop when there was a call on his phone from a Delhi number. It turned out to be the new junior investigator Shyamali Kundu, and she sounded excited. She had found out that Ranjana Ganguly lived in CR Park itself. But what was most interesting, she told Arjun, was that Ranjana's husband had been in Kolkata when Rohit had been killed.

'Are you sure?' Arjun asked her.

'Yes. I found out through their maid. She also works in the house of someone I know. Then me and Liza checked in the office and found out that he had taken a flight to Kolkata.'

'Interesting indeed. How long was he here for?'

'Three days. For a conference. He was there on the day Rohit's body was found. Left the next day.'

'Hmm. Alone?'

'Yes. Sir, I was thinking I should go and talk to Mrs Ganguly.'

'I'll do that when I'm back, Shyamali,' he said, and, to soften the blow, added, 'But well done. Very resourceful of you.'

'Thank you, sir!'

'I'll see you all soon. Bye.'

He hung up, and lit another cigarette and went out to the balcony. He was smoking too much, but told himself it was to help him think. Low grey clouds pressed down on the city: it looked like it would rain soon. Something vague stirred at the back of his mind, the way it had done at the canal. The wallet: but what about it? He decided to go out for a walk before it started raining.

Walking about in his boxers and sandals, he seemed like one of those people who owned or rented flats in the

Hindustan Park area, but only a keen-eyed observer would note the brisk stride and the steady watchful gaze, and further link that to possible professions, past and present. A hand-pulled rickshaw passed him, another reminder of China. Just before the entrance to a side street was a very old residence, double storied, with grey-painted walls, but not very wide, and close to the footpath. Past the narrow, raised veranda and the open front doors, Arjun saw a small sitting room where a frail elderly man in a vest sat on a chair, beside him a table with a stainless-steel glass on it and newspapers and books. The man's skin was pale, almost translucent, as though he hardly went out in the sun.

Further ahead, he came to Rashbehari Avenue again, and started walking along it. A tram clattered past on its lines. Past the saree shops another old building caught his eye, a decaying double-storeyed structure in a rubble-filled compound, creepers and branches poking out of the damaged façade, while on a rounded balcony on the first floor stood a middle-aged woman in a nightie, her hair left loose, her elbows on the balcony ledge, looking fixedly at something in the grounds. He went back in a circle through another street going down from the main road, the sweat pouring off him now, till he came to the dhaba from where he had bought the rolls the previous night.

He sat on one of the plastic chairs arranged in a line on the footpath and asked for a glass of tea, which was brewed and brought to him in a *kulhar* by one of the workers. The tandoor wasn't in use at the moment, and the workers were chopping onions and kneading dough inside. Arjun drank his tea and looked at the passing traffic and people and tried to think about the case which now seemed to be spreading in all directions, but his thoughts kept coming back to the elderly man inside the room and the lady on the balcony he had just seen. Stuck in their old houses, they seemed to capture a mood of the city—one of resignation: the rulers had left, and the natives had been unable to rise to the occasion. He had been in Kolkata before, when he had been in the army, but this was the first time he'd had the impression: maybe it matched something within him now. If Delhi exuded violence, then Kolkata was a tired city.

Halfway back to the guest house, it started raining heavily, and he had to run back. He walked down the covered side entrance to the reception area where he took out his wallet and phone from his pockets, both a bit wet. The receptionist Tapan was watching a Bengali movie or serial on his phone, and the old guard stood and saluted Arjun yet again.

'Dadu, why do you keep saluting me?' he joked with the guard in his imprecise Bengali.

'I was in the home guard once,' the old man said in a high voice. 'I can make out you are in the army.'

Arjun nodded. 'I was. Not anymore.'

He took his keys from Tapan and went up, his wet sandals making squelching noises on the steps. Back in his room he took a quick bath and dried himself, then opened the balcony door and poured himself a whiskey. The weather called for it. He stood outside, watching the rain slow down and then stop, remembering natural rhythms from his childhood deep within himself. Where was he, what was he doing: the old questions. He went back inside, put on the lights, and took out his notebook and noted down a few points: the printout, the number from Kolkata Customs, the wallet. It grew dark outside and the streetlights came on and he poured himself another drink. The television was on, tuned to a news channel with the volume turned low. His phone rang. It was Rhea.

'Know what I found out?' she asked.

'So soon? What?'

'That diamond pattern. On the wallet. I had seen it on Pinterest earlier.'

'And? Tell me.'

'It's pangolin leather. Cured pangolin skin. They have that pattern on their skin. Under their...'

'Under their scales, yes. I've seen that thing you know. In the North East.'

'Really?' Rhea said, sounding impressed.

'A very shy creature. Eats ants and insects, and rolls up into a ball when scared. Which makes it easy to catch and pop into a sack.'

'Oh. That's sad.'

'Yes. Anything else you found out?'

'Well, Taiwan was a big centre for pangolin leather earlier. They killed off almost all their pangolins. They would make bags for export, even boots for the US. Wallets and belts were made from leftover pieces from the legs and tails. Then the trade shifted to South East Asia. And North-East India nowadays. China is a big market, especially for the scales. They believe they're medicinal. And they've even found a replacement for pangolin leather.'

'Which is?' asked Arjun, as he wrote in his notebook.

'The araipama. It's a huge fish found in the Amazon. It has a similar diamond pattern on its skin which is thick enough to be tanned.'

'Wow. Fish leather. Do you think the wallet might be made of that?'

'No. This looks like pangolin leather. More *likely* too. So Rohit got it from China?'

'He might have. But in that case why bring it to Kolkata?'

'To give it to someone?'

'Could be,' Arjun said, yawning. 'I'm tired. It's this weather here.'

'Yea. I called Dadi, by the way. She said it was raining in Siliguri.'

Arjun realized with a twinge of regret that he hadn't called his mother yet. Strangely, she hadn't called him either. Was it a message from her?

'I'll call her later tonight,' he told Rhea.

After he'd hung up, Arjun looked at what he'd written in his notebook, flipped back a few pages. Then, on a new page, he wrote the following in a column: ROHIT VATS, WALLET, LEATHER, KOLKATA, LEONG. He almost exclaimed out aloud. How could he have missed it?

He tried calling his mother before he went to bed, but she didn't pick up. She must have gone to bed, he thought, and lit a last cigarette before putting off the lights.

17

At 10 a.m. the following morning, Prasenjit dropped off Arjun on Bentinck Street, not far from the Kolkata Police headquarters at Lalbazar. It wasn't police HQ that he was headed for though: the police and Arjun ran on different tracks, which was the way he preferred it. Occasionally there would be someone like SI Shankar Munda, a helpful individual, but mostly it was people he liked to keep at arm's length, for both professional and personal reasons.

Arjun caught a glimpse to his left of the large red-and-white colonial structure as he headed up Rabindra Sarani toward Tiretti Bazar. The road was crowded with traffic and people, and on either side were furniture showrooms and musical instrument shops, including a 'gramophone mistri': so said the sign above the small shop (more like a paan shop, in a blue-painted box), inside which sat a man in a blue checked lungi working on a gramophone placed on a plank just outside his shop. To the right branched off Sun Yat Sen Street, amid whose old structures were left a handful of Chinese, remnants of the old Chinatown from the days of the British.

His mother had called him just after 5.30 in the morning. They had gone to bed early, she told him, as she and Sunita were going up to Kalimpong for the day, to meet an old common friend of theirs. The weather was nice in Siliguri she told him, and asked cursorily about his work in Kolkata; not that he would have liked to tell her everything, but still, she had seemed different. *She's moved on*: the words came to him later, and he didn't know whether to feel sad or relieved. The thought had crossed his mind that he could go up to visit her; he could use the excuse of having to visit the Pure Life plant in Sikkim.

Past Sun Yat Sen Street he crossed over the tramline to the other side of the narrow road. Arjun looked up at the shop names even as he checked the map feature on his phone. Along the footpath interspersed among trim yet dusty Ashok trees were the ever-present street vendors. He was looking for a shop, one whose name matched the word on the printout: he had found it the previous night on the virtual street map, a shoe shop named Leong & Sons.

The insight that had come to him the previous night was so simple that he had felt like kicking himself for not thinking of it earlier: the city was known for its Chinese-run leather industry, so what if Leong was a shoemaker, or someone connected to the leather trade, someone Rohit might have been looking for? There it was now, a faded and dusty sign that said, 'Leong & Sons / Hand-made leather footwear / Calcutta 700073', with red Chinese decorations hanging under it, just after another Chinese shoe shop. Arjun stood before the shop he was searching for, a feeling of excitement growing within him. Such connections and discoveries were perhaps the rarest and most satisfying part of his trade. Still, he had to see what he could find out.

Inside, an elderly Chinese lady sat dozing on a wooden bench placed on the old yellow linoleum at a right angle to the entrance. Behind her were shelves packed with shoe boxes of various colours, while in front of her were a variety of shoes on display behind glass panes. There was a blue sunmica-topped counter inside, also a display case, behind which sat a middle-aged Chinese man reading a newspaper—probably the woman's son. Between the outermost display case and the inner one was a small altar with incense sticks and, a photo on the wall of a fierce-looking Chinese god, on a red background: the traditional colour of good luck and prosperity among the Chinese, and also, it went through Arjun's mind, the colour of Communism.

As he stepped inside, the woman opened her eyes and regarded him. He was reminded of an old cat: calm and wise with the experience of years. Arjun looked at the various types of shoes, harshly lit by tube-lights at the top of the display cases. He became aware of the pungent smell of cured leather. He hadn't really come prepared, and thought of how to broach the topic. Now he turned and looked around the shop, as if admiring its old interiors. Behind the newspaper-reading man was a working space cluttered with all manner of shoe-making equipment, a black-and-white Chinese calendar hung on the wall, and, in the corner, a doorway leading to what seemed like a storeroom. The upper level of the shop, in fact, had a series of small, square storage cabinets all around, also finished in blue sunmica. Arjun realized the man had lowered his newspaper and was looking at him. He had spiky grey-white hair and puffy eyes.

Arjun smiled at him, and said, 'Nice shop. How old is it?'

'Old, very old shop,' the man snapped, before letting loose a string of what sounded like bad-tempered words to the old woman, in what Arjun surmised could be Hakka or Mandarin: his ears couldn't pick up the difference. The woman didn't say anything, just blinked and looked at Arjun.

'I've come from Bombay,' Arjun said pleasantly, looking at both of them, and making it up as he went along, 'my father was from Calcutta. He used to talk about Tiretti Bazar, he had some Chinese friends here. Is Mr Leong still around?' He pointed toward the sign outside.

This time the man didn't bother answering. Instead he let off an even more irate sounding string of words at the old woman. She raised a pale blue-veined hand to placate him, and turned to Arjun and said in clear English, in a soft voice, 'You're here to buy shoes? Or are you looking for someone?'

'My father's friend, Mr Leong,' Arjun quickly said. 'I came to Dalhousie for some work, then thought I'd come to Tiretti Bazar and have something to eat. Then I remembered Mr Leong ... I asked a few people ... they showed me this shop.'

'How old is your father?' the woman asked.

'He's passed away.'

The words came out on their own, without him thinking, and he thought for a moment he had made a mistake before realizing it might have been the right thing to say. The man behind the counter raised his objections again, but the old lady silenced him with a few sharp words. Then she spoke softly once again to Arjun.

'Mr Leong is not here anymore. His father started this shop, then Mr Leong sold it to my husband. About ... twenty years ago.'

'Oh. So you mean ... Is Mr Leong dead?'

'No. He's still alive.'

'And where is he now?' Arjun asked.

'Chinatown. The other Chinatown. Tangra. He has a restaurant there.'

18

Arjun asked Prasenjit to pick him up from near the police headquarters, where he had got down earlier, and when the taxi driver said he would take around thirty minutes to get there, Arjun decided to go and get himself something to eat. There were a handful of old Chinese eateries in the Tiretti Bazar area, including one which he'd heard served a 'chimney soup' in old 'chimney bowls', but he didn't have time to sit and order, nor much of an appetite yet (and he would be going to a restaurant, he reasoned), so in the end he took a walk through one of the inner lanes of the area.

As he went in, the path turned even more dingy with rundown shops and crumbling old upper stories, some of which had saplings sprouting out of cracks in their masonry and clothes strung out on electric lines. Small green flags decorated with a crescent and a star were festooned over one section of the lane, and stray dogs waited with lungi-clad customers on the wet lane before butchers' shops. There were modest metalworkers' establishments as well, where men squatted hammering away at metal sheets to make baking trays and kulfi moulds.

The sight of the butchers had awoken hope, and he picked up the smell of grilled meat before coming upon the shop, a modest working-class eatery, its wooden tables and benches packed with people having a late breakfast or early lunch. There was an outer wall covered with tiles, on either side of which were openings: to one side was a smoky cooking area where kebabs on skewers were being grilled over coals and parathas were being fried on a large tawa, while to the other side was the entrance beside which sat the owner with his cashbox behind a serving area with curries in degchis. Outside, an elderly man kept an eye on the biryani and curries cooking over upright gas burners.

Arjun asked for a plate of kebabs, and was promptly served a few pieces from the current batch by one of the several stunted child workers who scurried in and out. He ate standing outside, enjoying the busy atmosphere of the place: the kebabs served on a small stainless-steel plate were charred and robustly flavoured, complimented by the onion rings and watery mint chutney served alongside them. The Chinese, and the Muslims beside them, here, and in Tangra as well, he remembered he had read somewhere, were symbiotically linked: the Muslims would trade in and slaughter the cows from which came the hides (and also meat) which the Chinese had needed for their leather products, and which they would tan with the help of the Muslims.

He had another helping before putting his plate into a basin filled with dirty plates for washing, wiped his hands with a square of newspaper, paid for the kebabs and went on his way. Up ahead, the lane turned to the right, and further ahead past shops selling varieties of tea came out on one of the crowded main roads. Arjun crossed over, dodging taxis and buses. A huge garbage dump lay before an old Chinese church, red- and white-bricked on the outside. Holding his handkerchief to his face Arjun squelched through the lane and turned right onto Sun Yat Sen Street, where he passed a Chinese sauce factory with high gates, a few old Chinese restaurants, women selling vegetables on the roadside and an ancient-looking Muslim fair price shop: a world away from the grand old buildings of Empire just nearby on the Hooghly, like Writers' Building. Once again, he felt touched by the mood of resignation: men strove, places rose, then declined, and then that energy dissipated and people went their way.

The taxi appeared on BB Ganguly Street (which cut through Bentnick Street) almost as Arjun got there, and after he had got in headed east in the general direction of Sealdah, on its way toward Tangra. The taxi driver asked Arjun if he was looking for a Chinese person.

'Something like that,' he replied, lighting a cigarette.

Following the directions Arjun gave him from the phone map, the taxi took the dusty road past two restaurants with red-fronted décor and red-lettered signs, abandoned buildings, and large residences and now-shuttered tanneries behind high brick walls, while outside them the open drains had a metallic-grey sheen with scum forming on the surface.

The taxi slowed down to allow a cycle cart to cross it; the man on it was lean and muscled and wore a dark blue lungi, while the back of the cart had streaks of blood on it. On their way here Prasenjit had told Arjun about Dhapa, the area beside Tangra, where the population were poor Muslims and low-caste Hindus who had come over, most of them long ago, from Bihar and Uttar Pradesh. Dhapa also served as a landfill for the tonnes of waste generated in the city every day. After some Chinese had moved to Tangra from the older Chinatown in the city and bought plots and started leather factories, many of the Chamars and Doms besides the Muslims from Dhapa started working for the Chinese, slaughtering cows and curing hides.

But new pollution regulations and an expanding city meant most of the leather tanneries had moved further east toward Bantala, the taxi driver had said, and besides, most of the Chinese had left Tangra for places like Hong Kong, Australia and Canada, places with better prospects for their children. It would explain, Arjun thought, why the area seemed so run down and melancholy, and besides, he hadn't seen any Chinese people on the streets yet. The taxi went deeper into Tangra, past two or three more restaurants and a Chinese printing press and a Hakka cemetery. Now there appeared some Chinese people, all elderly though, sitting just outside their buildings and smoking or talking, women walking home with vegetables. Here and there between the buildings and high brick walls Arjun saw trees and the odd overgrown vegetable garden, besides hides spread out to dry on the blackened asbestos roofs of some of the buildings—no doubt the tannery business hadn't all disappeared.

Prasenjit had to park the taxi ahead of a turning from where a narrow lane only accessible to two wheelers branched off to the left. Arjun got down and walked back toward the lane, an open drain with the same metallic lustre and scum on the other side of the road and old, crumbling buildings on either side. The lane was flanked by high walls discoloured by the tropical weather, only a few tree-tops visible above them, and Arjun had the feeling of entering a settlement from bygone days, a place where you stuck together and kept the world at bay.

'Shanghai', the restaurant the woman in the shoe shop had told him about, had its entrance in the form of an opening in the wall on the right, with an old signboard tilted at an angle above. When he entered, Arjun found himself in a sort of covered courtyard, with a kitchen in a room to the right, and the restaurant behind a wood-and-glass-pane door to the left. Up ahead was a brightly-lit open storage area under translucent roofing sheets, where a Chinese man sat at a table chopping vegetables. Empty utensils and plates were piled up under a tap. He could see people eating behind the coloured glass door, and three more Chinese men at work inside the kitchen, the cook tossing noodles in a wok over a high flame.

A young waiter, possibly Bengali, came out of the eating area carrying a couple of empty plates and bowls. Before he could go towards the storage area Arjun stopped him and asked him in Hindi where the owner Mr Leong was.

'Leong sahib? He's inside there, cooking.'

So that was Mr Leong. Arjun went and stood at the doorway of the kitchen. Mr Leong expertly transferred the noodles from the wok onto four plates, and barked at one of the two other men to take them away. Mr Leong then picked up a cigarette packet and a lighter from a shelf and came toward the doorway, and noticed Arjun. He was a thin, lightly-built man wearing grey trousers and a light-blue shirt on which there were splashes of sauce, and his thick black hair was combed back, a few strands hanging over his face, on which there was a frown now. Arjun stepped back. When the other man stepped out, Arjun asked if he was Mr Leong. The man lit a cigarette and looked at him coolly, responding to the question with only the slightest of nods.

'Actually I'm here regarding a missing person, Rohit Vats from Delhi,' Arjun said, reasoning that mentioning the word 'murder' wouldn't be helpful. 'He went missing here in Kolkata. I think he might have come to your restaurant? Did you know him?'

Arjun showed him a photo of Rohit and Kunal on his phone which Pinky had sent him, zooming in on the dead man's face. Leong blew out a stream of smoke through his nostrils and shook his head imperceptibly.

'No? Maybe he was looking for your shoe shop? The one you had in Tiretti Bazar?'

This time Arjun showed him a photo of the wallet he had taken at the Garfa station, whose diamond-shaped pattern Rhea had deduced came from a pangolin's skin.

'Do you know what this is?' he asked.

Leong looked at it, then started muttering to himself and shaking his head.

'You go now, you go from here, okay?' he said to Arjun. 'Leave now!'

With that he flicked away his cigarette and returned to the kitchen, saying something to one of the workers. Arjun stepped towards the doorway, unwilling to give up, but the worker then picked up a meat cleaver and came toward the door. Leong didn't look at Arjun, but turned on the burner under the wok and busied himself with his cooking again.

The muscular worker leant against the doorway, cleaver in hand, looking at Arjun with a flat, cold stare. In the end he had to turn away: a dead end.

He walked back to the taxi and got in and banged the door shut. Prasenjit raised his eyes to the rear-view mirror.

'Everything okay, sir?' he asked.

'Yes, all fine,' Arjun replied irritably.

'Where do we go now?'

'Take me back to the guest house.'

The driver went some way ahead and turned the taxi around, and then drove back towards the main road. Arjun's phone rang: it was SI Munda. He picked up.

'Hello Arora ji. Where are you?'

Arjun hesitated a moment before replying: 'Tangra.'

'Chinatown. Any leads?'

Again he hesitated before replying: 'I found Leong. He runs a restaurant here.'

'Not wasting time, I see. Anyway, some news for you. I called Anil Sinha.'

'And?'

'I'm going to Customs headquarters tomorrow morning. I can pick you up if you wish.'

'Sure. I'll come along.'

'Where are you staying?'

The call over, Arjun's mood improved somewhat. Mr Leong wasn't going anywhere. The Customs office telephone number was being looked into. While something inside him kept saying the real answer could lie where Rohit had returned from: China. He sat back in the seat and had a drink of water. Then he told Prasenjit there was a change of plans; he would be going to Park Street instead.

19

From Topsia More they headed west on the flyover across the city, before coming down beside the Park Circus maidan, and then going straight past the Arsalan and Shiraz restaurants to the Assembly of God Church on Park Street. Arjun paid, and told Prasenjit that he would get back to Gariahat on his own. He could feel the taxi driver's curious gaze on him as he got out opposite the church. And why not; from Garfa police station to Tiretti Bazar, and from Tangra to a Park Street place of worship, his passenger appeared to be taking a highly individualized tour across the city.

Once the taxi had driven off, instead of crossing the street, Arjun turned to his right and walked down the footpath along an old wall over which large tropical trees spread their luxuriant foliage. A short distance away were the pink-coloured walls of a gated entrance area, with a plaque that read: 'South Park Street Cemetery / Opened 1767 / Closed 1790' (though he knew that burials had continued till the middle of the 19th century). He bought a ticket from the office in the entrance area and walked in.

At once the city melted away and he was back in the distant past. Arjun walked slowly along one of the several paths criss-crossing the necropolis amid the fantastical shapes shaded by several varieties of ancient trees: a jumble of tombs, sarcophagi, cenotaphs and obelisks. A few of the monuments were being repaired with brick and mortar, most had a coat of green moss somewhere on them, and nearly all were discoloured by the heat and damp and sun, graves of people who had died far away from home: sailors, soldiers, scholars, administrators, and women and children too.

It was not just the past of Empire, but his own past as well. Her name was Rachel, a dusky Anglo-Indian singer at one of the Park Street nightclubs, a curvaceous girl with large eyes and curly locks, besides a sharp tongue. Arjun was then at Fort William, with his unit nearby at Alipore. It was before his marriage to Sonali, who was in Delhi, and truth be told, he was temporarily afflicted with cold feet the way most men are when faced with the prospect of setting up a family. He would go down to Park Street once or twice a week in the evenings, and it was at a nightclub there that he had come across Rachel, crooning *Besame Mucho* in a darkened room full of middle-aged men. At the bar he had approached her with the offer to buy her a drink, and she had responded scornfully: 'Not another one of you guys men.'

So, with a straight face, Arjun had told her that he was in the armed forces and that he was supposed to interview her as there were reports of her being a spy.

'A drink might make you less nervous,' he had suggested, to which she let out a delighted cackle. 'Okay officer, as long as you promise not to arrest me,' she had retorted.

It had been the beginning of a beautiful, but brief, friendship: he would come and have a few drinks and watch her sing, and later she would take him to the old, high-ceilinged family apartment nearby where she lived all alone, waiting for her papers to come through so she could go and join her parents who had emigrated to New Zealand. He knew from the start that he wasn't the only one, but that still hadn't kept him from hoping. One memorable weekend they had left the club late, being part of a group of revellers she knew, and gone back to her apartment where she had played her grandmother's old records on a gramophone—Jim Reeves, Hank Williams, Patsy Cline—while they had continued drinking vodka.

Then, she had taken his hand and led him down the steep steps of the ancient building and hailed a taxi to go the short distance to the South Park Street Cemetery, passing morning walkers on their way, where she had slipped a 10-rupee note to the chowkidar whom she knew to let them in. It was his first time there, and he had been mystified by it.

'What is this place?' he had asked her.

'My past,' she said. 'I come here sometimes when I'm in the mood.'

Then she had shown Arjun the rectangular tomb, a weathered plaque informing in faded block letters that it belonged to 'Elizabeth Warwick, taken away by God aged 22 years' in the year 1781; Elizabeth had passed away from malaria or cholera or something of the sort, but she had left behind a baby boy who remarkably survived—Rachel's ancestor. She told him the story as they sat in a cenotaph at the open area at the rear of the cemetery, a couple of huge old trees right at the back and new highrises visible in the distance, and still sipping on the vodka which Arjun had poured into a hip flask of hers.

She had also told him, he remembered now as he looked around for the cenotaph, that all the brick and mortar had been used so that the sicknesses that had carried the inhabitants away were well and truly buried. But he couldn't really decide which cenotaph it was they had sat inside, just as he hadn't been able to find the tomb of Elizabeth Warwick—maybe it was one of those being repaired. In the end he just walked around the melancholy cemetery, deserted except for the occasional teenage couple in a hidden corner, a tall foreign lady in jeans carrying a backpack and a camera, and a middle-aged Indian couple.

A couple of days later he had dropped by the nightclub unannounced, and seen Rachel with a Marwari trader who had been part of that group of revellers. Arjun had walked out, and gone to the nearby Oly Pub. He never returned to that nightclub again, and was married to Sonali a few months later. Rachel, he had thought, was somewhat unstable; only now did he consider whether she might have had some kind of death wish, a hidden desire not to go to New Zealand or some other white country, but to join her long-dead ancestor in these grounds?

He felt no need to find out where and how she was now: some things were best not revisited. Still, thinking about her made him think about his father, about Mr Leong: people carried about on the currents of life. And Rohit Vats: why had he come to Kolkata? After about twenty-five minutes he came out of the cemetery. He was both hungry and thirsty. Not too far away on his right were Shiraz and Arsalan. To his left, but a longer walk away, were the pubs and restaurants of Park Street. For old times' sake he turned left, telling himself he wanted to go see if Oly Pub still had the red-jacketed waiters doling out ice cubes with ladles from small buckets and if the steak with the fried egg was still on the menu. And as he walked along busy Park Street in the midday heat, he called Liza in Delhi and told her to get his visa application to the Chinese Embassy in New Delhi and look up flights to Shanghai.

20

The sub-inspector was outside the guest house at 10 a.m. the next morning. Arjun came down when SI Munda called him and got into the front passenger seat of the police Gypsy. SI Munda was driving and the constable accompanying him crept into the rear when Arjun appeared.

'Good morning!' the sub-inspector said heartily. 'How are you?'

Arjun put on his sunglasses. He still had a headache from the beer and whiskey at Oly Pub the previous day, followed by more whiskey back at the guest house.

'Good morning, it's a lovely day,' he replied, and lit a cigarette.

SI Munda looked at him, then started the vehicle. He was in civil dress today. They partly followed the route the taxi driver had taken the previous day, up along Ballygunge and Park Circus and Park Street, before cutting across Eden Gardens towards the river, from where the sub-inspector headed up Strand Road towards Custom House. Along the way he told Arjun about calling the Customs office number.

'I thought let me call and see,' he explained. 'One person called Biman Bose picked up. He's the Section Officer under Anil Sinha. Said Mr Sinha is out on tour.'

'Who are we going to meet then?' Arjun asked.

'Bose only,' the sub-inspector said. 'I felt he sounded a little nervous when I told him I was calling from Garfa thana.'

'Fair enough,' Arjun said.

It was worth a shot. He then told the sub-inspector how he had tracked down Mr Leong.

'Oh great! Real detective work.'

'But let him be. For the moment.'

'All right.'

SI Munda made some small talk about the weather and the traffic. When they stopped at a red light he returned to his question from the previous day.

'So Mr Arora, you are married?'

'Yes. One daughter. In college.'

It wasn't a topic he preferred to discuss. SI Munda shifted to first gear and stepped on the accelerator. The humid air enveloped Arjun, and he longed for some cold water.

'I'm married also,' the sub-inspector continued conversationally. 'One boy in class 3, one boy in class 7, and one girl in class 12.'

'That's nice,' Arjun said.

'She wants to go to college in Delhi,' SI Munda said. 'But is it safe there?'

'She just has to be a little careful, that's all.'

SI Munda nodded, looking thoughtful.

'Those links you sent me,' he said, changing the topic much to Arjun's relief, 'I went through them. He had some interest in wildlife, this Rohit Vats?'

'That's what it looks like.'

'Hmm. And that girl, did he meet her in China?'

'I don't know yet.'

Custom House was a long high building on Strand Road, another surviving relic from the time of the British so it seemed to Arjun. SI Munda drove past it, took a U-turn ahead, and then turned left onto Fairlie Place, which had wide towering old buildings on either side of the road. He stopped the Gypsy near a knot of yellow taxis, beside which was a roadside barber under a banyan tree, shaving a customer. They got down, and the sub-inspector asked the constable to wait in the vehicle. The two men walked back toward Custom House along the noisy road flanked by the grand old buildings of Empire which looked their age.

'You said you were at Fort William?' SI Munda asked Arjun.

'Yes. Many years ago, when I was still in the army. Why?'

The sub-inspector pointed to their left at an impressive three-storied colonial building in pale yellow with a high colonnaded veranda running around each floor.

'Eastern Railway head office,' he said. 'The original Fort William was here.'

'Really? This building?' It was something Arjun hadn't heard about before today.

'Yes, and no. Nawab Siraj-ud-Daulah captured it in 1756, before the Battle of Plassey in 1757. It was rebuilt more than a hundred years later as the East Indian Railway head office, which then became the larger Eastern Railway after 1947.'

'Interesting. I didn't know you were a history enthusiast.'

SI Munda laughed. 'I was a very bad student. Don't know how I managed to get into the police. But these last few years I've started reading a little about Calcutta's history. Gives me a ... what is that word ... perspective?'

'A good thing to have,' Arjun said.

They turned left onto Strand Road, the broad footpath taken over by myriad vendors with their plastic-sheet covered open stalls between the old, veined banyan trees. Arjun stopped to buy a bottle of cold water at one. Beside it was an eatery where a pot-bellied man was dipping pieces of vegetables in a besan batter and frying them in a bubbling cauldron of oil: the *telebhaja* loved by Bengalis. Arjun took a drink of water, passed the bottle to the sub-inspector, then wiped his face with his handkerchief.

'No one seems to be able to move these people,' he said, indicating the vendors.

SI Munda nodded, handing back the bottle to Arjun. 'It started after Partition, when the refugees arrived. Some of them have been around since then, children of their children.'

They carried on through the hurrying masses of people till they were at the entrance to Custom House. A brass plaque beside it said 'Indian Customs' with the Ashok sthamb below it, and then 'Calcutta'. Past the entrance was a desk with a couple of lower-grade employees chatting. One of them asked who they were and whom they were looking for. Arjun hung back.

'Shankar Munda, I'm here to meet Biman Bose,' the sub-inspector said, and in a low aside to Arjun, 'No need for them to know where I've come from.'

The man picked up the receiver of the phone beside him, rang a number and spoke.

'You can go up,' he said, putting down the receiver, and giving them directions.

They stepped out of the entrance area and went up a broad flight of stairs on the left, which carried on in a switchback up to the first floor. Arjun had a sudden moment of déjà vu: following Prem Tanwar up the stairwell of the building in Nehru Place. He saw the policeman's smashed face after he had shot him, and his father's body on the pyre in the gathering darkness—Arjun stumbled and held on to the polished wooden railing.

'What happened? Are you ok?' SI Munda asked.

'I'm ok,' Arjun said, breathing hard. 'Just the heat.'

They came out to the corridor that ran around the inside of the building, which was a U-shaped structure with the open end to their right; down below in the space before them was a parking area shaded by several stately trees. They turned left and walked down the airy high-ceilinged corridor, past several open tall green-painted doors (with slats on the upper level), through which Arjun saw people working at desks surrounded by tables piled high with files, under fans which came down on long metal rods. A man came hurrying around the corner and slowed down as they approached. With his glasses, half-shirt and trousers he seemed every inch the unremarkable civil servant. Except that he seemed agitated.

'Shankar Munda?' he asked.

'Yes,' the sub-inspector said. 'Mr Bose?'

'Yes. Come with me, it's better we talk outside.'

He walked hurriedly with SI Munda doing his best to keep up. Arjun followed them.

'Who's he?' he heard Bose say to SI Munda.

'My colleague from Crime Branch,' the sub-inspector said without missing a beat.

They came out of Custom House and crossed over to the other side of Strand Road. Bose turned to his right and kept up his brisk pace. Arjun followed a few steps behind. A little way ahead, the Customs official turned left past a crumbling old brick wall and they crossed the railway tracks and were in an open space before the Fairlie Place ferry ghat on the river. Bose looked back and around them, then walked towards the large trees by the river. The ticket office was a little way off to the right. Bose said something to SI Munda, who waited for Arjun to catch up.

'He wants to talk to me alone,' the sub-inspector said.

Arjun shrugged. 'Sure.'

He moved to the shade of a nearby tree and lit a cigarette. A slight breeze ruffled the murky green surface of the river. A ferry approached the jetty from the direction of the Howrah station across the river, while in the distance was the bridge of the same name, tiny buses crossing under its girders. He remembered his father's story about the boy who had disappeared in this river, after setting off from a ghat a little way upstream from where he now stood. And what had brought him here, a murder case, or something more cosmically arranged? He shook off the thought. Bose was talking somewhat agitatedly to SI Munda, but after the policeman spoke to him, seemed to calm down. Then he was off, walking back towards the railway line with quick steps. SI Munda came over and asked Arjun for a cigarette.

'What did he say?' Arjun queried, lighting the other man's cigarette.

'Anil Sinha is on tour. Jalpaiguri, north Bengal. Will be back after a couple of days.'

'He seemed upset about something.'

'I asked him if Anil Sinha handled wildlife trafficking cases, and he grew agitated. Said rumours were being spread by other people and that Sinha was a good officer.'

'Hmm. What does Sinha do?'

'He's an Assistant Director in Preventive.'

'Does his job involve looking into wildlife trafficking?'

'Yes, it does. All kinds of illegal cross-border smuggling, inter-state and international.'

'You found out?'

SI Munda nodded. Arjun looked at him, and smiled. 'Well done.'

'Oh, just a little background check.'

'So, the question is, is Mr Sinha clean or not? Mr Sinha and Mr Bose.'

'I'll keep track of them.'

'Great. In the meantime, I'll be going back to Delhi.'

The sub-inspector threw his cigarette into the river.

'Come, then let's have some tea before you go. I know a good place nearby.'

Arjun was about to suggest that they could go look for something stronger, before remembering that the policeman was on duty. No problem, he could wait a while.

21

Arjun was back in Delhi at midday the next day. It had rained at night and the air was muggy, just like in Kolkata, and the sky was a dirty grey. Passing through crowded residential/commercial areas with wet rubbish before them, and then stuck in the traffic because of the half-built flyovers, Arjun felt his mood darkening. He rubbed the bent metatarsals at the back of his hands: the humidity was making them feel uncomfortable. Delhi was hell, his own particular hell.

He made a call to his mother from the taxi. The house in Siliguri was noisy, with his mother's cousin sister's children and grandchildren, and the television and a barking dog. He told her he was back from Kolkata, and she asked him to go to her place if he had the time, and see if things were okay, with no rats running around. She told him about the trip to Kalimpong, meeting her old friend after decades, and visiting a Tibetan restaurant from her childhood where they had the thukpa—it still tasted the same. He told her it was good she was enjoying herself, and said she should stay on for some more time, maybe make a trip to Darjeeling as well.

After he had hung up, he smiled. She still hadn't given up. To go and have a look at his parents' place would mean getting the key from the girl from Shillong who lived above; in fact, his mother would have already asked her the same thing. After all this time his mother still had her hopes. Arjun had already told her long ago that she was too young for him. She was more of a friend to his mother than anything.

He got back to his flat in CR Park and ordered lunch from a nearby Punjabi restaurant, a heavy, oily chicken curry and a few tandoori rotis, which he ate after taking a shower. Post lunch he went into his 'office', Rhea's old bedroom beside the sitting room, where he took out his laptop and notebook from the locked cabinet and sat at his desk typing down his notes from Kolkata. It didn't take him much time.

After he was satisfied that he had his records up-to-date, he drove over to the agency. All four of them were there, busy at their desks, while Chandu seemed to be searching for phone numbers from someone's xeroxed phone bills spread out over the glass-top table. It gave him some satisfaction to see them like this. Even the television set up in the corner was tuned to an English news channel, but with the volume turned low.

'How was your trip, sir?' Liza asked him, looking up from her typing.

'Hot and humid,' Arjun said. 'But I found out a couple of things.'

Negi and Shyamali had come out on seeing him, and Chandu had put away the bills and gone to the pantry corner, where Arjun now noticed a tiny cylinder fitted with a burner.

'What's that?' he asked.

All of them smiled, and Chandu turned as he filled a saucepan with water from the tap.

'We make our tea in the office now!'

Arjun raised his eyebrows, playing the impressed boss. 'Great!'

As Chandu brewed the tea, Arjun proceeded to tell them briefly what he had found out in Kolkata: the printout, Leong, the Customs officer's secretary.

'So, it could be something connected to wildlife trafficking,' Negi opined.

Arjun nodded.

'Does Pure Life use ingredients from wild animals?' Shyamali asked him. 'Or test its products on them?'

'I asked Sahoo that, but according to him they don't,' Arjun said. 'Looks like there's a China connection to it.'

'You're going to China aren't you, sir?' Liza asked. 'I sent your documents to the travel agency, they've applied for the visa at the embassy.'

'Yes, that's what it seems like.'

'Could it be dangerous?' Negi asked. 'I mean, as you were in the army.'

'Not unless I go looking for trouble. Shyamali, give me Ranjana Ganguly's number please.'

As Arjun stored the number on his phone, Chandu came around with cups of tea on a tray. Arjun took a sip. Oversweet. Somethings never changed. He dialled Mrs Ganguly's number.

The Ganguly residence, whose address Shyamali had given him, was towards the rear end of CR Park, not far from the Kali Mandir and the police station and the modest-sized Market No. 2. Arjun walked from his place the next morning. He tried to think what he would ask of Mrs Ganguly. Something told him it wouldn't amount to anything much. Or was what he really wanted was to be on a plane to China?

The Ganguly family's building—they owned the entire three-storied building—was along a street where all the residences seemed to belong to rich and notable Bengali families, going by the décor and nameplates and cars parked outside. It was the sort of place that made Arjun feel like an intruder somehow. He rang the calling bell on the gate, and heard a faint echoing ring somewhere inside the house. The outer portion of the ground floor was filled with plants and creepers and flowers.

'Yes?' said a female voice from above, and Arjun looked up to see on the first floor a woman with short hair and glasses.

'Arjun Arora. I'm here to meet Mrs Ganguly?'

'Come up please,' the woman said, and withdrew.

Arjun opened the gate and went up the stairs in the left corner. The first-floor balcony was smaller than the outer portion of the ground floor, and had a couple of chairs and a coffee table, and a handful of potted plants. For some reason he had pictured Ranjana Ganguly as the usual plump CR Park woman, draped in a rustling sari, so it was a little bit of a surprise for him when the short-haired woman introduced herself by that name. She was slim, and wore an ordinary yellow and white salwar kameez with the sleeves of the kurta rolled up. It made her look younger than her face let on, he decided.

'So, what can I do for you, Mr Arora?' she asked. 'And why is a detective involved in this now?'

Arjun looked around. 'Could we talk ... inside?'

'Sure. Come in.'

The sitting room was large and decorated with handicrafts, wall hangings, carpets and low tables from all over India, no doubt an attempt at exhibiting secular taste, but which to Arjun seemed a confusing mismatch. There was a huge television on a low wooden table, and further back a maid was sweeping around a dining table. The sofa though was large, plush and modern, and Arjun sank into it while Mrs Ganguly, after turning on one of the ceiling fans, took a seat diagonally opposite to him.

'The Kolkata police haven't made much headway in the case,' he said, 'which is why Mrs Vats hired me to have a look at things. I've been talking to Rohit's friends ... and colleagues.'

'And which do you think I am?'

Before Arjun could reply she went on. 'I'm both. And maybe something more, if you've been talking to certain people.'

'Certain people? Like whom?'

They looked at each other for a moment.

'Like Kadambari, for instance. She thinks Rohit and I were having an affair.'

'Were you?'

Mrs Ganguly glared at him. 'It was a figment of her imagination. We were good friends, that's all. Do you know why I called you at this time, Mr Arora?'

'Because no one's at home?'

'Exactly. My two sons have gone to school and my husband's gone to office. Can you imagine me discussing this with them at home? I only agreed because Rohit is dead. Out of respect for his soul.'

'I appreciate that, Mrs Ganguly. And now Pinky, I mean Kadambari, needs to collect her husband's insurance policy—for herself and her children. Only problem is, the Kolkata police and the insurance company are treating it as a suspicious death. Which means that the pay-out has been held back. I need to find out what happened to him, find out who killed him. For the sake of his family. So, I would be grateful if you told me what you knew.'

'Have you considered Kadambari? Whether she might be involved? Since you're a *detective*.' She paused, then put a hand to her face. 'Oh God, I didn't mean that. Sorry.'

'Let's leave Kadambari out of this for the moment, shall we?' Arjun said gently. 'Tell me, how long had you known Rohit?'

'Oh ... six or seven years I guess.' She looked down at her hands. 'How time flies.'

'So you joined Pure Life after him?'

'Yes. Just a couple of months after him in fact.'

'Okay. What was he like? I mean, how would you describe him? As someone who knew him, a colleague and a friend.'

Mrs Ganguly angled her head up, looking at the ceiling. 'He was quiet and gentle, also stubborn and loyal. I respected him, you know.'

'What about his marriage? Was he happy in it?'

Now she took a deep breath and exhaled through her

lips. 'From the outside, yes. But, but ... there was some sort of vague dissatisfaction I could sense in him at times.'

It was a close, almost intimate observation. But Arjun didn't ask how she had come by it. Rather he asked her about Vivien.

'Did he ever tell you about his Chinese girlfriend from his time in London?'

The confusion on her face was apparent. Rohit had obviously never told her.

'Chinese girlfriend?' she could only repeat.

'Yes. She went back to China. Maybe he tried to get in touch with her? But he didn't mention her to you, did he?'

She shook her head, seemingly without anything to say now. What was it that Mr Sahoo, Rohit's boss, had said? *He was a private person. Kept to himself.*

'Let's talk about Pure Life,' he said. 'You're in the marketing team?'

'Yes, sales and marketing. I cover the western region.'

'And Rohit...'

'Sales and marketing too. Northern region, and international sales.'

'Ok. Did you ever go on tour together?'

A moment's hesitation, then she replied. 'Once or twice. Some years back.'

'Ok. Mrs Ganguly, would you say that Pure Life's products, the medicines, are strategic? As far as the country's security is concerned?'

'Well, yes. But at the same time, they're products, like any other. Speaking as a sales person. But why are ...'

'Let me interrupt you, sorry. Did Rohit seem to have

any special interest in wildlife? More specifically animal parts, or wildlife trafficking? Or maybe zoonotic diseases that jump from animals to humans? Anything of that sort?'

Ranjana Ganguly narrowed her eyes, and shook her head. 'Not that I recall, no.'

Arjun nodded, and moved ahead. 'Your husband was in Kolkata, wasn't he? At the time when Rohit was there.'

'Yes, for a conference arranged by his ministry.' Then it dawned on her. 'My God! Don't tell me you're ... He was busy the entire time with the conference! Stayed at the ministry guest house, was driven around by an office driver. He was around people all the time!'

'It's just a routine question, Mrs Ganguly. Suppose Rohit had wanted to meet your husband in Kolkata?'

'Why there?' she said, her voice rising. 'He could have very well met him here, in Delhi.'

The maid appeared now, and meekly asked Ranjana Ganguly in Bengali something about cooking the day's lunch. Mrs Ganguly lost her temper then, and shouted at the maid, about how she should be using her own brain to figure things out: if she had one. She turned back to Arjun, seemingly agitated.

'Well they were both there in Kolkata,' Arjun said. 'And I have to look at all the possibilities.'

'I'm sure you do. As long as they don't end up confusing you.'

'Mrs Ganguly, can I ask you ... what do you think happened? You must have given the matter some thought.'

'What do I think?' She shook her head. 'Something terrible happened. And believe me, it has hurt me very much.'

She sniffed and rubbed her nose, then took off her glasses and wiped her eyes.

'Now if you don't mind, Mr Arora ...' Ranjana Ganguly said and got to her feet. 'I've told you whatever I know. Now I need to get ready for work.'

Arjun stood up as well. 'Thank you for meeting me. Can I check with you in case I have ... other queries?'

'I don't see why not,' she snapped. 'You can show yourself out I believe?'

Arjun let himself out, and closed the gate behind him and looked up at the first floor for a moment before starting to walk back home. It was, he thought, more or less a dead end.

22

Poppy Barua had been on his mind since he'd called her that day from the railway station, or maybe even before that: when he had figured out from his mother's missed calls that morning that his father had passed away. It was just past 8 p.m. when Arjun entered the expensive restaurant on the upper level of one of the blocks in CP's inner circle and checked himself out in the mirrors: new black loafers, clean jeans, white shirt, dark-blue blazer, freshly shaved and hair shampooed and brushed. It was a vast improvement on his usually scruffy appearance. As a waiter led him to the table reserved for two by one of the large windows, he wondered if it—the preoccupation with Poppy, and not the outward signs of grooming—were the signs of a midlife crisis. He told the waiter he was waiting for a friend, and asked for a beer.

The parking area outside was full of cars, while more cars swept around the circular park at the heart of CP, or Rajiv Chowk as it was known now, with the metro station of the same name underneath. The waiter brought a bottle of chilled beer and poured a glass. Arjun took a long, satisfying draught and for a while followed a complicated operation by the parking attendants to extricate a parked Mercedes from among the swarm of cars. He himself had parked his Scorpio in a darkened alley between the inner and outer circles. Taking out his phone he messaged Poppy: an office car was dropping her off in a while. He drank his beer and looked up wildlife trafficking and the pharmaceuticals industry on his phone: a vast subterranean economy which most people had no idea of.

He had finished the beer and was considering asking for a second bottle when he saw her hurrying in and raised a hand. She raised her thin eyebrows as she neared the table, her heels clacking on the floor.

'Started already I see.'

'I don't believe in wasting time. Especially when waiting for a journalist.'

Poppy laughed her throaty laugh as she put her bag in the adjacent chair and sat down. She was wearing grey trousers and a cream-coloured half shirt which with her cropped hair gave her a gamine, cosmopolitan look. At the same time, the lines on her face seemed more prominent.

'Arjun,' she said in her husky voice. 'It's been ages. So sorry about your father.'

He nodded. She took out her cigarettes and lit one.

'What are we drinking?' she asked him.

'Beer?'

'Whiskey yaar.'

He ordered two scotches on the rocks.

'Is it your birthday or something? What happened to the Blender's Pride?'

'Why not?'

'All right.' She looked around them. 'We've come quite a way, haven't we Mr Arora?'

Like him, she too had a failed marriage caused in part by the demands of her job, and like him she had been an unwilling migrant from the North East as well.

'The long and winding road. Speaking of which, I was in Shillong last year.'

Poppy nodded. 'Your daughter told me,' she said, and, seeing the expression on his face, went on. 'When I had come to the hospital to see you. They didn't know whether you would wake up.'

'As you can see, I have. When did you last go?'

'Shillong? Oh, more than a decade ago. I saw the traffic jams and the buildings and the crowds, and I thought, I can't do this anymore. Not that there's anything there, my parents moved to Guwahati in 1980. I'm happy with my childhood memories of the place.'

'Eating oranges around a coal fire in winter?'

Poppy nodded. 'As the poet said, enough if in our hearts we know ...'

'... there's such a place as Yarrow,' Arjun completed it for her.

She smiled, and they said cheers and clinked their glasses together.

'But how are you, Arjun?' she asked, leaning forward and studying his face.

He shrugged. 'I'm alive. I'm getting by.'

'Cheers to that.' She paused, struck by a thought. 'How's your mother?'

'She's ok. She's a strong woman. In fact she's in Siliguri now.'

'Siliguri?'

'She went after the funeral. To meet a cousin sister.'

'Good she's taking a break from Delhi,' Poppy observed.

Arjun nodded. 'Anyway, how's work? Your boss Banerjee still giving you a hard time?'

She gave a high-pitched laugh that turned a few heads. 'He was sacked by management. And guess who they picked to replace him? Vani Shetty!'

The blank look on his face seemed to irritate her.

'Arjun! Don't tell me you don't know who she is?'

'I don't think I've heard of her.'

Poppy touched her forehead with a palm in mock despair. 'Hai re. She's a famous academic turned journalist, was in the US for several years. An authority on women's issues.'

He drank his whiskey. 'I see.'

'And she has such *great* ideas on how we can enhance our coverage on women. Especially to show how they're affected by the times we live in.'

So that was the academic-turned-journalists' angle; why didn't they say what was really on their minds, that they wanted the present government out, and a return to the good old days? He didn't say that of course, but just commented, 'It's still a poor, patriarchal country where women get a raw deal. Do you need to go to the US to learn that?'

'Arjun Arora, cynic par excellence.'

'Just a requirement of my profession.'

She smiled, and the moment passed. But later he would look back at it as his first mistake of the evening. She said they should order, and Arjun waved at the waiter. They ordered, and asked for a repeat of their drinks.

'What's up with this current case of yours, tell me,' she said once the waiter had left.

He gave her a condensed version of the case, along with details of what he had found in Kolkata, and added that he would be headed to China very soon.

'That'll be a first, I guess? An international case?'

'Yes.'

'Have you been before? China?'

'No. You?'

'Ages ago. On a junket from the newspaper. It was ... more like a separate world than another country. Oh but we ate so much!'

'Something I'm looking forward to.'

'But strange, isn't it? What was he doing in Kolkata, this Rohit?'

'That's what I'm hoping to find out in China.'

'Might you be making a mistake though? In trying to link the Chinese girl and his death in Kolkata. Couldn't they be two separate things?'

Arjun nodded. She had a point there.

'I've been thinking of that too. Then there's the wildlife angle. The pangolin leather wallet.'

'Yes, why would he be looking up rhino horns? Could he have been planning to deal in them?'

'Who knows? It's a lucrative business. Have you heard of cordyceps sinensis?'

'Wait, the caterpillar something, isn't it?'

'Caterpillar fungus. Or keeda jadi in Garhwal, yarsagumba in Tibet. Collected in the high Himalayas during summer. Do you know how much it can fetch in China? 100,000 US dollars a kilogram, even more. Costlier than gold.'

Poppy let out a low whistle. 'That's a lot of money.'

'There are reports of it being collected in Arunachal, in Bhutan and Sikkim, Nepal. Maybe he was trying to get his hands on some. Who knows?'

'Who knows indeed. Ah, here come the starters.'

Their waiter placed a plate of sesame-seed covered chicken wings on the table. Arjun asked for a repeat for both of them. Poppy speared a wing with a fork and placed it on her side plate, then picked it up with her fingers.

'I don't know about you, but I'm using my fingers.'

'Me too,' Arjun said, and picked up a wing directly from the plate.

It was a long boozy dinner, the whiskey and food ingested slowly as they talked about the North East, about their former spouses, about their children (Poppy had a daughter as well, who lived with her grandparents back in Guwahati), and it was past 11 p.m. when they stepped out into the now-deserted colonnades of CP's inner circle.

He had dropped hints after dinner about the bottle of orange liqueur back at his place, and now asked her if she would come over for a nightcap, adding that she could get a taxi to get home. She agreed, and he felt a surge of anticipation as he turned the Scorpio onto the outer circle of CP. Unwilling to inflict Led Zeppelin upon her at such an hour, he turned on the FM radio, and as if by magic, there was Phil Collins taking them back in time. Arjun sped through the deserted yellow-lit roads, and Poppy turned to smile at him.

When they got to his flat, he turned on the sitting-room fan and opened the sliding doors to the balcony, and then, more out of habit than anything else, switched on the news—later he would see it as his second mistake of the evening. He poured out the liqueur into two small glasses and they sat down on the sofa. Arjun didn't care much for liqueur, anything in fact apart from his usual Blender's Pride, but tonight was different. He made a joke about something and she laughed, the alcohol bringing colour to her face and making her all the more desirable.

He refilled their glasses. Things were going well. On the news there was a debate going on about Hindu terrorism. A panellist said it was a dangerous phenomenon.

'What rubbish,' Arjun muttered, sinking back into the sofa. 'Bloody idiot.'

'What?' he heard Poppy say, and turned to see her looking at him in disbelief. 'Arjun?'

'What what?'

'You think he's talking rubbish? Really?'

'Oh come on, the last I heard Hindus weren't blowing up people all over the world.'

'But in India? You recognize the climate that surrounds us?'

Now it was his turn to look at her in disbelief. 'What are you going on about? I'm out on the streets almost every day. And I don't support any political parties, you know that.'

'Maybe that's the problem. In times like these you need to make a stand.'

He looked at her, and slowly shook his head.

'What?' she demanded.

'Poppy, listen to yourself. Is that you speaking, or is it Vani Shetty?'

'What the hell are you talking about?' she hissed, and put down her glass on the table. 'You know, it's time I left.'

The sweetness of the liqueur turned bitter in his mouth. He had hit close to home, but it brought him no satisfaction. He watched as she called a taxi; instead of trying to placate her, which he could have done, he went out to the balcony and lit a cigarette. Too similar, he told himself yet again, they were too similar in temperament. He stood there, lighting a second cigarette and stubbornly refusing to look back, even when the taxi appeared below and he could hear her getting up.

'Bye.' A pause. 'Have a good trip.'

He raised a hand without looking back, turning around only when he heard the front door closing. Going back inside, he had to resist an urge to throw the liqueur bottle at the television. Instead, he turned off the television, put the liqueur bottle on the dining table, and, after a moment's reflection, went to the kitchen and poured himself a large Blender's Pride.

23

He woke the next morning with the customary hangover, but decided he wasn't going to brood over the events of the previous night: what had happened had happened, and he was who he was. After a shower and breakfast and the newspapers he set out for the nearby M-block market in GK-I, a place he usually avoided, but which at this morning hour was thankfully free of the usual idle rich whiling away their time by shopping or eating. Here, at a toy store he remembered from when Rhea had been little, he picked up a rattle and a basic toy car, which he hoped would do for a six-month-old boy. On his way out he passed his old friend Harry Bains' jewellery store Amritsar Jewellers; the heavy and expensive pieces on display behind the thick bulletproof glass the perfect distillation of the desires and fears of this Partition-scarred city.

Next he drove to Nehru Place, where he managed to park in one of the dusty parking lots scattered around the old office towers. He made his way up to Computer Baba's cramped little office in one of the buildings. One of the two usually unseen repair workers was at Baba's desk, fiddling with a dismantled laptop. Baba was on his way, he said. Arjun decided to wait outside the cluttered shop, leaning out of the corridor as he smoked a cigarette, looking at the hive of activity far down below. He was a part of it too, this eternal maze. Checking his phone, he saw a message from Liza and called her to say he would be at the agency soon. She let him know that the travel agent had told her Arjun's visa was done, and that she had asked him to book Arjun on a flight for tomorrow night.

'Can't wait to pack me off to Red China?' he told her.

'I can postpone the ticket if you want.'

'No, tomorrow night is fine. Thanks, Liza.'

He hung up and was stubbing out the cigarette butt on the cemented railing when Baba's voice rang out.

'Oh, Arjun ji! Hope you haven't been waiting here long?'

Baba came hurrying along to the end of the corridor, as well-groomed as the last time, with a fresh tika on his forehead, proving that his transformation wasn't a temporary event.

'No problems, I just got here,' Arjun said.

But Baba paid no heed, instead proceeding to give his employee an earful.

'You don't know who this person is? Why couldn't you get him some tea?'

Grumbling, the employee climbed up into the cubicle above with the dismantled laptop. Baba's mood improved though when Arjun gave him the toys for his son.

'So kind of you Arjun ji! But why did you bother? Very kind of you! Will you have some tea? Breakfast? Bread pakora? I can call one of those restaurants down below.'

'Nothing, Baba. I'm here for the CDRs of that number. Done?'

'Yes, of course. Just let me find that printout.'

He placed the toys on top of a stack of printer boxes and opened one drawer after another in his desk.

'Where is it gone? I thought I had kept it right on top here. Sorry to keep you waiting Arjun ji, it's just that I had to take my missus and the baby to the temple for blessings.'

Watching him rummage through the junk inside his desk, it struck Arjun that Baba was moving in the opposite direction that he himself was, from a somewhat seedy solitary character to a contented family man. It wasn't a comforting thought. Baba held up a printout.

'Ah, here it is. I knew it was somewhere here.'

Baba handed the stapled printouts over to Arjun, who quickly went through them. He could make out a couple of numbers: Pinky's and Kunal's numbers, Ranjana Ganguly's just once or twice, while in the last four days of his life, in Kolkata, there were just a handful of calls and texts—a call to Pinky every morning and night (except the last night) just as she had said, and a landline number which took Arjun a few seconds to recognize. It was the number on the back of the printout Rohit had left in the Kolkata guest house, the office number of the Customs official Anil Sinha.

'Thanks, Baba. This will be covered with the next payment, okay?'

'Sure, sure. But have some tea at least Arjun ji.'

'Some other time.'

On his way back to the car he had a mausambi juice with powdered sugar and masala in it to fortify himself. At the agency they were all at work. Arjun updated them on the Vats case, telling Shyamali about his visit to Ranjana Ganguly.

'Doesn't sound like too much of a link,' Liza commented.

'Yes,' said Arjun, 'but I don't want to leave the husband out of it just yet.'

'So what do we do?' Shyamali asked.

'Try and find out more about him, his past life etcetera. And I'll ask SI Munda to go over his movements when he was in Kolkata. Though he was supposed to be around people all the while. Yes, Chandu?'

'Tea, sir?'

'Not for me. Give these people. Negi, what's happened to your missing wife? Is she in Jaipur?'

'Ah, looks like she might have gone out of the country. I'm working on it.'

'Really, out of the country? Resourceful woman. Anyway, get back to work, I'll see you all tomorrow when I come by to get my ticket.'

It was early afternoon, and CR Park had sunk into a somnolent quiet; Arjun was looking forward to a short nap after lunch, but as he eased his Scorpio into its spot by the low park fence he saw a familiar face loitering about nearby. When he got down, Kunal Mendiratta approached him. The property executive seemed hesitant, but Arjun waited for him to make the opening.

'Hi, uh ... I thought I'd come meet you at home.'

Arjun nodded, not saying anything.

'Anyway, it was about the girl. Vivien. Could we talk?'

Arjun suggested that they take a walk to the nearby Market No. 3.

'The day Pinky came to meet me at home ... it was you who drove her here?' he asked.

'Yes,' Kunal said, then cleared his throat. 'I've been helping them out.'

'Rohit's father said that I should talk to you. Any special reason why?'

Kunal shrugged. 'We were friends...'

'So you would know, wouldn't you? If he was having an affair with Ranjana Ganguly?'

'I really ... I mean they were colleagues ... apart from that ...'

They had crossed the road to the shops that made up the small market. Arjun stopped and studied the chubby-faced man before him. Instead of Rohit and Ranjana, was it Kunal and Pinky who were having an affair? In which case...

'What about Vivien?' he asked. 'Rohit met her in China, didn't he?'

'How ... how did you know?'

'What else could it be about her? Come, let's have some tea.'

A little way into the market was a small shop that sold chops, cutlets, rolls and sweets, the kind of snacks loved by Bengalis. Arjun asked for two teas, and looked at Kunal.

'Do you want anything to eat?' he asked.

Kunal inspected the contents of the counter with its smudged glass pane.

'I'll have a chicken cutlet.'

Arjun asked for two chicken cutlets. Kunal looked around curiously.

'All Bengalis here, isn't it?'

'It's a Bengali colony. EPDP colony: East Pakistan Displaced Peoples' colony.'

'And you like staying here in this area?'

Arjun shrugged. 'It's not bad.'

It would take too long for him to explain to this youngster that this was one of the few places in Delhi which put him in mind of where he'd grown up. They took their tea and cutlets to a small table outside the shop. The market was deserted, shopkeepers nodding off to sleep in the midday heat.

'Why didn't you tell me the first time?' Arjun asked gently.

'I don't know,' Kunal said, raising his hands halfway up, 'Maybe I was worried about what you might think of him.'

'That's not relevant. I'm only concerned with his wife getting the policy money.'

Kunal took a deep breath and exhaled. 'He told me over the phone after he was back that he had met Xiaomei.'

'Xiaomei?'

'Vivien's nickname.'

'Where? How did he find her?'

Kunal shook his head. 'That was all he told me. He said he would tell me the rest when we met.' He shook his head. 'But that never happened.'

'Was he in touch with her?'

'No. Like I told you, the last time he saw her or spoke to her was in London.'

'Hmm.'

Arjun ate a piece of the cutlet, then drank some tea to take away the taste of the oil and masala. Rohit finding the Chinese girl, and then ending up dead; were the two linked, or, as Poppy Barua had suggested, not connected? The night's episode rose up in his mind again, and he pushed thoughts of her aside. He put his elbows on the table and leaned forward.

'I still don't know how he found her, and what he was doing in Kolkata.'

'No ... guesses, or hunches ... at all?'

'A couple of things. Which is why I'm going to China.'

'Oh, I didn't know. When?'

'Tomorrow night. Is there anything you can remember about her? Hometown, family, relatives? Anything at all.'

Kunal scratched his cheek, thinking, and said, 'A name of a school for some reason, that's what I remember her telling Rohit once.'

'What was it?'

'Hangzhou school. Maybe Hangzhou primary school.'

'But where?'

Kunal shrugged. 'That's all I remember,' he said, then added, 'she was a very private person, didn't talk about her past.'

'Like Rohit?'

'Yes.'

Arjun nodded, drank his tea. 'Are you married, Mr Mendiratta?'

'Yes. Why?'

'Children?'

Kunal shook his head. 'My wife has ... problems.'

'Sorry. You know, I never asked you where you were on the night Rohit died.'

'He died in Kolkata! Why ... wait, what are you trying to say? I was here, in Delhi!'

'Do you remember what you were doing?'

'I was either at office or at home. Where else could I be!'

'Well could you try and remember? And let me know?'

'Sure, I will. *Detective*.' Kunal snorted, and shook his head. 'I don't know why Pinky chose you.'

With that he got up and walked away. Arjun just watched. He wanted to see what reactions would emerge out of this meeting. He finished his tea, then stepped into the nearby Punjabi 'Chik-Inn' restaurant to order tawa rotis and mutton curry for his lunch.

24

Arjun's interrogation of Rhea's new boyfriend the Kashmiri youth had been set up due to Arjun and Sonali's efforts, but Rhea had managed to get her parents agree to her picking the venue. It was a café in Khan Market, and only when he had squeezed into a spot in the parking area in front and got down that he realized the café would be dry. The prospect of coming face-to-face with a potential son-in-law without a preparatory drink or two inside of him was so frightening that he hurried to a ghastly sheesha bar in the inner lane, on the upper level. Thankfully he was early while Rhea said they were running late on the way back from college. That gave him time to knock back two large vodka tonics with ice. The place was deserted at that hour except for two men near him drinking beer and discussing setting up a restaurant. Arjun listened disinterestedly; he'd been there, done that.

His flight to Shanghai left from the international airport after a couple of hours; he still had to get back home and pack. He checked his phone: no word from Poppy Barua, but he wasn't going to be the one to call her first. The previous evening, he had sent a text message to Kadambari Vats, informing her about his upcoming trip to China and the need for some interim payment; she had then turned up in the morning in person with the money. And as he had expected, she knew about his conversation the previous day with Kunal.

'Don't tell me *Kunal* is a suspect now!' she had said to him.

'That's a strong word,' Arjun replied. 'I just wanted to know where he was that day.'

'But why?'

He didn't answer, just kept looking at her, and she understood. She sat down on one of the chairs, looking shrunken all of a sudden.

'He was with me, all right? So he couldn't have been in Kolkata at the same time.'

'Where?' Arjun asked harshly.

'At a coffee shop. In GK-2. We met and talked, that's all. I was worried about Rohit.'

'And from there?'

'I came home.'

'How?'

'I took a taxi, ok?' She shook her head with a wan smile. 'Kunal was right. You're wasting my time.'

Arjun had suddenly tired of these relationship games.

'You can remove me right now,' he said. 'I'm not interested in finding out who's sleeping with whom, only in clearing Rohit's name, so that you and your children get the insurance money.'

'We're friends! And Rohit could be ... secretive at times. So I would talk to Kunal. I'm not sleeping with him, I'll tell you that.'

'I could tell you the same thing about Ranjana Ganguly.'

She looked at him for a while, then stood up and moved towards the balcony, looking outside, then turned back.

'Are you married, Mr Arora?'

'Separated.'

She nodded, as if confirming some private theory of hers.

'Mrs Vats, I mean Pinky, did Rohit tell you what sort of work he was doing in China?'

'Meetings mostly, he said it was very dull. Everyone was polite all the time. Most of the time he was with his Chinese liaison, went out with him too a few times for drinks.'

'Chen Song,' Arjun said.

'Yes, that was his name. He invited him to India.' She gave a small laugh.

'One more thing, did he have any flight detours? Hong Kong maybe?'

Pinky shook her head. 'No. He went straight from Delhi to Shanghai. While returning he had a layover in Bangkok, the flight from Shanghai was delayed and he missed his flight.'

'He stayed the night there?'

'Yes, in the airport. He had called me.'

'You said on the phone that Rohit was looking into the wildlife trade and animal viruses?'

'Yes. Do you have any idea why?'

She shook her head. 'Unless it was for work.'

'That seems unlikely.'

'And you think you could find something in China?'

'Yes.'

'If ... you find something, some evidence. How are you going to bring it back?'

'Don't worry about that,' he had said to her. 'Let me get there first.'

But now as he drained his second glass of vodka, he admitted he was a little worried. An ex-Indian army man carrying out an investigation in Communist China; what was he thinking? His phone rang. It was Rhea.

'Where are you?' she said. 'We're waiting outside the café.'

'Coming,' Arjun said, and took a last drag on his cigarette before stubbing it out.

He saw them out at the front of the market, laughing and joking outside the café. The boy was taller than Rhea, and looked like a six-footer. The sight of Rhea, unselfconscious in her teenage confidence, awakened within him for a moment a father's sadness—and pride—for his now-grown-up child. Then she saw him among the other pedestrians.

'Hey, there you are! You were here already?'

'Yes, I was just looking up something,' he said, maybe a little too quickly.

She tilted her head as she smiled, and he knew she suspected. She knows me well, he thought, again with a measure of pride.

'Dad, this is Bashrat.'

He shook hands: a large palm, soft. The boy was slightly taller than Arjun, and typically Kashmiri with a sharp nose, light-coloured eyes and fair skin, along with a light stubble on his cheeks.

'Hello, sir,' he said in a soft voice.

'No need to call me sir,' Arjun mumbled, embarrassed.

Rhea laughed. 'You can call him Mr Arora. Ok, Dad?'

They went in, took a table for three. It was one of those places with a self-conscious air of being chic that made Arjun feel uneasy, and even more so under the present circumstances. Rhea, he observed, was in charge of the proceedings, prodding the two men to go through the menu and make up their minds. Bashrat followed Rhea in ordering a burger and fries, while Arjun thought a pasta would be the safest bet.

'What time's your flight, Dad?' Rhea asked, then to Bashrat, 'I told you na, he's off to China to solve a case.'

'Wow, China,' the boy said.

'Past midnight,' he told Rhea, and then to both of them, 'Sort of a research trip really, to find out some things.'

'So what's it about, this ... case?' Bashrat asked him, in perfect sincerity it seemed.

Arjun briefly looked at his daughter before replying; she hadn't told Bashrat everything.

'Someone from Delhi died in Kolkata. He had been to China before that.'

'He was murdered, you mean?'

'Yes. Now there's some problem with his insurance his wife wants me to look into.'

Bashrat looked genuinely alarmed; Arjun felt he'd hardly had any experience of death and violence close up, which would mean he'd probably grown up outside the Kashmir valley.

'The food's going to be great there!' Rhea said, and

looking at her, Arjun suddenly realized she was the tougher of the two. Maybe it was something which the Arora women had, he thought.

The waitress, a petite girl from the North East, brought their orders. As they ate, Arjun gently queried Bashrat about his background. He had been born in Pulwama in south Kashmir, his father was a politician, and he had done his schooling in Delhi, living with a relative in GK-2. He had an elder sister, married and living in Dubai, while his parents were in Srinagar.

'Rhea said that you were in the army?' he asked hesitantly at one point.

It was something he had been expecting, and with Bashrat studying him, Arjun gave the answer he had already prepared: 'That was a long time ago. I didn't like it and I got out of it.'

'See, I told you,' Rhea piped up, dipping a large fry in mustard.

Bashrat nodded. 'Did you ever serve in Kashmir?'

There was something in the query, something about the tone, which Arjun didn't like. Or maybe he was just imagining things.

'No,' he said curtly.

Bashrat nodded. 'You could visit sometime,' he suggested.

'What do you say, Dad?' Rhea asked him.

Arjun shrugged. 'Sure, why not.'

Rhea beamed at him. With that out of the way, the rest of the meal proceeded uneventfully. Arjun got up to go and pay the bill once he had eaten. Rhea told him she didn't need a lift; Bashrat would drop her home.

'Has your mother met him?' he asked her once they were outside and he was lighting a cigarette.

'Yes.'

'And?'

'She would have preferred someone more, mainstream, I guess.'

'Well, give her some time.'

Rhea nodded. 'He's not coming up to the flat.'

'Keep me posted.'

'You too. Safe journey.'

They embraced, quickly, awkwardly, then Bashrat shook his hand again and they were off, to look for an auto from the road outside, while Arjun headed for his car. Driving back to CR Park, he called Sonali and told her what he thought, which was that their daughter's new boyfriend was decidedly unthreatening, especially when measured against the normal in-your-face Delhiite youth.

'Yes, but the *father*,' Sonali said, always tenacious about the focus of her attention, 'what about him?'

'Politician, stays in Srinagar, sent his son to study here. I can't go to Srinagar to find out more about him you understand? But I can ask around, ok? Even though I'm really not in touch with my old colleagues.'

'Ok. There was that intelligence guy, what was his name, Abbas? Your friend.'

'Yes him or someone else. I'll make a call before I leave for China.'

'Thanks, Arjun. When do you leave?'

'In a few hours.'

'I'll see you when you're back.'

Arjun hung up, and, moving through the early-evening traffic, thought about why she had said that. He thought about Rohit Vats and the Chinese girl, how she had disappeared from his life all of a sudden. We can't let go, he said to himself, of those who mean something to us.

Back at the flat, he took a shower, packed a suitcase with the clothes he had set out earlier in the day, poured out a large Blender's Pride, and called a taxi for the airport. Before turning off the lights he took a look around the sitting room with its sofa and dining table and bookcase, and knew what he would miss was the familiarity of it all: the boundaries of his life had shrunk over time. There was no time though to follow this melancholy train of thought, for as he turned the corner of the park—where the Durga puja pandal was coming up, along with bamboo framework along the outer edges of the field—and headed for the waiting taxi a voice called out to him from a parked car.

'Arora ji! Where to?'

In the front passenger seat of the Tata Safari was a short, bald man: Prince Kapoor, the crooked detective cum property dealer. Arjun crossed the road to the vehicle parked on the side of the other, smaller park. Kapoor was in a tracksuit as usual, looking like a knockoff version of a New Jersey wise guy, while his companion from last time was in the driver's seat with another shifty-looking character in the back. What were they doing here?

'Going out of station for a while,' Arjun said.

Between the two men in front he could see plastic glasses and a paper plate with kebab pieces and onion rings; they had been here for some time.

'I was just about to come and check on you,' Kapoor said.

'Any work?'

'No, just that we haven't seen you at Prem Tanwar's place.'

Arjun looked towards the waiting taxi; his patience was wearing thin. Kapoor's two henchmen reminded him of a pair of dogs.

'I've been busy working on a case,' he said.

'We all have work,' Kapoor said, 'but we should remember old friends too, isn't it?'

'Yes. I'll drop by his place, don't worry.'

'I know you will,' Kapoor said with a shifty smile. 'So, where are you going?'

'China.'

Kapoor raised his eyebrows. 'International khiladi,' he said.

'I'm late,' Arjun said. 'See you, Kapoor.'

Prince Kapoor raised a hand. Arjun walked ahead to the taxi. As he opened the door he looked back and saw Kapoor staring at him fixedly. He swore as he got in and shut the door.

An hour later he was in one of the airport bars at Delhi airport's T3 terminal along with Bunty Chawla. Outside, in the darkness, planes took off and landed, while saccharine canned music played from a nearby restaurant. Chawla drummed his large fingers on the table top.

'Like I said, don't worry,' he said, and took a noisy gulp of his whiskey. 'Bastard must have needed a place to drink and was just sniffing around your place.'

Arjun, contemplating his glass, nodded.

'And the police have a suspect, did you know?'

Arjun looked up. 'Who?'

'Devraj Punj, a builder from Noida. Apparently he had threatened to shoot Tanwar in a bar a few weeks prior to ... that.'

'Tanwar was a popular fellow.'

'So the investigation is moving in that direction now. Kapoor? Forget that chutiya.'

They sat in companionable silence for a while in the empty bar.

'What about your mother, is she back?' Bunty asked.

'Not yet. I called her. It's good for her, this break.'

Bunty nodded.

'At my father's cremation,' Arjun went on, 'you seemed a little ... lost?'

'You know why.'

Arjun sighed. 'I felt something like that too ... for a while. It's only natural. But only for a while. Don't you see, there's no connection. What I do, what you do, what happens. None of it makes any sense. The universe doesn't care, things just happen. Don't you see?'

Bunty stared back wordlessly at him, a little afraid even it seemed to Arjun. Maybe he had overstepped the mark with his friend for whom home and family were everything. Bunty then drained his glass and straightened his back.

'Ok *kancha*, I better get moving,' Bunty said. 'Have a good time in China.'

'I'll try my best.'

They separated after a quick hug, Bunty heading for the exit, and Arjun making for the customs area. After queuing up, he was questioned by an ex-military type sitting in one of the open booths, and a brief look of recognition passed between both men. He headed for the boarding gate, but the China Eastern flight was delayed by over an hour. There were no free seats and a sleepy Arjun decided to forego appearances of dignity and found himself a place to sit on a platform below the glass windows. He had to catch some shut eye but before that tried calling SI Shankar Munda. The Kolkata policeman picked up after a couple of rings. Arjun apologised for calling so late, but Munda said he was still up, watching an old movie on television. Munda said that Anil Sinha was back in Kolkata, but that he hadn't approached him yet. Arjun asked him to hold off for the time being, and gave him Subir Ganguly's details to check on. At the end he informed the other man that he was in terminal 3 of Delhi Airport, waiting for his flight to Shanghai.

'I had a small request Arjun ji,' the policeman said, after wishing him luck for his trip. 'Could you please get me an original copy of Mao's Red Book?'

'I didn't know you were a Communist,' Arjun said.

'I'm not. It's just for my historical perspective.'

Arjun said he would get him a copy. After he'd hung up, it occurred to him that he had possibly, after many years, made a new friend, and the thought made him smile. He scanned the waiting passengers. The airport had started feeling noisy and stuffy to him. The fair-skinned Chinese were a group apart, almost all of them wearing windcheaters, and with hard-shell suitcases and small backpacks on top of the suitcases leaning against the extended handles—uniformity even in travel. Arjun yawned and shut his eyes.

25

On the plane, though, he couldn't sleep, and kept raising the cover of the window beside him to look out. He was too wired, hadn't even asked the airhostess for a drink: everyone in the plane had leaned back their seats and spread out their blankets when they boarded after midnight. So he had looked out, imagining how he was following in the footsteps of his client's late husband: at first darkness, then pale cloud cover, later a view of green hills under wispy clouds (maybe over Myanmar or Yunnan), then shining ribbon-like roads over low green hills, at one point under the clouds a vast flat brown plain, then the Yangtze River delta, neat and orderly like some European country with its rectangular blocks of farmland and factories. Breakfast was served; Arjun observed the Chinese passengers. There was none of the boisterousness of Indians in them. Then the aircraft was banking over the brown, wrinkled sea, with only a lone ship in view and a shipping jetty extending out into the water, before flying through light cloud cover over the Huangpu river and domino-like apartment blocks stretching in all directions.

They landed in a light rain, in what seemed to Arjun to be a nondescript airport, and then for some reason they couldn't deplane. An announcement was made in Chinese. Most of the passengers took out their phones and were soon lost in their WeChat accounts. Only the handful of Indians, Arjun noticed, kept standing up in a show of impatience. He looked out at the rain and the flat grey buildings, cursing the delay. Finally, after an hour, they were let out. The customs staff were quick and efficient, and it was then that the mystery was solved: because the flight had been delayed, it had been diverted to Shanghai Hongqiao, the older airport. He collected his suitcase and then changed some money (each yuan or principal unit of renminbi costing him almost 10 Indian rupees) before going to a pre-paid taxi counter to get himself a taxi for downtown Shanghai.

It was early evening, the rain continued to fall from a grey sky; speeding cars passed them on the elevated expressway and he could see highrises everywhere—in his tired and jet-lagged state Arjun felt as though he were in a dream. Making an effort, he opened the map of the city he'd brought with him and, after some finger pointing and sign language with the driver, managed to work out that they were headed east across the city on the Yan'an Elevated Road. Yan'an: the name seemed familiar, and then he remembered. The place with the almost-mythical Communist Party base before they had seized power in China. In India it might have been the name of someone connected to the freedom struggle against the British. Two countries, two different roads.

The taxi came down from the elevated road, passed through a commercial centre with large luxury brand showrooms, crossed the towering Jing'an Temple, then waited at a traffic light before steering onto the tree-lined Yuyuan Road and dropping Arjun off at his destination. It was a sixteen-storied highrise, halfway up which could be seen several floors with curtained windows: the service apartments where Rohit Vats had stayed. Across from it were a line of eateries. Arjun paid the driver and walked up the steps to the open lobby of the building. Two security guards eyed him from behind a high desk. Pulling his suitcase behind him he walked to the elevators, waited, and got into one and pressed 16; along with him were a middle-aged American man and a Chinese delivery boy carrying plastic bags with food packets in them.

The door to the WorldView Apartments office on the top floor was open; it was one of four doors along one side of the building after exiting the elevator area, in a corner. That told Arjun that there were sixteen apartments on each floor. Just past the entrance was a single chair and a tiny table jammed beside a desk, around which were drinking water canisters, toilet paper packs, detergent and soap cartons, and a fish tank with ornamental fish. To the right of the desk was a sink; the part of the interior he could see had the look of a cluttered flat, with a single bed in a corner and a copying machine. Through the windows was a view of glistening highrises and tile-roofed houses, and above the desk were photos on the walls of past guests and employee get-togethers. It felt very American to Arjun, or maybe that was just how the whole world was nowadays. He called out, 'Hello?'

An office worker in a white polo tee appeared out of

the part he couldn't see. Arjun produced his passport and a print-out of his booking, and was asked to sit and fill up a form. The worker took his passport to the copying machine. When he returned Arjun handed over the completed form.

'What's my room number?' he asked.

The worker produced two swipe cards and handed them over, along with a WorldView Apartments visiting card and a wi-fi password slip.

'Room 1113. Your room cards, keep them carefully.'

'Thank you. Could you check something for me?'

'Yes please?'

'A friend of mine from India by the name of Rohit Vats, he was staying here some time ago. Could you tell me which room?'

The worker made a few clicks with the computer mouse.

'What his name again ah?' he asked.

Arjun told him, along with the dates.

'Ok, ya. Ro-hit. Room 1201.'

'Could I have that room, if possible?' Arjun said, then added, 'My friend said it had a nice view.'

'Ya,' the worker nodded. 'Jing'an Temple. You know it was moved, the whole temple? When they make the road bigger?' He made a few more clicks with the mouse. 'Ok, sorry ya. Now is booked. But you can move there after ... three day.' He held up three fingers.

'Ok,' said Arjun.

'Ok,' the worker replied with a grin.

Arjun looked down at his passport, then up again. 'How long was he here? Rohit? Ten days right?'

The worker looked at the computer screen. 'Yes. Ten day.'

'He didn't go anywhere, right? I mean, out of Shanghai?'

'Just one day he was out. Came back next day. Went to Shaoxing.'

'You're sure?' Arjun asked, suddenly interested.

'Yes, Shaoxing.' The worker sounded faintly annoyed now. 'I tell him where to go and book the train ticket.'

'Why did he go to Shaoxing?'

'He say to me he want to meet a friend.' The worker tilted his head. 'You can go check your room now?'

'Yes. Thanks.' Arjun stood up, then extended a hand. 'Arjun.'

The worker looked at him for a moment before extending his. 'Tommy.'

Arjun took the elevator down to the eleventh floor. Room 1113, like the office, was in a corner. The red-and-blue carpeting along the corridor didn't look too clean and an unidentified smell of cooking hung in the air. On an impulse he went back to the elevator area with his suitcase and up the steps through the emergency exit to the twelfth floor just to have a look at Room 1201, which was again in a corner. He came back down, swiped a card on the lock and entered 1113.

The layout was similar to the office above: an electric cooking range and sink to the right with a storage area above them, a washing machine and fridge and cupboard to the left, and then the room with a large bed and sofa to the right and a table and drawers and a television to the left. At the far end of the room the top to bottom windows looked out over the tile-roofed apartments and highrises he had already seen from above. Arjun went to the windows to pull the curtains: down below he could see people walking past the eateries, while the top row of flats in the building opposite were being renovated by workers. He washed up in the small bathroom, put his suitcase into the cupboard, and his passport and money in the safe at the bottom of the cupboard, then sat down on the sofa and switched on his phone and connected to the building wi-fi network.

The VPN or virtual private network he'd downloaded and signed into in Delhi caught on, and he checked his e-mail and saw that Chen Song had replied to his mail along with his phone number saying they could meet: he replied saying that he'd reached Shanghai and would call Song after getting himself a connection. He also sent a mail to Pinky Vats, saying that he'd reached and would keep her updated. Next he looked up Shaoxing on Google: it was a city to the east of Zhejiang province (which included Shanghai too), known for its canals and yellow rice wine, the writer Lu Xun and the East Lake. Why had Rohit gone there? To look for Vivien? And why had he returned the next day itself? Arjun got up and walked around the room. He was in another country now, but essentially the same: a lone man in a flat. He decided to go out to buy a couple of things.

It was cool outside and the drizzle had stopped. There was a convenience store around the corner, past a bank and a row of ATMs; a chime rang and the glass doors slid apart for him. Inside, it was air-conditioned and antiseptic smelling, and he picked up bread, milk and cheese—expensive—and some beer—cheap—and eggs before heading to the counter, where a uniformed middle-aged woman with short curled hair watched impatiently as Arjun counted out notes and coins. He went back and looked at the eateries on the other side of his building—a pizza place, a Uyghur restaurant, a Chinese soup and dumplings outlet, and a Shaanxi restaurant—and because it seemed the busiest entered the last one, made his way through the diners at the low tables, and managed to gesture in sign language with the owners and get himself packed some dumplings and fried rice. He could already pick up the insularity of the people, something which would have been further conditioned by Communism.

By the time he was back in 1113 his eyelids were drooping, and he managed a bottle of beer and some food before crawling into bed and pulling the covers over himself. His last thought before he fell off to sleep was that he was searching for a needle not in a haystack but in a field full of haystacks.

26

He came awake in the darkness of the room, disoriented from a dream of meeting a south Indian girl in a train travelling across the Tibetan plateau, endless miles of nothingness all around them. Pulling the thick curtains apart he saw it was an overcast day. Cars and scooters silently moved along a traffic roundabout amid the anonymous highrises, and in the distance towards the west a flight was taking off as if in slow-motion, most probably from the Hongqiao airport, where his flight had landed.

It was just before 10 a.m., but the time here was two-and-a-half hours ahead of Indian time, so it seemed to him that he hadn't been too badly affected by jet lag. He shaved and took a shower, then made himself breakfast which he set on the table and ate even as he checked Google on his phone for a Hangzhou primary school in Shaoxing: there was just one record for a Hangzhou Baoshan school in that city. By the time he left the apartment it was almost midday. The sun was breaking through the clouds and a cool breeze came down the street as he walked up towards the Jing'an temple. A black Mercedes and then a dark blue BMW came out of the car park of a sleek highrise, a uniformed attendant with a baton waving them through, while outside on the pavement a line of electric scooters from food delivery services waited, their young drivers slouched on them and engrossed in their phones.

Arjun went across to a line of shops, looking both ways along the side street for traffic and for a possible tail, but he had already noted the CCTV cameras pointing down at the streets from all angles. He crossed an outlet selling bao or steamed buns, a fruit stall, a pharmacy and a spacious barber's shop (with both men and women customers inside) before coming to the China Mobile store where he had to take a token and wait for his turn. He looked at the others waiting with him: an elderly woman, a shabbily dressed middle-aged man, a stylish young couple, both slim and fair. The promotional standees and posters were of a generic type, only everything was written in Chinese. When his turn came, he went up to one of the three counters where a young female executive entered his passport details into a tablet where he had to sign too before she produced a SIM card which she helped him insert into his phone; she was serious and unsmiling throughout, he didn't know if it was because he was a foreigner. Organization and efficiency: he was getting an idea of the PRC.

He came out of the store and made his first call, to Chen Song's number. Rohit's liaison picked up after a long time and answered in Chinese. When Arjun identified himself, he switched to English. Politely putting aside Arjun's suggestion that he could visit the offices of Zhejiang Huashang, Chen Song asked him where he was staying, then said he would come to a nearby coffee bar in the evening. Just a phone call, but Arjun nonetheless hung up with a feeling of having accomplished something.

The street led on to a large traffic intersection, on the other side the wooden balconies and golden roofs of the structures that made up the Jing'an temple, and he let himself be carried by the crowds along the zebra crossing. The traffic waited without honking, all around rose sleek highrises, and the people walked silently and with purpose: he felt what he supposed all visitors from India would feel, a sense of shame at having been left behind, as well a grudging admiration. Faced with this, what moral could be discerned? That political parties were a hindrance? On the other hand, what price could one put on the freedom to say what one felt?

The rear of the temple had a spacious restaurant and a bakery outlet; across the road from it were more eateries, including a Japanese crab restaurant with a large red plastic crab outside, and an American burger place. He turned right and strolled along an open space between the temple wall (where there were a couple of shops, tour operators and tailors) on one side and trendy coffee outlets including a Starbucks on the other. Arjun soon reached the entrance to the temple behind stone lions and high wooden gates, while on the opposite side was a large mall with an entrance to the Jing'an metro station below. He waited with the crowds on the pavement and once the green pedestrian sign appeared, crossed over again. Everyone seemed busy on their smartphones, and the young ones typed fast with one hand while walking.

An even bigger mall rose up a little distance away to his left, with huge international fashion hoardings inside it, but directly in front, across the road from the temple entrance, was a small park. After walking in a little way past a café and a fresh juice and an ice cream outlet he came across people seated on benches under trees; further ahead a group of elderly women, some in bright trackpants, were group dancing to what sounded like an old pop song. To his left, in a separate area, a couple of card games were going on, keenly followed by knots of observers, mostly all of them white-haired retired men.

Arjun took a bench where a young man sat scrolling through his phone with one hand, a takeaway cup of coffee in his other hand. He took out his Indian cigarettes and lit one. An elderly couple walked past, between them a small girl, their granddaughter probably, in a pink jacket with two long braids who held on to their hands. The one-child policy, dating back to 1979, had now started to produce an older population in the country. As he sat there, no one paid him much attention, and he thought with amusement that many of the tall and fair Shanghainese might take him to be a rural migrant from somewhere far away in the interior, albeit a slightly better dressed one. His cigarette over, he walked back the way he had come.

He thought it was better he had lunch somewhere outside, and on an impulse while returning walked up into the restaurant spread across the rear of the Jing'an temple. It was full of the daytime lunch crowd—Arjun supposed people here generally ate early—and amid a hubbub of voices the customers, mostly older people, slurped down noodles at long tables with plastic sheets spread over the tablecloths. He waited in line for a token; in front of him were two young girls, one possibly an American tourist, the other a Chinese girl.

'I've heard *so* much about this place!' the American girl said, and her Chinese friend smiled back at her.

Like elsewhere, almost everything was written in Chinese, but he managed to make out from an advertising standee that it was a vegetarian restaurant, part of a Taiwan chain: possibly a link to the Buddhist Jing'an Temple. When his turn came, he looked at the photos above the counter and ordered mushroom noodles and *cha ye dan* or tea boiled egg, then moved to another counter to collect his order. His food came on a tray, the noodles with soup in a bowl, and two pieces of melon for dessert. He found a place and started eating; the noodles were firm and chewy, and the soup with mushrooms in it delicately flavoured. The shells of the hard-boiled eggs were stained by the tea, but there seemed to be no discernible flavour as such; he wondered if it had its roots, in such a practical people, in eggs being boiled in the tea as a way of saving extra effort (and fuel).

With the meal over, he sat back with a full stomach, observing the crowd and the babble of voices rising up from them. Here he was, walking around and eating on his client's money—it made him feel guilty. He took out his phone and put on the mobile data; it caught on, and his VPN, his link to the outside world, which he had been told never to sign out of, came on as well. He checked his mail: there was one from Rhea, asking if he'd reached, and another from a Vivek Kaul with the subject line 'welcome to China'. Who was this person? The mystery was solved when he opened the mail. Over the course of the recent dinner with Poppy Baruah, she had happened to mention a former colleague who was now in Shanghai, and said she could put him in touch with Arjun, something to which he had agreed. So, she hadn't forgotten. He didn't know how he felt about that. For a moment he considered deleting the mail, then remembered where he was, and his position. Any help would be welcome. He opened the mail, a brief one, and replied to Kaul, saying he would be glad to meet up.

On his way back he stopped at the fruit stall, after the barber shop and the pharmacy, and from the couple manning it bought some apples and a 20s pack of a local cigarette called 'Double Happiness'. The packet was red with a pictorial character repeated twice—presumably happiness times two. The jovial husband taught him how to count from one to five in Chinese, but Arjun felt that could be a way of covering up the fact that his wife had overcharged the man from Yindu, or India, for the apples.

The WorldView literature in the apartment said smoking wasn't allowed, but there was an ashtray on the table before the sofa, and he had smelt cigarette smoke along the carpeted corridors outside, so now Arjun lit a Double Happiness and stretched out on the bed. Through the windows in the distance he could see another flight climbing above the city in slow motion. The sky was starting to clear up. He called his mother to say he had reached—Gita Arora told him that she had got her return ticket to Delhi—and then called Rhea to tell her the same.

'How is it over there?' she asked.

'Well, it's fine. Interesting.'

'You sound tired.'

'Disturbed sleep I guess.'

'Take a nap. How's the case going?'

He told her that he had got in touch with Rohit's liaison and would be meeting him in a while, and also about Rohit's trip to Shaoxing.

'Where's that?'

'A small city about three hours to the east of Shanghai.'

'Will you go there?'

'I might. Let's see how it goes with Chen Song.'

'Great work.'

'What d'you mean?'

'Well, you've hardly been there a day and you've already made two connections.'

'I suppose so,' Arjun said, and after a pause: 'But what am I doing here?'

Rhea sighed. 'Take a nap, Dad.'

27

The glass-fronted coffee bar was on one of the streets radiating out from the smaller intersection which Arjun could see from his window. It had a section that sold cheeses, cold cuts and bread, and also served beer and wine—half price till 6 p.m. Arjun checked his phone: it was half-past-five. He stood on the pavement outside and lit a Double Happiness; he was starting to enjoy the taste. People were walking home from office carrying their shopping in bags, and taxis and electric scooters zipped past. There was a decidedly western feel to the city, Arjun thought.

He had flicked his cigarette butt onto the roadside—he had seen people do that—and was looking around when he saw a bespectacled man in a light sports jacket on top of his work formals approaching, a leather satchel slung on one shoulder. He approached Arjun hesitantly.

'Mr Arjun?' he asked.

'Yes. Chen Song?'

They shook hands, and took one of the inside tables. There were no other customers around, and Song, after asking Arjun what he would like to have, ordered two coffees from a waitress. Then he sat back in his chair and smiled.

'Welcome to China.'

'Thank you.'

'So, you're Rohit's friend?'

'Family friend.' Arjun thought it was better he didn't mention the word 'detective' while in China.

'His boss, Sa-hoo, he mail me. What happened to Rohit?'

'Well, there was an incident. In Kolkata. That's what Calcutta is called now,' Arjun explained. 'He was found dead. This was just after he had returned from China.'

Song frowned. 'You mean, it's a murder?'

Arjun nodded. The waitress came to their table with their coffees. They waited till she had left. Song shook his head.

'He had a wife. Two children.'

'Yes.'

'So you're here for...'

Arjun leaned forward on the table. 'There's a problem with the insurance company. They need to find out what exactly happened.'

Song stared at him for a while before speaking. 'But why here? Shanghai? He just came for work.'

'Yes, yes. I'm here just for a ... background check. Routine stuff.' He added, 'As a family friend.'

Arjun could see Song was starting to get worried about the whole thing, maybe wondering why he had agreed to a meeting in the first place. You stayed out of trouble as far as possible, in a country like this. He needed to get his information fast.

'So, Rohit was here for ten days.' Arjun said. 'He went to your office every day?'

Song sipped his coffee. He appeared to be thinking. Then he looked at Arjun.

'Yes, every day. He went by the metro.'

'Your office is in the Pudong area, isn't it?'

'Yes.'

Arjun nodded. 'I'm staying where Rohit stayed, by the way. WorldView Apartments.'

Song just looked at him without saying anything, eyes blinking behind his glasses. Arjun took a deep breath and ran his fingers through his hair.

'Look, I'm not here to cause any problems,' he said. 'I just have a few questions, that's all. Think about his wife and his children. *They* need the insurance money.'

'Okay,' Song said grudgingly.

'What did Rohit do at the office? Did he meet a lot of people?'

'He didn't have much to do. Go through reports. Sit at meetings.'

Pinky had told him the same thing too. It sounded like a confidence-building trip more than anything else to Arjun.

'So he would mostly talk to you?' he asked.

Song nodded, and added, 'I was his official liaison at Zhejiang Huasheng.'

'Did Rohit's company, Pure Life, did they have any other suppliers in China?'

Song shook his head. 'Our company was their sole supplier.'

'Did your company supply any other companies in India?'

'Yes. Shri Vinayak Pharmaceuticals. It's in south India. Benga...?'

'Bengaluru?'

'Yes. Bengaluru. We supply them too.'

'What did you usually supply Pure Life?'

'APIs mostly. Active Pharma...'

'I know what it means. And would any of your people visit India? The Pure Life and Shri Vinayak offices?'

'Sometimes. The sales managers.'

'You've never been?'

'No. Rohit invited me to Delhi. He said I could stay with him.'

Arjun nodded, took a sip of his now lukewarm coffee. A middle-aged couple talking in French entered and asked the waitress for two glasses of wine. He checked his phone, and to his regret saw that it was almost 6 p.m. No happy hour beer for him, at least not today.

'You should come,' Arjun said, then, 'How was he when he was here? Rohit.'

'His boss ask me the same thing,' Song said. 'I told him, he was normal, happy.'

'Happy?'

'Yes. He liked China. Said he want to come back and visit other places.'

'I see. His boss, Sahoo, he said Rohit was applying for permission for Pure Life to sell their products in China?'

'Yes. With the authorities. But...' Song shrugged, 'we knew nothing would happen in the present time.'

'Does your company use wildlife products in any of your medicines?'

'Wildlife? No! We are a pharmaceutical company.'

'Nothing at all?'

'No. Just some traditional ingredients. For our herbal products.'

'Ok. And was Rohit interested in wildlife products? Things like tiger bones, rhino horns. Did he ask you anything?'

Song shook his head. 'No. he never say anything about the wildlife.'

Arjun unzipped one of the pockets of his windcheater and took out the photo he had found in Rohit's house. He laid it on the table and pointed to the girl.

'Do you know who she is?'

Song looked at the photo, then looked up and shook his head.

'No. Who is she?'

He seemed genuinely puzzled to Arjun.

'A Chinese friend of Rohit's from London. When he was studying there. It seems he met her here. Vivien, I think, is her name. Did he say anything to you about her?'

Song shook his head again.

'Did you know he went to Shaoxing for one night? He returned the next day. By train.'

'Rohit?'

'Yes. I found out from the apartment staff.'

'Shaoxing? No, I don't know he went there.'

Song seemed bewildered by these two Indians.

'You didn't meet him every day, did you?'

'No ... on the weekend. There was no office. He told me,' Song broke off once, then resumed, 'he told me he had visited places in Shanghai. Qibao, Yuyuan Gardens.'

'Looks like he was in Shaoxing instead,' Arjun said grimly.

Song looked stricken, confused. He wiped his forehead with the edge of a hand.

'Did you go anywhere with him? Outside the office?'

'Just ... restaurants, for dinner once or twice, drinks. To a pub once to have beer.'

'Where were these places?' Arjun asked, a little too sharply.

Song looked at him for a moment. 'Pudong, near the office ... and Nanjing East road. The restaurants. Where we had dinner. The bar, not far from here. Hot Spot.'

'Where?'

'Julu Road. It's walking distance. Rohit wanted to go there.'

'Do you remember him asking you about a school? Hangzhou something?'

'School?' Song shook his head, flustered now. 'What are you asking me?'

He took a quick gulp of coffee and checked his phone.

'I'm sorry, but I have to go. I'll pay, please.'

He left without saying goodbye, paying at the counter and hurrying off with his bag. The Frenchman glanced at Arjun, who then slowly got up and went out. Standing on the pavement he lit a Double Happiness and looked around. Chen Song had disappeared into the night.

28

He walked back towards his building. The four restaurants opposite the building were all busy, and there was a lively scene outside the Uyghur restaurant in the corner where people were out on the pavement at small tables on which were beer and kebabs and naan. At the restaurant's outdoor grill they were threading lamb and chicken pieces and offal on skewers. Arjun asked for two lamb skewers and a bottle of beer and had them standing up. The beer was from Xinjiang, weak like other Chinese beers, while the lamb pieces were succulent and juicy, grilled to perfection and dusted with chilli and cumin.

At the table nearest to him were three Americans, two boys and a girl. One of the boys was holding forth loudly on ales. Across the road, near the steps rising up to the front of the building, sat a fair Turkic-looking man in an easy chair, possibly the restaurant's owner, for he had presence and kept shouting over at the two boys manning the grill. As Arjun had his meal, he ran over in his mind the encounter with Chen Song.

Song had naturally been alarmed by the line of questioning, but Arjun hadn't expected him to leave so quickly. There seemed to be little hope of a second meeting now. What had he learnt, Arjun thought. That Rohit had liked being in China, and that he had kept his Shaoxing trip a secret from his Chinese liaison? That he hadn't asked Song about wildlife products (or so Song claimed)? And why had Song seemed flustered when asked about the school? He supposed he would have to go to Shaoxing and look up the school—maybe it still had a link to the girl Vivien.

He stepped inside to pay for his beer at the counter. It looked like a family-run place to him, with the head of the family keeping an eye on things from across the street. As Arjun sorted his notes and coins, the boy at the counter asked him in broken English where he was from, and when told he was from India, gave Arjun a thumbs up and said 'Shah Rukh Khan!'. Arjun gave him a thumbs up too, and stepped out. It wasn't late, and he decided to go and have a look at the pub where Song and Rohit had gone. He checked the route on Google Maps, again via his VPN app, and set off.

The route he followed was the same one he'd taken that morning, around the rear of the Jing'an Temple, but instead of crossing the street to the park he carried on left past the large mall and the subway entrance. Soon he came to a spacious intersection and turned right onto Changde Road; large malls with showrooms of international brands were followed by highrises with the offices of multinational companies and towering hotels like the Shangri-La, but in between there was also an eight-storied apartment in the Art Deco style which harkened back to Shanghai's glamorous past. Arjun waited at a red light, then walked past a crossing under the elevated roadway, the same one the taxi had taken from the airport.

Song had said that Rohit had liked China, and Arjun was starting to feel that way too; Shanghai seemed like a first-world city. The cleanliness and lack of littering, the discipline on the streets, were what one noticed. At the same time, Arjun knew there were other things which were not visible. The city was what China wanted the world to see. He went down Fumin Road which had more of a residential character with red-brick apartment buildings, their blocks sealed off with gates similar to what he had seen near his building, and then he came to Julu Road which cut across Fumin. He checked his phone and followed the way shown to the pub. He passed fruit vendors and cigarette shops and restaurants, a few of which were housed in old wood-plank structures, as well as newer-looking departmental stores. All along the street there were smooth-barked trees he had noticed earlier in the day near his apartment.

Just before his destination he came across a bookshop with large wood-framed windows through which he could see book shelves and book displays, neatly arranged, and on an impulse he pushed in the heavy wood-and-glass door and entered. It was chilly inside from the air conditioning and a bespectacled assistant turned to look as he entered; the only other customer was a woman looking at one of the book displays on a table, a bouquet of flowers in the centre, while a wooden staircase at the rear led up to a café. Arjun was reminded for some reason of the glossy Soviet magazines in the library of an upper Assam school, and photographs in them of the glorious deeds of socialism. The books were all in Mandarin, some of them beautifully produced, but there was a slim shelf of translated titles in English, and from them Arjun, again on something like a whim, selected a novel by a celebrated female author, described on the back cover as a tragic love story spanning the changing decades of Shanghai. He paid the assistant, who put the book into a small paper bag for him.

Hot Spot was a little way ahead, on a dimly-lit stretch of Julu Road. It was across the road, while directly opposite to it on this side was a tattoo parlour with a red neon-lit dragon on a vertical signboard. Arjun crossed the road and walked through the open door, beside which were three tables out in the open inside a low enclosure. At one of them a European-looking man in his late middle-age was sitting with a slim young Chinese girl. Being a weekday there weren't too many people inside. A large flat-screen television on the wall by the bar was showing a Premier League game with the sound turned off while '80s rock played over the sound system. Arjun sat at one of the rough wood tables and looked around. A girl in a lime green dress sitting at the bar studied him. A waiter appeared, Arjun asked him what beer they had, and settled on an Asahi. He remembered it from a trip to Thailand ages ago. Rhea was a small girl then, and had loved the beaches at Chon Buri.

Arjun followed the game for a while: a corner kick and then City scored. He noticed the middle-aged couple behind the bar looking at him; more than Chinese they seemed vaguely Thai. Taking out his phone he opened the WeChat app, which was like China's WhatsApp, and messaged Poppy's friend Vivek Kaul to set up a meeting. His beer was almost done when the girl from the bar approached him.

'Hi! You want to buy me a drink?'

It was said in a friendly bantering way; Arjun thought about it and nodded.

'What would you like? A beer?'

'No, G&T,' she said, pulling out a chair and sitting down beside him.

Arjun raised a hand at the man behind the counter, and the girl said something to him rapidly in Mandarin. He asked for another beer for himself.

'Thanks!' she said, turning to Arjun with a smile.

'You're welcome,' he said.

The G&T was poured at the bar, and the waiter brought it over with Arjun's beer. They said cheers and the girl took a sip of her drink.

'What's your name?' she asked him.

She was duskier than the pale willowy girls he had seen so far, who seemed to float by as they typed into their phones, and more lean than slim: probably a migrant from a far-off province.

'Arjun,' he said.

'Arjun,' she repeated. 'You have nice ears.'

'Nice what?' he said, laughing.

She touched one of her ears. 'We Chinese say big ears lucky.'

'Oh ... I see.'

'Where you from, Arjun?'

'India.'

'You don't look like Indian.'

'Well, there are many different types of Indians. What's *your* name?'

'Me? Angela.'

'Angela? Is that a Chinese name?'

She laughed. 'You can't remember my Chinese name. That's why I have American name.'

She asked him what he was in the city for, and Arjun said he was on holiday. She was pretty in a hard-faced sort of way. No doubt she would leave with him if he asked. But the Poppy Baruah business had left a bad taste in his mouth, and he couldn't forget what he was here for too.

'So you come here how? To Hot Spot. You know about this place?'

'Yes. A friend of mine from India had come here. He told me. Did you meet him? His name was Rohit. He came with a Chinese guy.'

Arjun described Rohit, but she shook her head. Her attention was now elsewhere: a stocky man in jeans and a black half-sleeved shirt hanging loose had bustled in; he gestured and spoke to the couple behind the bar, and also kept glancing towards Arjun's table. He realized the girl had gone quiet. Slowly he finished his beer and then told her that he was leaving.

'Where you staying?' she asked.

'Nearby,' he said.

'You want me to come with you?'

'Some other time maybe,' Arjun said, and gestured to the waiter for the bill.

She seemed thankful, and Arjun felt for some reason it could be because of the man in the black shirt. He had a crew cut and seemed commanding in a way Arjun hadn't seen among people here yet. As he walked out the man followed him with his eyes, and said something to Angela. She came to the door and said bye to him. There was a look in her eyes: fear, it seemed to Arjun. Across the road, the red neon-lit dragon glowed in the dark.

29

The next evening, on his third day in Shanghai, Arjun met Vivek Kaul. The journalist worked for a media company whose office was in the Changning district, and near the large Zhongshan Park. Like Song he said he would meet Arjun at a coffee shop not far from the service-apartment building. Accordingly, Arjun set out at half-past six after a quick shower and change of clothes: he had been out most of the day. He had woken early, his body now in sync with the local time, and after his physiotherapy and some yoga and freehand exercises he had gone out and bought potstickers and fruit from a nearby street; close to those shops was a sort of traditional bakery selling moon cakes and dried herbs and fruit, and a cigarette wholesale outlet. At the bottom of a commercial highrise not far from the Jing'an Temple was a Ferrari showroom and he spent some time checking out the two sports cars on display. Out of habit, he had also kept an eye out for anyone following him.

Back in the apartment a restlessness had come upon him, and he decided to explore a little of the city before his evening appointment. He took the metro from the nearby Jing'an station, which had a supermarket and shiny fast-food outlets around its underground exits, and rode the line till the East Nanjing Road station, where he got out and then walked through crowded streets past shopping malls and hotels on his way toward the Huangpu riverside. Before the main waterfront road he crossed the imposing old stone-clad Custom House with a clocktower high above it. The waterfront area, the Bund, swept around a curve of the grey-brown waters of the Huangpu river, and people milled about here too, tourists both local and foreign most of them. Arjun lit one of his Chinese cigarettes, leaned on the thick metal railings skirting the embankment, and looked around. Across the water, in the Pudong area, rose up skyscrapers glinting in the morning light, among them the iconic Pearl TV tower and the new Shanghai Tower, while behind him were the sober stone-clad buildings which in the colonial era had housed banks, trading houses and hotels. There was a symbolism there: the new towers of steel and glass looking down on what had been created by the old masters.

A long flat barge carrying a huge load of coal came around the bend from the left, from the direction of the Yangtze river, while a mid-sized ship came up from the other way, and he watched them cross each other. Calcutta, and now Shanghai: two cities of the British Empire on great rivers, but the world had changed since then. There were two swarthy men nearby smoking as well whom Arjun thought might be Delhi-ites, but when he spoke to them it turned out they were from Pakistan, here for a trade exhibition.

He walked back past the historic bulk of the Peace Hotel and along Nanjing East road, the old shopping district of the city which now had enormous malls and commercial buildings with showrooms and restaurants, and crowds of people—here and there down the smaller side streets were glimpses of an older Shanghai in the small noodle shops and hotels. At a pedestrian intersection among the buildings a woman approached him asking if he wanted a massage; declining her offer Arjun made his way back to the East Nanjing Road station.

The previous day he had picked up a couple of brochures from the tour operator beside the Jing'an temple and gone through them, and now he went back to the People's Square station—one of the largest in the world apparently—where he changed the line and went two stops down to Laoximen. The metro trains and stations were spacious and clean, as good as, if not better, than the London Tube, he felt, and the passengers orderly, most of whom were glued to their smartphones. Just near the station and the commercial buildings on the main street were the lanes of an old neighbourhood. Elderly people played mah-jong inside cramped rooms or lay outside on recliners; Arjun passed eateries and salons, also a store with rice wine in earthen jars, and a photo framer with framed illustrations of Mao and Zhou Enlai on display. The Confucius temple he managed to find on Wenmiao Street was nothing much, and there were hardly any people around, but with its rock formations and pond (and handwritten prayers tied to the temple posts) it was quiet and peaceful while the view of the highrises in the distance—even the futuristic Shanghai Tower across the river—made for a pleasant contrast.

From the temple he made his way to nearby Xuegong

Street and the Kong Yi Ji restaurant, where he took a seat at a table for two and ordered glazed pork and drunken chicken from a pictoral Chinese/English menu: they obviously had tourists here. Amid the general hubbub of the restaurant with people entering and waitresses serving (there was another inner area with larger tables for groups), Arjun sipped yellow rice wine as he waited for his food, turning the case over in his mind. What might have happened to Vivien? Two countries of over a billion people each, and not on very friendly terms: a dead person in one of them, and a girl to be traced in the other.

The rice wine came in 250 ml jars, and was an aged and complex drink, a product of Shaoxing. In fact, the restaurant served Shaoxing food; Arjun had chosen it with the vague idea that it might somehow help him. But more and more it felt like a hopeless case to him. The food, which was excellent, served to distract him though. After lunch he wandered around the Laoximen area and through to the Huaihai Middle Road district, before catching the metro from Lujiabang Road station back to Jing'an for his meeting with the journalist.

Vivek Kaul had picked an outlet of a coffee chain in the lobby of an office building off Changde Road, near the route Arjun had taken the previous day to Hot Spot. Nearby, young couples and parents with children strolled around a flat fountain with several water jets, while officegoers with briefcases were walking out into the evening. Apart from the coffee outlet itself the lobby was curiously empty; a tall man with a hooked nose and sparse greying hair unfolded himself from a sofa and approached Arjun with an outstretched hand.

'Arjun Arora? Vivek Kaul. Nice to meet you. Please, sit.'

Kaul insisted on getting them coffees. Arjun watched him across the coffee shop (which was empty too) and idly wondered if he had ever gone to bed with Poppy: it seemed unlikely. Kaul returned, and they chatted over the coffee. Arjun asked the other man how he was perceived here as an Indian. Kaul laughed. He had an easy, relaxed style.

'Most people think I'm Uyghur or something!'

Arjun smiled. 'There's a Uyghur restaurant opposite where I'm staying.'

'Opposite the WorldView building?' Kaul asked.

'Yes. Food seems to be good.'

'It is.' Kaul lowered his voice. 'And you can get grass and hash there if you want.'

'Thanks, but I don't smoke. Don't they get into trouble?'

Kaul shrugged. 'The owner knows how to take care of things.'

Arjun recalled the fair man sitting in an easy chair across the road from the restaurant, keeping an eye on the grill and the customers as he drank from a bottle of beer.

'So how long have you been here?' he asked Kaul.

'Oh, six-seven years. Came here from Mumbai. It's a decent place to stay. Just me and the wife now. Son's in the States.' Kaul cocked his head. 'What do *you* think about it?'

'Impressive. When you come from India. But under the surface...'

Kaul nodded. 'Hidden currents. You need time to read them. The language too. How's Poppy, by the way?'

'She's good,' said Arjun: there didn't seem to be anything more to the question.

'We were working together in Cal. Mid '90s. Great times. Speaking of Cal ... Poppy mentioned you were here investigating a case with links to Cal?'

Arjun cleared his throat and looked around, then moved a little closer to Vivek Kaul.

'I'm here to find a girl,' he said. 'She may be in Shaoxing.'

Kaul nodded, a look of caution suddenly coming upon him.

'I suppose I don't have to tell you to be careful?' he asked.

'Of course.'

'What are the ... particulars, if I may ask?'

As briefly as he could, Arjun sketched out the details of Rohit Vats' death and his search for the girl Vivien. When he finished, the journalist pondered in silence for a while, drinking his coffee, before speaking.

'So going by the story Rohit's friend Kunal told you ... this girl was selling pirated DVDs in London, while the Chinese fellow Rohit saw at the flat ... he seemed to be something of a tough guy?'

'Yes, that's right.'

'Then she could be involved in the black market, or the grey market at least.'

'That's a possibility, yes.'

'You also said Rohit was looking up the wildlife trade.'

'He was. How could I find out more about it?'

'Hmm. Well, there's someone I know who may be able to help you...'

Kaul took out his phone, and Arjun watched as he quickly typed out a message on WeChat and sent it.

'A friend of mine,' Kaul said. 'Let's see what he says.'

'Rohit seemed to be interested in SARS and that stuff too. I've been trying to see if there's a link between that and their suppliers in China, but nothing so far.'

'You mean Zhejiang Huasheng?'

Arjun nodded. 'Rohit's liaison was afraid to talk.'

'Oh most of them are like that. Not like us Indians, shooting off our mouths.' Kaul scratched the back of his neck and grimaced. 'I doubt you'll get anything out of them. And talking of SARS ... I've been hearing some stuff latcly.'

'Like what?'

'Have you heard of Wuhan?'

'It's a city here somewhere?'

'Yes. Central China. A transport hub. Lots of foreign companies there, especially French companies. Anyway, the French helped the Chinese build a bio-security lab there. For experiments. From what I've heard they've built up quite a collection of bat viruses.'

'Where do they get them from? The bat viruses.'

'Yunnan. Guangdong. They want to beat the Americans you see. As in all other things.'

Kaul's phone pinged, and he picked it up and checked the message, then looked at Arjun.

'What are you doing tonight?' he asked.

30

They ended up at the flat of an Indian couple whom Kaul knew, and his friend, who turned out to be a Chinese businessman called Stephen Wu, was already present there. Arjun and Vivek Kaul had taken the metro to Hanzhong Lu station just two stops and one line change away from Jing'an station, and from there walked to a tall apartment block, one of several in a quiet and anonymous area of Chang'an Road. From the balcony of the flat at the top of the building there was a view across the Suzhou creek of the lights and highrises of downtown Shanghai, the Shangri-la Hotel rising up among them.

They were drinking scotch provided by their host Monty Vaswani, a stylishly-dressed garrulous Sindhi expat. Apart from Arjun, Kaul, and the Chinese man, there were two more Indians: Dasgupta, the China head of an Indian IT firm, and Joseph, an Indian Embassy official. Mrs Vaswani was in the kitchen cooking with the help of an elderly Chinese amah while the Vaswani children, a boy and a girl, were busy on the PlayStation in the sitting room. Kaul introduced Arjun to Wu, a genial man with a crewcut wearing a casual cream summer suit.

'Anyone for a cigar?' Vaswani asked, and went in for

one. He was wearing ripped jeans and a yellow blazer, his thinning hair slicked back with gel.

'So where in India you from?' Wu asked, turning to Arjun. 'I been there few times on business.'

Arjun shrugged. 'I live in Delhi, but I grew up in ... the North East.'

'Ah. Arunachal Pradesh! Sensitive region.'

'Yes.'

'When I was in Mumbai and Delhi,' Wu said, 'people thought I was from Manipur or Nagaland!'

'And here we're,' Kaul said, indicating himself and Arjun, 'mistaken for Uyghurs. Steve, Arjun wants to find out something about the wildlife trade. Can you help him?'

'Wildlife? You want to buy something?'

'Just ... looking around,' Arjun said.

'Anything specific?' Wu asked, looking at both of them.

'Tiger bones maybe,' Arjun said. 'Rhino horn.'

Wu laughed. 'You'll get those cheaper back in your country than here!'

'Still, just find out?' Kaul said. 'It's important for him.'

Wu nodded. 'Will do. There was a guy I knew once ... let me see if I can find him.'

'Here, this is for you guys,' Vaswani interrupted, clipping a cigar and handing it to Kaul to light. 'Cuban stuff, enjoy.'

'Do you know what I liked to drink in India?' Wu asked Arjun.

'Kingfisher beer?'

'That too. But I liked Old Monk rum. Good drink.'

'Cheers to that,' Arjun said.

They puffed on the cigars while Vaswani refilled their glasses. His wife, whose name was Honey, came out with a plate of chicken pakoras for them. Vaswani asked her if she wanted some wine.

'Give me a glass please. Dinner in an hour, ok?'

'All depends on Monty,' said Dasgupta the IT man.

'Arre Dasgupta babu, think of it as your own house,' Vaswani said. 'Have dinner whatever time you want!'

He went in to pour his wife the glass of wine, and Dasgupta followed him. Both men returned after about twenty minutes, and Joseph, the man from the Embassy, asked in a knowing way: 'Deal *ho gaya*?'

'Even here business?' Kaul said in a mock complaint. 'Relax yaar, Monty.'

'Arre I learnt from the Chinese. Right Steve?' Vaswani said. 'C'mon ganbei!'

Vaswani did a bottoms up, followed by Stephen Wu, and Arjun had a feeling it was going to be a long night. A while later he was in conversation with Joseph and Dasgupta while their host discussed a new restaurant in town with Kaul and Wu. The man from the Embassy wanted to know what he was in Shanghai for, to which Arjun said that he was there on some personal work. From the look Joseph gave him, Arjun was sure he would try to find out more from Kaul later on. Talking to Dasgupta he found that the computer engineer had spent part of his childhood (as Arjun had done) in Shillong, before making his way out into the larger world. They spoke about Shillong for a while—Arjun had been there just the previous year, in connection with the case of a girl from Nagaland who had been murdered in Delhi—before the talk turned to China.

'It's a very difficult society to understand,' Arjun observed.

'You're right about that,' Dasgupta said.

'So what's going on at the moment? What's the big story?'

'There are a lot of strong currents moving under the surface,' Dasgupta said, in what seemed to Arjun to be a very Chinese-sounding statement. 'Many government officials being hauled up for corruption. In fact, under the new guy things in general have gotten a lot stricter than before. And my reading is, there's more of it to follow.'

It took Arjun a moment to work out whom he meant by the 'new guy'.

Two days later, Arjun was on a bullet train to Shaoxing. It lay some 200 km to the west of Shanghai: the high-speed CRH train would cover the distance in just an hour and a half. He had taken the metro to the Hongqiao railway station, supposedly the biggest in Asia, found the waiting area after checking in (almost like an airport), went out the platform as the gates opened twelve minutes before departure, lined up according to the coach number on his ticket, and got in after the sleek train pulled in.

He had woken up late the previous day, after having got back past midnight in a Didi cab hailed for him and Kaul by Vaswani. Arjun had managed to get out of the journalist that their host was a broker for Indians who came looking for products in China, especially from Shenzhen and the market city of Yiwu, while Stephen Wu was into real estate, restaurants and electronics. The rest of the day had been taken up by going to the nearby train-services office where he bought a round ticket for Shaoxing, and then shifting his stuff up to 1201, the room Rohit had stayed in.

As Tommy, the office staff from the WorldView office upstairs had mentioned, it had a good view of the Jing'an temple, the golden pagoda visible through the surrounding highrises. Arjun had taken a couple of photos of it through the windows with his phone, to send to Rhea. Then he started searching the room thoroughly, the cabinets and drawers, under the bed, in all the cracks and crevices, in the slim chance that Rohit might have hidden away something. But, as he had half expected, there was nothing.

Now as he watched the urban landscape outside giving way to farmland, his thoughts turned to the curious encounter from that morning. He had woken early and gone out for a walk, taking the wide Wanhangdu Road that went up in a north-west direction from the Jing'an Temple, passing storefronts and apartment blocks and administrative offices, before turning back and having a breakfast of hot scallion pancakes from a roadside vendor, and then carrying on till he was back at the temple, and crossed the road at its front to get to the park again.

Sitting on the same bench as on his first visit, Arjun had called his mother and then Rhea, and as he talked, watched an elderly Chinese man nearby dipping a large mop-like brush into a bucket of water and then quickly drawing Chinese characters on the wide pavement stones—elaborate characters which also evaporated quickly, a sort of Zen-like exercise that seemed to touch upon transience and perfection. At some point someone had come and sat next to Arjun on the bench. Preoccupied with observing the water calligraphy he hadn't paid the person any attention, but upon sensing he was being watched, had turned, and saw a middle-aged man who gave him an awkward smile. The man was slightly haggard looking, had a darker complexion than an average Chinese, and wore a denim half-jacket and sneakers. Arjun had smiled back and greeted him. 'Hello. Where you from?' the man responded, and they spoke for a while.

The man said he was originally from Nepal, but had been in Shanghai for three decades, and had a Chinese wife. He said he was into the pharmaceutical business, and visited south India regularly. In turn, Arjun only volunteered that he lived in Delhi, and that he was here on personal business. The man (Arjun didn't ask him his name) turned out to have some sort of a chip on his shoulder about India, starting to complain about how Indians thought they knew China when they had no idea about the country, and how China had moved far ahead of India. Arjun listened, slightly bemused, and when he observed, only half-jokingly, that the absence of political parties seemed to be a benefit, the man faltered. It was then that Arjun had realized the man's unease throughout the conversation. He quickly bid Arjun farewell and hurried off.

Only now did the thought come to him: was he being tailed, had the encounter been an approach of sorts? In a coach full of Chinese passengers he acutely felt his foreignness, and the fact that he was headed to an unknown destination based on the slimmest of leads did nothing to assure him. He got up from his seat at the head of the coach and slowly walked up the aisle, looking at the passengers scrolling through their phones, eating instant noodles, or working on their laptops. At the toilets at the end of the coach he turned and pretended to be busy with his phone, as if waiting for one of the toilets to be free, then looked up to check if anyone was looking back. No heads were turned towards him, but once the suspicion was in his mind it was hard to ignore it. He entered one of the toilets, washed his face, and returned to his seat.

They were crossing farmland now, vast orderly fields of ripening paddy, and wheat too. The fields were intersected by canals, transmission lines, roads and raised traffic intersections with cars and trucks speeding along them. Here and there were run-down factories and abandoned projects, as well as shiny new housing projects. Arjun caught a few glimpses of what looked like the past: a crumbling white house with black tiles over which creepers were spreading, a man fishing in a canal, an old lady riding a cycle on a path between the fields. He saw plantations of fruit trees too, orange trees maybe. The same scene as he had seen from the air of the Yangtze river delta, only now from the ground.

As they neared Shaoxing he saw in the distance storied pagodas on the top of low hills. The journey was like an illustration of how thousands of years of human settlement had resulted in every inch of the land being worked upon all over the eastern coast of China, producing a landscape of highrises, malls, airports, highways, warehouses, factories, large-scale farms. There were hardly any birds to be seen anywhere, except for small flocks of pigeons, some of which were used for racing. Was this landscape the future of mankind, Arjun wondered.

Shaoxing Bei or Shaoxing North station was a vast open structure; as he walked along the platform headed for the exit one level below, he saw on the opposite platform across the tracks a group of soldiers in uniform. He took a taxi from the station, showing the lady driver a printout of the hotel that he had booked. The sky was overcast and it had started raining. When the taxi stopped at red lights the driver would pick up her phone: there was a photo of a little girl on the lock screen, and the lady would look up pizza delivery. Gazing out into the rain Arjun thought of Rhea, and felt an overwhelming sense of futility at his investigation. Where in this city would he find Vivien, assuming she was here in the first place?

The hotel was beside a canal, near a bridge that spanned the waters. There was a red China flag in front of the hotel, which had a shiny pre-fabricated look to it that reminded Arjun of similar hotels in Gurgaon. The check-in took a long time, the plump, shiny-faced receptionist not knowing or unwilling to talk in English, and after it was done Arjun called Vivek Kaul and asked him—the journalist spoke Mandarin—to tell the receptionist that he wanted a taxi that would take him to the location of the Hangzhou Baoshan school, which didn't appear to be marked on Google Maps. He handed the phone to the receptionist, and she listened as Kaul spoke, nodding, and then handed back the phone to Arjun.

'I've told her, and she said yes,' the journalist told him.

'So you'll get me a taxi to the school? Shwe–shiyao?'

he asked her after he'd hung up, trying to pronounce the Mandarin word for school.

The girl nodded briskly, and said 'Deng dai, deng dai,' which, when Arjun looked it up on Google Translate, meant 'to wait'.

Arjun gave her a thumbs up and headed to his room, which, though on the third floor, had an 8 at the start of the room number: 8326. The Chinese considered the number 8, along with the colour red, as being lucky. The room was comfortable with a low wide bed and muted brown colours in the carpeting and walls and an oversized chair. From the windows he could see the bridge over the canal, wooden pavilions along the pedestrian walkway on its sides giving it an appearance of antiquity. The rain had stopped. He washed up, then went down to the deserted restaurant where he had a lunch of fried chicken wings, a bottle of beer, and a large bowl of soup with what turned out to be omelette, tofu, cabbage and tomato in it. A thin man with a slight paunch and red eyes came in smoking a cigarette, followed by a woman balancing herself on her heels. Arjun noticed his car keys in a belt clip. After his meal he went back to the reception to ask about the taxi. The response from the girl was the same: he had to wait. Annoyed at the delay, Arjun decided to go out and see if he could get a taxi by himself.

31

He came out of the hotel and started walking north toward the central part of the city. As he waited to cross a road intersection, a man with a decidedly rural look riding an electric scooter came and stopped near Arjun, and started talking in Mandarin, seemingly asking for directions. Arjun shrugged, said in English that he didn't know, and moved on. Ahead lay a Communist Party assembly hall of sorts, followed by a police station, while on the other side of the road was a big open-plan mall. He crossed over and approached a taxi from which a young couple had just alighted, and tried to make the driver understand through a mix of English and Google Translate Mandarin that he wanted to go to the location of the Hangzhou Baoshan school. The other man listened impatiently, then muttered something in Mandarin and drove off.

Past the mall was a line of small shops and some old houses, then a larger street. He approached another taxi, with the same result, then crossed the street. Some distance ahead was a garden with a pagoda-like tower. He stopped a youth in a basketball jersey and tried to explain where he wanted to go and that he wanted to get a taxi, but the youth listened to him and shook his head, and only said, 'no, no school' after he'd heard about the Hangzhou Baoshan xuexiao or school. Arjun watched him walk away, and lit a cigarette. A mood of disgust came upon him: here he was, a detective, unable to even get himself a taxi! Why had he even agreed to take on the case, why had he agreed to come here?

As he stood there smoking, he checked Google Maps on his phone, and saw that the old residence of the writer Lu Xun, along with his memorial hall, were nearby: the restaurant serving Shaoxing food he had visited in Shanghai, Kong Yi Ji, had been named after one of Lu Xun's stories, about a failed alcoholic scholar with the same name, and it had even served the cold and sweet kidney beans which the scholar ate in a tavern in the story. On an impulse he decided to make his way there.

Following the map on his phone he entered a narrow lane and walked past old houses and apartment buildings till he came to an open area where restaurants were being made with old-style wooden facades and touts were trying to peddle boat rides on the small canal winding through the area. As he turned onto a cobblestoned street the number of tourists became apparent, and the buildings were all shops, made in the traditional style, and selling souvenirs like inscribed folding fans or different sorts of food items and varieties of Shaoxing rice wine. There were Chinese people everywhere, old and middle aged and young and some children, entering and exiting the various tourist spots: the old residence of the writer, the new memorial hall, and the Sanwei or 'three flavour' study. At one point they hadn't been allowed to move around without a valid reason, but now they were being encouraged to travel and spend in order to boost local economies. Arjun hadn't counted on so many tourists, or the fact that Lu Xun would be so popular. In the canal, boats took tourists wearing lifejackets for rides. When Arjun reached the front of the street he saw a mural at the entrance with images of Lu Xun and realized that he had entered from the rear. On his way back he bought a rice-wine infused ice cream from a shop and sat on a concrete bench around a tree observing the tourists. The ice cream with the yellow rice wine in it tasted nice, smooth and subtle. In spite of the crowds around him he felt at peace for a while.

When he got back to the hotel, he saw a green-and-white taxi waiting outside the main entrance with a man in crumpled black trousers and blazer leaning against the hood and smoking. He squinted at Arjun through the cigarette smoke, and when Arjun went in the receptionist jabbed a finger at the taxi. So he went back out and approached the driver, a middle-aged man with a round face and thinning hair.

'You'll take me to the school?' Arjun asked him. 'Hangzhou Baoshan xuexiao?'

'Yes, yes,' the man said in English, and opened one of the rear doors for him to get in.

The driver got in and they set off. At the road intersection from where Arjun had gone north earlier, the taxi now turned toward the west. Arjun looked back at the intersection, remembering the man on the scooter who'd asked him directions earlier in the day. Now it struck him: had it been a random encounter, or was someone trying to check whether he knew how to speak Mandarin? As before, it was hard to get rid of the suspicion once it had appeared. The driver turned left off the broad tree-lined road and took a bridge over a small river—the Fengze according to Google Maps on Arjun's phone—and then passed through the orderly buildings of a university campus as the taxi continued moving west across the city.

Shaoxing was a city of canals and waterways and rivers, as he'd seen since. Arjun wondered if it ever got flooded, or if the waterways were an ancient method of avoiding flooding. Now they were passing through a flat landscape of warehouses and small factories. He leaned forward to tap the driver on his shoulder.

'How far? To the school?'

'Near, near!' the driver said, pointing ahead.

What would he do once they were there? Show people the photo and ask if they recognized the girl? Close to his destination, the absurdity of his plans became apparent. Still, he had made it this far, and who knew what luck he might have. The taxi climbed onto a broad highway, passed rows of warehouses on one side and apartment blocks on the other before crossing another longer bridge over the same river. Across the bridge, on either side, were rows of new highrises, part of the ceaseless churning of China in its quest for development. The driver slowed down and then halted by the side of the road and pointed outside. Arjun looked out, but all he saw were more highrises, new and unoccupied housing units all of them.

'What's this?' he said. 'These are flats. Where's the school?'

'There, there!' the driver said, repeating his words as usual.

Arjun got out of the taxi. Cars and trucks sped past behind him on the highway. Before him, past a high fence, were symmetrical rows of dark brown towers with empty steel-and-glass clad flats within them. There was a large signboard nearby with the image of a family of three—father, mother, child—with the same towers in the background. A new residential development, maybe even part of the countless empty projects across the country undertaken only to make use of all the cement and steel, and labour too, being pushed out into the market. The driver had joined Arjun now, lighting a cigarette.

'I told you I was looking for a school. Xuexiao! These are flats. People's houses! Where's the school? Hangzhou Baoshan xuexiao!'

The man shook his head. 'Meiyou, meiyou,' he said in Mandarin.

Then Arjun understood. 'It's not here anymore? It's gone?'

The driver nodded. 'Yes, yes. No more.'

'When? Which year?'

The driver scratched his head and thought. 'Ten-twenty year. Gone.'

So that was it. How stupid of him to have imagined that things would have stayed the same in China, of all places, the one country where the past had been turned upside down. He accepted a cigarette from the driver, then took out his phone and called Vivek Kaul.

'Arora ji. How's it going? How's Shaoxing?'

'Confusing. I need your help again.'

'Tell me.'

Arjun explained what had happened. 'Could you talk to him for me?'

'Ok, give him the phone.'

As the driver spoke to Kaul, Arjun smoked and waited, vehicles rushing past the taxi all the while. An elderly man with a wrinkled, decidedly rural face driving by in a three-wheeler delivery cart (with what looked like cement sacks in the back) smiled at Arjun as he passed by. The strangeness of the situation, of the location, with the towers of empty flats spreading away from him, gave him a vaguely dreamlike feeling—like being driven into downtown Shanghai the day he had reached China. The driver nodded and handed back the phone to him.

'So what the guy is saying is,' said Kaul, 'that the school was there, where the buildings are now, but several years ago. It was closed down in the '90s and a factory came up in its place, then a real estate company bought the area a few years ago. He's a local fellow, so I think he knows what he's talking about.'

'Ok, but why didn't he tell me that?'

Kaul chuckled. 'Must have wanted the fare. Could have happened in India too. *Hai na*?'

'I suppose you're right.'

'He told me, "Your friend wanted to come, so I brought him." Man has his logic too.'

'So this school, was it moved elsewhere?'

'No, just closed and torn down. You know how it is here. There was a stabbing incident apparently, before it was closed. Several kids killed by a disgruntled chap who'd lost his government job elsewhere in the city.'

'I see.'

'It'll be a near impossible task to dig out stuff about this school, do you understand?' Kaul sighed. 'Go and see the East Lake instead, take a nice boat ride.'

'I'll think about it. Thanks, Vivek.'

He hung up, and told the driver the name of the hotel, and pointed back with his thumb, indicating he wanted to return. The driver turned around up ahead, and Arjun watched the empty towers pass by and then disappear.

32

Back in his hotel room, Arjun lay on the bed in the growing gloom, with the curtains open, the room lights unlit. His once-fractured meta-carpals in both his hands had started throbbing again. The end of the road: for the case, and, he felt, in his current state, for him too. Truth be told, he hadn't taken on the case out of purely altruistic reasons; there had also been his need to get out of Delhi for a while. He couldn't keep the images at bay any longer and they rose up in his mind again: Prem Tanwar's bloody face as the policeman lay dead on the floor of the dark corridor; his father lying asleep on his hospital bed as the life ebbed out of his once strong physique. Arjun sat up and with shaking hands lit himself a Double Happiness cigarette.

Then he picked up his phone from the side table and called Rhea.

'Are you back in Shanghai?' she asked.

It was a relief to hear her voice. He said, 'No, I'm still in Shaoxing.'

'No luck with the case?'

'No.' He knew she had heard it in his voice.

'Hang in there. It was always going to be tough.'

'I know. I was just thinking, could you look up the girl Vivien on Facebook? Long shot, but still...'

'Will do. Any other leads?'

'Maybe a last one once I get back to Shanghai,' Arjun said, thinking of Stephen Wu. 'There's a guy who's supposed to find out something for me.'

'Ok. Don't lose hope. Just go through the angles in your mind again.'

Feeling better after he had spoken to her, Arjun did just that, lying in bed smoking and thinking till it grew dark. And out of all that had happened since he'd set foot in China—the meeting with Chen Song, visiting Hot Spot, the journalist Vivek Kaul, the night at Monty Vaswani's, and the trip to Shaoxing and standing at the site where the school had stood—out of all of that he felt, or rather vaguely sensed, something that was significant but which wasn't apparent to him just yet. What was it? In such a situation, he knew better than to push it; it was more useful to stop thinking about it, and let the subconscious take over. In time things would get clearer.

He put on the room lights, pulled the curtains, took a shower and changed, then went out. From the hotel a short walk took him to the mall he had crossed in the morning, a large open-plan place with a playground for kids out front and people generally milling about.

Arjun entered a nearly empty restro-bar that was playing karaoke videos of Chinese pop songs. He had two beers while watching the overly-sentimental videos, and picked up two more to go. For dinner he ordered chicken from a fried chicken place he had seen earlier and walked back with a paper bag and beer to the hotel. In the hotel's restaurant he tried to get some ice or 'bing' for his hands from a waitress wearing shorts, without any luck, and instead had to buy a can of cold Coke from the visicooler. In one of the private rooms in the restaurant a group of men sat eating and drinking in a cloud of cigarette smoke, among them the thin, red-eyed man Arjun had seen the previous day. Back in his room, he applied the cold can to the backs of his hands while he drank the beer and ate the chicken. That night he slept fitfully, sweating even with the air conditioner on.

He was woken at 4 a.m. by a worker scraping cement in one of the pavilions on the side of the bridge outside the hotel. Outside, it was grey and overcast with a faint layer of mist over the canal waters, and he made himself a cup of instant coffee which he drank sitting in the oversized chair beside the windows. He felt a desire to get home, to be free of the burden of the case. No new insight had come to him. A strange restlessness had come upon him. There was time till he had to leave for the train station, so he took a shower and went out for a walk.

A path led down to the canal, and as he walked alongside it and went under the bridge a slim, middle-aged woman in a swimsuit climbed out of the misty waters like some sort of an apparition. He looked at her pale face as she went past him towelling her hair: could *she* be Vivien? A few steps led up to a garden where a couple of old ladies were moving through their tai chi exercises. He came out to the road intersection near the hotel. A three-wheeler delivery cart driven by an old woman in a padded jacket went past; in the back were crates of eggs. Arjun crossed the road and walked ahead and then took a left, headed for the garden with a pagoda-like tower he had seen the previous day.

Around the boundary of the garden labourers with rough rural appearances were hauling earth and breaking stones. Inside the garden, with paths and pools and bamboo groves, old people were exercising, maybe a habit from after the revolution. He walked up a winding stone path but the pagoda gates weren't yet open. He went back down and kept walking through the morning streets. Following Google Maps, Arjun came to the Zhou Enlai memorial hall and ancestral home, which had just opened. Zhou, a son of Shaoxing and a contemporary of Mao's, had been involved in the setting up of the CPC, the PLA, and the PRC, and had been a legendary survivor in Mao's court. A low entrance by the road led into an open courtyard where a grey statue of Zhou in an overcoat stood under the grey sky, a bright red Communist flag beside it.

On his way back to the hotel, Arjun stopped at a small eatery on a tree-lined street. The owner was friendly, and he quickly cooked fresh noodles which he then tossed in peanut sauce and garnished with spring onions for the man from Yindu: a simple and tasty breakfast. For a moment he could have been on holiday, exploring a new city on foot. Back in his room at the hotel Arjun packed his things then sent a message to Liza Thomas at the agency that he would call once he was back in Shanghai: India time was two-and-a-half hours behind.

It was raining by the time he left the hotel in the taxi they called for him, and once he reached the train station, he bought two squat red bottles of Shaoxing rice wine from a souvenir shop and had a filet-o-fish burger at the McDonalds before settling down with his novel in the vast waiting hall: everything seemed to be built in larger-than-life scale. The boarding gates to their platform opened in a while, 12 minutes before the train arrived, and as he walked along the spotless platform looking for where coach no.2 would come and stop, a white bullet train went whizzing past on the next line.

A while later he was in a comfortable window seat watching Shaoxing recede from him. The man on the seat beside him was typing an e-mail on his laptop, 'I had a meeting with the manager Mr Huang which was very helpful...', while next to him was a girl stretched out on her seat and engrossed in her phone. Arjun looked out, watching the journey unspool in reverse, and tried not to think of the e-mail report he would have to send to Kadambari Vats once he was back in Shanghai.

The train pulled into Hongqiao railway station punctually at 12.32 p.m, and it took him another hour to get to Jing'an station on the metro line. As he bought some items from the underground supermarket, he reflected that he would miss the convenience of it all once he got back to Delhi. Outside there were blue skies and a blustery wind blowing, and walking back to the apartment his spirits were lifted somewhat. At 2.30 p.m. he called Liza from his cell phone to get an update on what was happening at the office, including on the Rohit Vats case. Shyamali Kundu had looked into Subir Ganguly, his secretary told him, but there seemed nothing amiss with him: an excellent student, he had cleared the civil services at his first attempt and had risen quickly within the Delhi bureaucracy. There was a mention in the police files though, an arrest following an incident of reported assault which had happened on the road after a minor collision with another car: nothing surprising for Delhi, and there was the probability that the other party had started getting physical.

Next, he called Shankar Munda. The sub-inspector had traced Subir Ganguly's movements in Kolkata, and said they all checked out.

'From guest house to conference hall every day, and all the time people with him, I have checked.'

Just as his wife had said. Still...

'Ok,' said Arjun, 'however there's the possibility...'

'That he might have arranged it? Yes, I am looking into that side as well. I have got his mobile phone number.'

'Well done, Shankar. And what about Anil Sinha?'

'He's back from tour. I'm finding out about him too. Some things are emerging.'

'That's great.'

'What about you? Is your work getting done?'

'It's been ... difficult,' he confessed. 'I'll be back soon. We'll talk.'

'Don't forget to get what I asked!'

'I won't.'

Last of all he called Vivek Kaul, to ask if there was any word from Stephen Wu. Not yet, said the journalist. He was at work. After asking Arjun when he would be leaving, he said he would try to meet him before he left. Arjun didn't particularly mind; Kaul—and Wu—were under no obligation to help him. The mood of the previous evening returned: he was done. Another day, and then he would be flying out of China. It was time to send the e-mail admitting failure. He logged into his mail account on his phone, then hesitated. Never before had he given up on a case. What was his intuition trying to tell him?

Arjun paced the room restlessly, smoking one Double Happiness after the other: what had he overlooked? Down below electric scooters halted at the traffic roundabout, then started moving again, people headed somewhere. Kaul's words over the phone when Arjun had called him from the taxi now came back to Arjun, telling him what the taxi driver had said: 'your friend wanted to come, so I brought him'. The school. And what had Chen Song told him? He stopped in the middle of the room, the ash on his cigarette growing longer. Suddenly he knew where Vivien could be.

33

Arjun waited till it was dark before heading out. It would be one last throw of the dice for him. He got there walking. On the other side of the road, the red neon dragon shone on the signboard advertising the tattoo parlour. A young girl in a white dress stood outside smoking, her face lit by the glow of her raised phone.

It was the weekend and Hot Spot had considerably more customers than the last time Arjun had been here: foreigners, tourists, Chinese girls. He looked around and didn't see who he was looking for, so he approached the bar. The music was loud techno-pop this time and the flat screen television was showing an NBA game with the sound muted. The same middle-aged couple was behind the bar, and Arjun beckoned the man and asked for an Asahi draught. The beer came, and as he paid, he asked the man: 'Where's Angela? Is she here?'

The bartender looked at him for a moment. 'She coming. Wait.'

Arjun nodded, and took his beer to one of the smaller tables. More waiting. And as he waited, the certainty of midday faded: he was clutching at straws here. What chance did he have of finding one woman among a billion plus people?

He had almost finished his beer when he saw Angela walk in. She was wearing a dress in pastel pink tonight with her hair done up. Arjun raised a hand and caught her eye, and she walked over.

'Hi, you came back!' she said with a smile.

'Of course. Can I buy you a drink? A G&T?'

She said yes, so he went to the bar and returned with a gin and tonic for her and another Asahi for himself. They clinked their glasses and drank.

'I thought you gone back to India,' Angela said.

'Not yet,' he said, studying her. 'Looking good tonight.'

'Thank you!'

'How come you drink G&Ts?' he asked. 'Did you have an English boyfriend?'

She laughed. 'No. Beer make me feel very, how to say, full?'

'Yes, it does that.' He looked around: no sign of the stocky crew-cut man from last time. 'So were you here earlier? Or you just got here?'

'I just came. You?'

'Five minutes before you.'

'Great!' she said, looking deep into his eyes now.

'My friend told me about this place, I told you, remember? You sure you didn't meet him? His name was Rohit.'

'No, I don't think so.'

'He was in Shanghai end of August, he would have come here around the 27th.'

'End of August? Oh, I go back home then. To Dongyang. Near Yiwu. You heard of Yiwu? Many Indians come there.'

Arjun nodded. 'The largest market in the world.'

'That's right. Dongyang next to Yiwu.'

'You have family there?'

'Yes, parents, my brother and his wife. Their kids.'

'You like it there?'

'Yes. But here is better.' She seemed to search for the words. 'Because, every day in Shanghai is new.'

She was young, just a few years older than Rhea, and was still untouched by cynicism. He suddenly felt very old.

'Here's to Shanghai,' he said, raising his glass, and she lifted hers too.

He leaned towards her over the table. 'There's something I want to ask you, Angela.'

'Yes?' she said, her eyes widening slightly.

Arjun took out the photo from his jacket pocket and placed it on the table.

'This is my friend who came to Shanghai,' he said, pointing to Rohit, then moved his finger. 'Do you know her? Vivien. Look at her face.'

Angela looked, then looked up at him, and he willed himself to stay calm. She knew her! Now she looked at the bar, a worried look on her face.

'Angela, listen to me, you know who she is, don't you? Who is she? Here,' he took out several notes from his wallet, rolled them and pressed them into her hands, 'take this. Now tell me. Who is she?'

She hesitated, turning the roll of yuan around in her fingers, then took a deep breath.

'Yes, I know her.' A pause. 'She's running this bar.'

Arjun sat back in his chair and tried not to show his surprise. His hunch had been correct. 'Is she here?'

Angela shook her head.

'Can you call her here?'

'She'll be coming. On Saturday she always come. You wait.'

'Ok. What time?'

Angela shrugged and started to get up. 'She'll come, you wait.'

He watched as she went and started talking to the couple behind the bar: all three of them looked at him. He hoped they wouldn't call her and warn her off. He drank his beer and waited, then got himself another beer. Angela started talking to an older European, an expat probably. The place was packed now, the volume of the music had risen, and several times Arjun had been asked if the seat opposite him was free. To all of them he said he was waiting for someone. He messaged Rhea, and she told him what she wanted him to get for her from Shanghai. Just after 9 p.m., the stocky crew-cut man from Arjun's previous visit swaggered in, followed by a short woman wearing silver heels and a leather jacket. They headed for the bar, and Arjun got off his chair and approached them. He could see Angela's eyes following him across the room.

She was the same person—older, her hair cut shorter—but the same person as in the photo: he was sure of that. The crew-cut man was talking loudly to the couple behind the bar. She noticed Arjun when he was standing beside her.

'Xiaomei!' he said loudly. 'Hi, how are you?'

Vivien looked at him with a frown.

'I'm Arjun, from India,' he continued, extending a hand, 'I'm Rohit's friend.'

She turned towards him then, ignoring his hand.

'You remember Rohit? Rohit Vats?'

'What you talking about?' she demanded.

'Your friend from London, Rohit. He was here in Shanghai.'

'I don't know what you talking about yea?'

The inflection was pure London, he noted. How to get through to her though? The crew-cut man turned towards them now, and said something harsh sounding, but Vivien raised a hand, indicating that she could handle it herself. There was only one way, Arjun thought.

'Do you know that Rohit is dead? He was killed, one week after he returned to India. In Kolkata. You haven't heard from him, have you?'

Her mouth opened in an involuntary show of surprise, then she regained control of herself.

'Your friend, Rohit! Whom did he meet here? He was killed as soon as he got back!'

'Listen, I don't know what you talk about, ok? You better leave now!'

She had raised her voice, and people turned to look, including Angela. The crew-cut man had a shifty grin on his face now; Arjun wondered if he was the man Rohit had seen with Xiaomei, only he wasn't tall and didn't have a scar on his face.

'You never knew Rohit? Can you say that? He's *dead*, Xiaomei.'

She stepped up to him now, her face taut with anger.

'Just leave, ok?' she hissed. 'Just leave!'

The crew-cut man made a comment, and this time she

turned on him and gave him an earful. Looking offended, he went towards a side door behind which he disappeared. Xiaomei deliberately looked away from Arjun, who, up against a dead end again, slowly walked out. Angela glanced away when he looked at her.

He stood on the pavement outside and lit a cigarette. Across the road, the red neon dragon glowed outside the tattoo parlour. He wondered if it also doubled as a massage parlour. What could he do now? Find out where she lived and make his way there? So close and yet so far! He heard footsteps behind him, a woman's heels, then a familiar voice: 'Can I have a cigarette?' He turned around, offered her one, and lit it for her. Vivien took a drag, looking up and down the long street.

'What happened to him?' she finally said.

'He was killed. It was a murder. A week after he got back. In Kolkata.'

She pursed her lips and took a deep breath, looked around again.

'Why?'

'I don't know. I'm trying to find out.' He took out the photo and held it before her.

She looked at it and her features softened for a moment. 'And who are you?'

'My name's Arjun. I'm a ... family friend. Listen, I need to talk to you.'

Vivien dropped the cigarette and stamped it out. 'Where are you staying?'

He told her, and handed her a card from the apartments.

'Go back and wait for me. I'll be there soon.'

'I could wait here...'

She shook her head, and glanced back. 'Not here. Not safe. You go, I'll come.'

Arjun nodded, and watched her go back inside, then started walking to the apartments.

34

An hour later, he was still waiting, drinking from a can of Asahi and looking out from the windows of his room at the golden pagoda of the Jing'an Temple shimmering in the lights—he had put on just a table lamp, pulled the curtains apart, and opened the door; all ready for Vivien a.k.a Xiaomei. But where was she?

Down below, around the corner, they had been playing a game of mah jong outside the soup and dumplings restaurant, the building supervisor enthusiastically taking part as well, while in the nearest highrise opposite he could now see three men and a woman playing cards at a table in one of the flats, the windows opened maybe for the cigarette smoke. Arjun was considering going back to Hot Spot when he heard the click-clack of heels. They stopped, then started again, and he turned around to see her standing in the doorway.

'Come in,' he said, moving forward. 'Please, come in.'

She entered and looked around, slightly disapprovingly it seemed to him. He went and shut the door and came back, then moved toward the switchboard on the wall.

'Let me put on the...'

'Let it be,' she cut him off. 'It's fine. What are you doing in Shanghai?'

'Let's sit down first,' he told her.

They sat opposite each other at the table beside the television set, and, after he had asked her, Arjun poured her half-a-glass of Shaoxing wine. He put his packet of Double Happiness with the lighter and the ashtray between them. The dim light within and the glittering lights outside the windows gave the room a strangely surreal feeling. For a moment Arjun was reminded of the ghostly woman rising out of the misty canal waters in Shaoxing.

'As I said,' he started, 'my name is Arjun, and I'm a family friend of Rohit. His ... family asked me to come here and see if I could find out something. About why he had been killed.'

'A detective,' she said, and helped herself to a cigarette.

He lit it for her with the lighter. 'You could say that.'

'And you found out anything?'

'I found you.'

She sniffed and looked away from him. 'Rohit told me he would come back. What happened to him?'

'The police haven't found out. But there seems to be a link to the Chinatown in Kolkata. A man who runs a restaurant there. Mr Leong. Do you know him?'

'Maybe. Leong, he must be Hakka Chinese, from Hong Kong, or Guangdong. I grew up in Hong Kong.'

'Then went to London?'

She nodded, took a sip of wine, looked at the glass.

'Tell me about you and Rohit. The last time you saw him in London, the tall guy with the scar who was present. I think the answer might lie somewhere there.'

'Who told you about the tall man?' she asked sharply.

'Kunal. Rohit's roommate. Who is he? Is he here in Shanghai?'

'No, he's not here. He is my husband. He is also *jianghu*. You know what that is?'

'No.'

'It means he's a ... gangster.'

As Arjun absorbed this piece of information Vivien took another sip of the wine.

'Where did you get this?' she asked him, lifting her glass.

'It's from Shaoxing. Where I went looking for you. Rohit had gone there too. Hangzhou Baoshan school, right?'

'How do you know? Kunal?'

'Yes.'

She nodded again, reflectively, then said, 'I studied there as a child. For a few years. Rohit must have remembered that. Then my mother had a second daughter. But, you know, the one-child policy. Soon afterwards my mother's cousin came from Hong Kong, she didn't have children of her own. Her father had moved there after the liberation. So I was sent with her, somehow it was managed for me to travel with her. After that I grew up in Hong Kong.'

'And they gave you a new name?'

'Yes. Vivien Chan.'

'What was your real name?'

'It doesn't matter now. I wasn't happy in Hong Kong though, I resented my aunt for taking me away from my real family, and she said I was an ungrateful child. By the time I was a teenager I was a rebel, not coming home sometimes. That was when I met my husband, Sheng Li.

His parents had a small restaurant in Quarry Bay. Have you ever been to Hong Kong?' she asked him.

Arjun shook his head, lit a cigarette. She continued.

'He was a troublemaker even then. But I thought it was cool.' A bitter laugh. 'One day we got married, a registry marriage. I moved out of my aunt's house, she was furious. But soon after he was arrested by the police for the first time. For smuggling. He was locked up. I had to go back to my aunt's house. Life was hell for me then. I decided to get out. There was some of Sheng Li's money, and I used it to get to London, to start a new life. I was studying and working at the same time. That was when I met Rohit. I was always interested in India. Then Sheng Li got out of jail and came looking for me. I was staying with a woman from Hong Kong, it wasn't hard for him to find me. He told me to come back with him. I didn't want to, but I had come to the UK with his money.'

Vivien drank the rest of the wine and held out the glass for a refill. Arjun got up for the bottle, and helped himself to another beer from the fridge: he had bought half-a-dozen from the convenience store around the corner on his way back. She made him pour a full glass this time. He sat down and asked her, 'How did you meet Rohit?'

'I was selling some stuff then.' She looked at him, then added, 'pirated DVDs. Kunal must have told you. There was a Chinese guy who made them, I took them from him to sell. He was the one who told Sheng Li about where I was.'

'Kunal told me, yes. He also told me Rohit met Sheng Li.'

She shook her head and sighed, helped herself to another cigarette. After he had lit it and she had taken two puffs she continued.

'Rohit came looking for me. I hadn't contacted him for some time because my husband was there. There was a fight. I told him to leave.'

'And Rohit never saw you again, till he met you here.'

She nodded, a far-away look on her face now.

'How did he find you? He went to Shaoxing before that?'

'Yea, looking for the school. You went there too, yes? But this is China, every ten years everything changes. Nothing stays the same. Not even memories. He sent me an email before he left from India, to my old email address. I hardly check that anymore, I wouldn't have even seen his mail. But one day I logged in, to look for a mail regarding my UK classmate. And then I saw Rohit's mail. I told him to come to Hot Spot, it was not far from this apartment. So we met again, after ten years.'

'Wait, he came alone to meet you? At the bar?'

'Yes. I reached there quite late that night.'

'I thought he went to the bar with someone.'

Vivien shrugged, as if to say she hadn't met anyone else.

'He had mailed you several times while he was in London but you didn't respond?'

'I thought I would never see him again. I thought better he forgets me.'

'How many times did you meet him? I mean, how long did you spend with him?'

'Not much time, he left after two days. He had to go to office too.'

She drank her wine, and Arjun considered if they had spent the nights together.

'He told you he would be back?'

She nodded, and for the first time looked tearful, lowering her head and bringing a hand to her mouth. Arjun got up and went to the window and lit a cigarette. That morning when Kadambari Vats had come to his flat came back to him; a different city, in another country, but it could have been the same scene. Two women, the dead man, and what was he doing in-between, did any of it make sense? He shook the thought out of his head. Some distance away in the opposite flat the gamblers were still throwing down their cards, totally intent on their game. That was one of the 'olds' Mao had been unable to eradicate.

'What happened to him?' she asked. 'How did he die?'

'He told his family he was going to Mumbai on work, but he took leave and went to Kolkata. His body was found in a canal, strangled. Not a nice way to go.' Arjun came back to the table and sat down. 'Why was he in Kolkata? What could he have been looking for?'

'That man you said, Leong. What does he do in Kolkata?'

'He runs a restaurant. Before that he had a shoe shop.'

'Sheng Li has an uncle in Kolkata. I think maybe it's the same man.'

'Really?' Arjun picked up his phone, scrolled through the photos till he came to the pangolin-leather wallet, and showed it to Vivien. 'Recognize this?'

'Where you got this?'

'You recognize it, don't you? It was in Rohit's suitcase which he took to Kolkata.'

She nodded. 'I gave it to him. I mean, he took it from me, when I showed it to him. It was the only sample of my husband's I had, a couple of those wallets from a long time ago.'

'I don't follow you.'

'He stayed at my place. Rohit. I told him about Sheng Li, our marriage, how I returned with him to Hong Kong. He started dealing in drugs and after a while was arrested again. After that I came to Shanghai. He came looking for me again when he got out, but this time I told him to get lost, told him that I would go to the police. He knew the Chinese authorities would lock him up or throw him out. He's stayed away from China after that. Bloody bastard,' she added with venom.

'Why did Rohit take the wallet?'

'I think he wanted to help me.'

'I don't understand.'

She shook her head, smiling sadly. 'He was quiet, very sensitive. I told him Sheng Li hadn't given me a divorce, and the authorities still troubled me sometimes asking me where he was. He asked me what Sheng Li was doing at present and I told him, that he has a trading company in Bangkok and also deals in smuggled wildlife items. Some of it comes from India, Kolkata too. I think Rohit was trying to get information on Sheng Li.'

'And do what?'

'Have you heard of Operation Fox Hunt?'

'What's that?'

'How the Chinese government gets back corrupt people who have run off with lots of government money. They can get them back from anywhere in the world. The US and Australia are difficult though. They get back gangsters and crooks too. Just before he left, Rohit asked me for more details of Sheng Li's trading company, and what I knew about his uncle in Kolkata.'

'What do you know about his uncle?'

'I just knew the name of the shoe shop, Leong & Sons. I remember Sheng Li mentioning it once.'

'That's the name of the shop Mr Leong used to run. So ... you think Rohit was trying to find out about Sheng Li so that he could inform the Chinese authorities about him?'

'Yes, I think so.'

'And then he would come and see you again,' Arjun said, more to himself.

'How did you find out about me?' she asked. 'Kunal?'

'The photo I showed you. I found it in Rohit's house, he had hidden it.' Arjun took out the photo from his jacket pocket and gave it to Vivien, who looked at it with a sad smile.

'It's strange how our lives turn out yea?' she said. 'Can I keep this?'

'Sure. Thanks for talking to me.'

Vivien shrugged, drank the rest of her wine. 'But *why* are you here? Why come all the way to China? What you get from talking to me?'

'Hopefully I can clear his name. So that his wife and children can get the money from an insurance policy he had done for them—right now it's a suspicious death, and the insurance company isn't paying. Did you know he was married?'

'Yes, he told me,' Vivien said briskly. She checked her phone. 'I have to go.'

He saw her off to the door. She said she was going back to the bar. He asked for her number and she gave it to him.

'Why did you ask me not to wait there? Who was the guy with the short hair?'

'The owner's guy. Keeps an eye on everything, including me. I didn't want him talking to you. He's mixed up with all sorts of people. People who ... anyway, I hope whatever I told you was helpful.'

'I'm sure it'll be. I might message you if I have any more questions.'

'Do that,' she said. 'Bye Arjun.'

'Bye Vivien.'

He watched her walk away and turn toward the elevators. A faint flowery fragrance hung in the air after she was gone. Her words came back to him: *It's strange how our lives turn out.*

35

'What time is it over there?' Rhea asked.

Arjun groaned, put his feet down from the bed and looked at his phone.

'Nine in the morning. What time is it there, 6.30 a.m.? Why're you calling so early?'

'I'm going for a run. Thought you might be going out. Late night?'

'Yes. I managed to find her, Rhea. She was right here in Shanghai.'

'Really? Wow! I knew you could do it.'

'Thanks.'

'So what's next? You're returning tomorrow, right?'

'Yes, back to Delhi. I'll have to see after that. Maybe Bangkok or Kolkata. We'll talk when we meet.'

'Sure. Listen, I called because I spoke to a friend who's been to Shanghai. There's a jacket I want. Please? She said you could look in AP Plaza, near the Shanghai science museum, or in Nanjing road. I've sent you a photo of the jacket on WeChat. Please, Dad?'

Arjun sighed. 'Sure. I'll get it for you.'

'Thanks, Dad. See you after you get back.'

Arjun hung up, then went to the bathroom where

he looked at his haggard face in the mirror. Bangkok or Kolkata, what did it matter he thought, it was all pointless in the end. The previous night after Vivien had left, he sat on the bed watching the card game in the opposite high-rise as he thought about the strange story of her life, and had finished all the beer in the fridge. But now after a hot shower and a shave and a cup of tea he felt revived, and re-motivated.

He went up to the WorldView office to see Tommy, and found him at the desk inside the front door, talking to someone on the phone in English.

'Yes, yes, I do that don't worry. Yes, Xian, Nanjing and Beijing. I will get the tickets done. Thank you, have a good day!'

He hung up and explained to Arjun, 'Old customer. How can I help please? You want to travel some place?'

'I'm leaving tomorrow,' Arjun said, and the other slapped his forehead with a palm.

'I forget, sorry. When you leave you return the room card, ok? Office is open twenty-four hours.'

'I'll do that. Listen, I wanted to ask you something. About my friend Rohit who was here, also staying in room 1201.'

Tommy nodded, even as he started typing on the computer in front of him.

'Did he talk to you about his return flight or anything?'

'Oh ya,' Tommy said, 'I change his ticket for him.'

'Changed his ticket?'

'Yes, I cancel his Shanghai–Delhi ticket and book two new tickets, Shanghai to Bangkok, and Bangkok to Delhi.

He tell me he had some work in Bangkok.'

Arjun nodded. 'And the Shanghai–Delhi ticket was done by...'

'By his company.'

'Did he mention anything about coming back?'

'Yes. He said he wanted the same room. I told him no problem, you just mail me.'

'Well, thanks.' Arjun got up to leave.

'If you meet him tell him I say hi, ok?' Tommy said.

'Ok,' said Arjun.

Of the two locations Rhea had mentioned, Nanjing East road was closer, but Arjun decided to go to AP plaza which was across the Huangpu river in Pudong (the side he was on was Puxi). He took the metro from Jing'an station, going by the green line he had used to get to the Bund a few days earlier, and carried on to the Lujiazui, Donchang Road and Century Avenue stations, getting down at the last one.

He came out of Century Avenue station to a wide road bordered by commercial highrises with manicured grounds over which towered a group of three immense skyscrapers; the tallest, a spiralling structure called the Shanghai Tower, still had work going on right at the top. Walking around, Arjun found the building he was looking for, a shiny black office highrise, and bought a cup of coffee from a snack bar at the bottom and sat down with it on one of the concrete barriers beside a garden with a small pond and a bamboo grove. The building before him was where the offices of Zhejiang Huasheng Medicine Co. Ltd. were housed, where Chen Song worked, but Arjun wasn't there to meet him;

he had just wanted to retrace Rohit's route to work while in Shanghai, to see if it told or suggested anything to him. So Rohit had stopped by Bangkok; the only reason Arjun could think of was Sheng Li's trading company.

The coffee and a cigarette over, he retraced his steps back to the station and from there went one stop ahead on the same line, to the Shanghai science museum station. AP plaza was below Century Square, accessible from the metro station itself. It was a vast underground market, a warren of shops selling all kinds of items, from silk (which could be tailored there) to fake Lego to childrenswear to souvenirs to electronics. Arjun found the jacket Rhea had wanted, in her size, added two knockoff Super Dry t-shirts for himself, and managed to bargain to 300 yuan below what the saleslady had quoted. Twice as he walked around, he noticed behind him when he looked back a man in black trousers and jacket seemingly loitering in his trail. He took no notice: by this time tomorrow he would be at the airport, checked-in into his Delhi flight.

Arjun came out of the market with a large plastic bag in hand, and walked to Century Square—a raised, landscaped area with flower beds and fountains, and a direct line of sight through them to the skyscrapers of Pudong—before going along Century Avenue again: down to Century Park. He walked past the entrance towards the large Jingtian lake, where a cold wind was picking up off the grey water, scattering the yellow leaves from the same maple-like trees. There were hardly any people about, and he felt the mood of sadness and resignation that had come upon him in Kolkata: it was time for him to return.

Walking back to the metro station along an underground route lined with shops (half of them were shuttered: they reminded him of the empty apartment blocks in Shaoxing) he stopped to have a passable lunch of duck and noodles, Miao or Sichuan food, with the taste of Sichuan peppercorn in it, what they called mejenga in Assam he remembered. Like in India, places where lots of officegoers went to have lunch seemed to be a better bet. He headed back to the other side of the city, but on an impulse got down at the People's Square station. The station was immense, one of the largest in the world he supposed, and he came out onto the wide Renmin Avenue.

Arjun went leisurely along the avenue, then turned around the Grand Theatre and walked over to Nanjing West road with its cinemas and old hotels; to one side was People's Park, and he went in and sat down on a bench amid a rustling bamboo grove listening to a jazz guitarist performing while he had an ice cream. He tossed in some coins into the busker's guitar case on his way out, and then rode the metro one stop from Nanjing West Road station back to Jing'an Temple station. He was walking back along the side of the temple, skirting the outdoor tables of the coffee shops, when out of the corner of his eye he saw someone approaching him from one of the temple side entrances.

'Excuse me, you have a light?'

It was a middle-aged Chinese man, slim, with a lined face that hinted at some past hardship. He was wearing trousers and a plain dark-blue jacket and had a crewcut. Something made Arjun look around, and siting at one of the tables, apparently busy with his phone, was the man in black from AP Plaza. So, they had decided to make contact.

'How did you know I smoke?' he asked, to which the other man just shrugged.

He took out his lighter and gave it to the man, who lit a cigarette from a packet and then offered one to Arjun. He took it and the man lit it for him.

'Thanks,' the man said, smiling and showing yellow nicotine-stained teeth. 'Where you from?'

'India,' Arjun said, 'Yindu.'

The man nodded, still smiling. He handed back the lighter.

'So, what are you doing in China?'

'Travelling. Sightseeing.' He raised the plastic bag. 'Shopping.'

'Good, good,' the man said. 'Can I buy you a coffee? You're our neighbour, you helped me, so I should do something for you.'

'How did I help you?'

The man raised his cigarette.

'Well, you gave me a cigarette too.'

'One good turn deserves another,' the man said. 'Isn't that what they say. Come, please. Don't worry.'

Arjun followed him to a round table under a glossy brown awning; it was a different shop from where the man in black sat, facing them.

'Sit,' the man said to him, 'I'll go and get the coffee.'

He sat there wondering what it was all about. He was calm—there was nothing illegal he had done, and he was flying out in less than twenty-four hours—but a small voice of caution told him to stay alert: he had no way of knowing who these men were exactly. The man returned holding a tray with two cappuccinos on it and packets of sugar and stirring sticks. He set the tray down on the table.

'Is it okay?' he asked, still standing, and Arjun nodded.

'Or maybe I should have got tea? You Indians drink a lot of tea.'

'So do the Chinese,' Arjun said. 'But we drink milk tea.'

The man sat down, a delighted smile appearing on his face.

'Just like our two countries,' he said, spreading his palms. 'Two different systems.'

How they loved their symbolism, Arjun thought. The man extended a hand.

'You can call me Zhang.'

'Arjun Arora,' Arjun said, shaking the other's calloused hand. 'But I don't have to tell you that, do I?'

Zhang shook his head, stirred sugar in his coffee, and took a sip.

'We know you are ex-army, we know you are a detective, and we know you are going back to India tomorrow. What we don't know is why you're here.'

'I told you what I'm here for.'

'What's your interest in Vivien Chan?'

When Arjun hesitated, Zhang went on: 'Rohit Vats came and met her. Then you meet her. What is the purpose, I'm just curious.'

Arjun sighed and looked at the people walking past. It was starting to get dark and a chilly wind had picked up.

'Who sent you?' he asked Zhang in return. 'Sheng Li?'

Zhang stared at him, then burst out laughing. The man in black looked up from his phone.

'Sheng Li? *We* are after Sheng Li. You understand?'

Something clicked in Arjun's mind. He asked, 'Operation Fox Hunt?'

Zhang nodded. 'Exactly.'

'I guess I can call you Agent Zhang then?'

'As you wish.'

'So, what's his crime? Is he an enemy of the revolution?'

Zhang smiled coldly. 'Times change, but a criminal is always a criminal. A *jianghu*.'

Arjun pushed his coffee aside and leaned over the table. 'Rohit Vats knew Vivien from London, many years ago. When he came to China, he was looking for her. Soon after he got back to India, he was killed. In Kolkata. I'm trying to find out what happened, so that his family can claim an insurance policy. *That's* what I'm doing here. Am I in any trouble, Agent Zhang?'

'You seem honest, that's good. No, no trouble. In fact, why we not help each other? You think Sheng Li is connected to this death, yes?'

'Yes.'

'We've been after him for a long time. If you could lead us to him...'

'What do you mean?'

'He visits India, Kolkata. The Chinese settlement there. We cannot operate in your country. But we have an embassy there ... you understand?'

He understood, and it astonished him, but he hid his surprise well.

'You get Sheng Li, what do I get?'

'Like I said, one good turn deserves another. In the future, I could be of use to you.'

'Maybe.'

'Consider it, ok? We are two old civilizations, it would benefit both our countries if we cooperated. You and I could make a small start.'

'I'll think about it.'

Agent Zhang stood up to leave. He placed a piece of paper on the table, just a telephone number and an e-mail address written on it.

'Have a safe journey home, Mr Arora.'

With that, he was walking away towards the rear of Jing'an temple. The man in black had already disappeared. Something struck Arjun then, and he called out, 'Hey, Zhang!'

Agent Zhang stopped, and walked back. Arjun stood up.

'I was just wondering,' he said, 'would you know where I could buy a copy of Mao's red book?'

Agent Zhang raised his eyebrows.

'Don't worry, I'm in no danger of becoming a Communist,' Arjun said. 'It's for a friend.'

'You should get one for yourself too. You'll get it at Yuyuan Garden, in the shops.'

'Will they be open now?'

'If you hurry you should be able to make it. Three stops east on line 14.'

'Thanks,' said Arjun, pocketing the card and heading for the Jing'an metro station.

When he got to the entrance he looked back, but Agent Zhang had disappeared as well.

36

The taxi sped past highrises and over the river, then past the administrative areas and the warehouses and canals in Pudong to the international airport: two terminals facing each other, planes rising up into the sky every few minutes, then the vastness of the terminal inside, with stern-faced security men keeping a watch. Later, glimpses from the window: brown farmland stretching out to infinity, a silvery canal running through it in an arrow-straight line; undulating mountains of a dry green colour with winding roads and scattered settlements. Arjun was gripped by a nostalgia for places he would never go and people he would never meet.

Now that he was leaving, he could finally admit to himself the grudging admiration he felt for this opaque country, the sheer bloodymindedness that had been required to take it over and then turn it upside down in the pursuit of a new society. *It's strange how our lives turn out.* He thought of Vivien and Rohit, of Sonali and himself and Poppy Barua. They weren't serving drinks on the flight, and Arjun watched a Russian science fiction movie followed by a Chinese crime melodrama involving two brothers; it could well have been a Bollywood movie. He raised the window blind to see the sun setting towards the west and turning the horizon a deep pink even as the clouds below them darkened into night.

Delhi seemed shabby and dusty, the infrastructure inadequate, the wretched urban poor huddled in corners. This should have been China, Arjun thought peevishly, they would fix it all in a week. But it was thankfully cooler, and he was glad to be back in his flat. Down below in the park there were stacks of bamboo poles, wood planks, and tin sheets waiting to be carted away; he had forgotten that Durga puja had come and gone. There was some Blender's Pride left in a bottle and he made himself a drink, opened a packet of Double Happiness from the two cartons he had brought with him, and sat outside on the balcony thinking about how to go about the Vats case.

He called Rhea and told her he was back; she said she would come over the next day to get her jacket. For dinner he ordered tandoori roti and chicken curry from the Punjabi dhaba in Market No. 3. As he ate while watching the news on a Hindi channel, his mind was preoccupied with the offer Agent Zhang had made him. A quote from Mao's little red book, which he had gone through on the flight, came to his mind: *Just because we have won victory, we must never relax our vigilance against the frenzied plots for revenge by the imperialists and their running dogs (the Chinese reactionaries).* It actually seemed to Arjun more like something from Sun Tzu.

By 10 a.m. the next morning, he was at the office updating his employees on the Vats case: he had woken early and already updated his own notes. The four of them listened to him with attention, Liza Thomas taking down notes in a pad. When Arjun had finished his account, Ujjwal Negi was the first one to put forward a question.

'Was Rohit looking for Sheng Li in Bangkok?'

'I think so. I found his legit company through Google, they have an office in Yaowarat, Bangkok's Chinatown. Phoenix Trading.'

'But why?' piped up Shyamali Kundu. 'What would his *motivation* have been?'

Arjun looked around at them. Liza spoke up.

'Not something straightforward,' she said, 'he must have been looking at somehow trapping Sheng Li ... thus helping Vivien. Remember, the last time Rohit had seen Vivien in London, Sheng Li had tried to chase him off. Revenge, a favour for an old flame. Like I said, not straightforward.'

'Yes,' Negi agreed, 'that seems the most probable motive. Looking at his profile, one can see he wasn't really the criminal type.'

'And that led him to Kolkata,' Arjun added.

Shyamali raised a hand. 'Okay, assuming that's true, how would it help for *us* to go after Sheng Li?'

'I doubt he would have carried out the killing himself,' Arjun said. 'Find the killers, and Mrs Vats and her children get the insurance money.'

'And how will you do that?' Shyamali asked.

'The sub-inspector. And Mr Leong, I think I'll have to go see him again. He knows something. And, talking about Sheng Li,' Arjun paused, having not told them yet about his encounter with Agent Zhang, 'there's something I guess you all should know.'

After he told them there was silence for a moment. Then Negi spoke up.

'They want you to help extradite him? That's ... crazy!'

'Not extradite ... just help them catch him. In Kolkata, where he would least expect it.'

'But ... how will they get him out?' Liza questioned. 'It's impossible!'

'I'm sure they'll think of a way,' said Arjun. 'A flight. Getting to Nepal by road.'

'It sounds dangerous!' Shyamali was flustered now.

'Then again, it might help us too,' said Arjun, and, almost to himself, 'the sub-inspector is the key to it all.'

No one spoke. The murder investigation was veering off into a far darker place now. Arjun reached for his backpack on the glass-top table before the sofa, opened it and took out a couple of souvenirs and duty-free chocolates for his employees.

'How was it, sir?' Shyamali asked. 'How was China?'

'How was it?' He recalled what Poppy Barua had said, that night, about it being more like a separate world than another country. She had been right. He wondered whether he should call her.

'Yes, how was it, tell us,' Liza Thomas chimed in.

'Well, the first thing is,' said Arjun, 'that it's more like a separate world than another country.'

'One question Arjun ji,' Chandu interrupted in Hindi. 'What language do they use over there?'

'A standard form of Chinese. Mandarin. Do you want to learn it?'

He shook his head. 'No. So they don't use English over there?'

Arjun glanced at Liza; it seemed the language war wasn't over yet.

'Not much, but a lot of people learn it, even in school.'

Chandu nodded gravely, as though confirming an important point with himself.

'Go make us some tea, Chandu,' said Arjun.

While Chandu went over to the pantry corner to make tea on the stove, Arjun started telling them about his journey on the bullet train to Shaoxing.

Later in the evening, when Rhea came over to get her jacket and a few things he'd bought for her—a tracksuit, chocolates, cosmetics—he tried to tell her about his trip, but she was more interested in his method of deduction.

'I thought you had given up,' she said, as they sat on the sofa drinking the coffee she had made. 'What changed your mind?'

'I had given up. But then I ran over everything I knew, and what struck me was something Chen Song had said. He said Rohit *had wanted to go* to Hot Spot. And *that* was set off by what the taxi driver told Vivek Kaul about me: "your friend wanted to come, so I brought him". Regarding the place where the school had been.'

'But *wanted to go* ... maybe he had read about the place on the internet?'

'Yes, but I also thought ... maybe he wanted to check out the place with a local first, and then return when Vivien was there?'

'A tenuous connection,' sniffed Rhea.

'But I proved it, didn't I? Listen, *everything* about this case has been tenuous so far.'

Rhea laughed. 'I know, going to China because you found a hidden photo!'

'Now if I can just work out the Kolkata endgame...'

Rhea's face suddenly turned grave. 'You'll be careful, won't you? Rohit was killed by these people.'

'I will, don't worry. Let's order something for dinner, then we can watch the movie.'

'Let me look at the menu cards,' she said, and got up and went over to the dining table. 'What a mess, you should clean this table!'

'Too late for that.'

He watched her, content that she was there, glad that she would stay the night in her old room. From a small child to a grown woman; how quickly time had gone by! His father's story of the boy drowning in the Hooghly suddenly came to mind, and he felt guilty at the thought of how few times he had thought of his father these past few days.

'Pasta, followed by cheesecake. Ok?' asked Rhea.

'Sure.'

The movie was a relatively new Chinese one called *A Touch of Sin* by Jia Zhangke; he had picked up the DVD from a store on one of his walks around the Jing'an area. Four visceral stories set across a changing China had both father and daughter engrossed, and its animal motif—snakes, a monkey, cattle, a horse—indirectly reminded Arjun of his case. Sheng Li was getting animal parts out of Kolkata through someone: that was the key to tracing him.

After the movie they had their dinner which had been delivered, and as they ate at the dining table—he was dry tonight, drinking only the Coke that had come with the pasta—Rhea brought up an unexpected topic.

'Dad, how long has it been since you and Mama have been apart?' she asked.

He coughed. 'Not long. Since we've been divorced.'

'In total. From the start.'

'Oh ... four years. I think.'

Strange how it didn't seem to matter anymore, he thought.

'You know ... it's okay if you ... like ... have someone around, you know? You could use the company.'

'You're there if I want company.'

'You know what I mean.'

'Yes. Noted. Ok? Some more pasta?'

If anything, it had suddenly and uncomfortably reminded him of Agnes Pereira, the young girl from the missing Bollywood actress case. Rhea would have forgotten about it though: moving on, the privilege of the young. Me on the other hand, I'm a dinosaur, he thought as he stood out on the balcony afterwards smoking a cigarette. He thought of Poppy Barua, thought of calling her, took out his phone, then decided against it. He wasn't going to give in just yet. Or was he? In the end he sent her a text message: BACK IN DELHI. SORRY ABOUT THAT NIGHT. He couldn't think of anything more to say, and sent it.

37

Two days later, early in the evening, he was sitting in a sweet shop in Kalighat, not far from the temple there, drinking tea and trying an assortment of sweets which SI Shankar Munda insisted on ordering.

'This one, try this one, Arjun ji. Unique flavour!'

Arjun, not too fond of sweets, dutifully spooned a bite and said it was good. Even the owner and the child workers were looking on. He had reached Kolkata at midday and checked into the same guest house in Gariahat. The sub-inspector had asked him to come to Kalighat, saying it was nearby, and wait in this particular sweet shop, and had turned up himself a while later in his police Gypsy. Now he was leafing through the pages of Mao's red book of quotations which Arjun had got for him, chuckling to himself as he did so.

'What a genius,' he remarked. 'Listen to this, Arora ji. *Every Communist must grasp the truth, "Political power grows out of the barrel of a gun."* From "Problems of War and Strategy", November 6, 1938.'

'Yes. See the one at the end of page 233, about investigations.'

SI Munda turned to the page, and read out: '"*Investigation may be likened to the long months of pregnancy, and solving a problem to the day of birth."* Ok, I will keep that in mind!'

'Now, regarding *our* investigation,' Arjun said, 'let me give you an update.'

Arjun proceeded to tell the other man about tracking down Vivien Chan in Shanghai, and what she had told him about Rohit Vats. For the time being he kept quiet about Zhang's request.

'So that means Rohit must have contacted Mr Leong?' SI Munda said.

'I think we can assume that. I'll go and talk to him again. What about Anil Sinha?'

'Mr Sinha is an interesting fellow. Seems there was an inquiry against him two years ago. Suspected dealings with wildlife traffickers. But nothing happened to him. I'm planning to bring him in for questioning.'

'When?'

'Tomorrow. When are you going to see Mr Leong?'

'Tomorrow morning.'

'I'll pick up Sinha from his office tomorrow at midday.'

'Arrest warrant?'

'I'll get a bailable one. From a magistrate who owes me a favour.'

'Based on?'

'Anil Sinha's phone number. That'll be enough to hold him for twenty-four hours.'

'Twenty-four hours?'

'Ok I'll try for forty-eight hours. You can come see him too after you're done in Tangra.'

Arjun nodded. 'Ok. Hopefully tomorrow we find out

the link between these people and Sheng Li.'

'Don't worry, it will work out,' said SI Munda. 'Acha, we've not had dal puri yet? Ei, chotu, get us some radhaballabi! And more tea!'

At half-past eleven the next morning, Prasenjit drove his taxi through the inner lanes of Tangra and stopped near the entrance to Shanghai restaurant. Arjun asked him to wait up ahead and got down. He walked past the high discoloured walls and went through the doorway of the restaurant. Standing in the covered courtyard, he saw in the open storage area under translucent roofing sheets the workers and Mr Leong at a table, smoking and chopping vegetables. The young waiter from his previous visit was washing dishes at the tap set at ground level. In the kitchen a worker attended to a steamer set on the stove, while the restaurant's coloured glass-and-wood door was open, no customers inside yet. Then they noticed him, and Mr Leong got up and came over. He had a lit cigarette stuck in a corner of his mouth and was dressed in the same work clothes as before, his sleeves rolled up.

'You! What you come again here for?'

Arjun considered him; today he wasn't going to beat a retreat.

'The restaurant is open, isn't it? I want to have some noodles. And I want to talk to you about your nephew, Sheng Li. I met his wife Vivien in Shanghai last week.'

Arjun indicated that the other man join him, and walked into the restaurant, where he sat down at a table in the far corner. Mr Leong followed him inside slowly. He placed two pale, veined hands on a chair and looked down at Arjun, then drew the cigarette out of his mouth.

'Who are you?' he asked in his raspy voice.

'Arjun Arora. I've come from Delhi, I'm a detective.'

'Just now you said you came from Shanghai.'

'Shanghai to Delhi, then to Kolkata.' He held up the photo of the pangolin-leather wallet in his phone once more. 'I think someone called Rohit Vats from Delhi came and met you and asked you about this wallet? He was killed here in Kolkata some time back.'

'Make up your mind man,' Mr Leong growled. 'Last time you said he was missing.'

'It was my first time meeting you, I didn't want to alarm you. Now I feel like I know you better.'

Mr Leong snorted and took a drag on his cigarette. Arjun placed a plastic bag on the table.

'Which is why I brought you something from China.'

Mr Leong picked up the bag and looked inside: there were a couple of packets of Double Happiness cigarettes. A thin smile appeared on the man's face.

'Sit down, please,' Arjun said. 'I just want to talk.'

Mr Leong then turned and yelled out something in Chinese. For a moment Arjun was worried about a worker appearing with a chopper, but it was only the Bengali waiter. Mr Leong spoke rapidly to him before sitting down. The waiter hurried away.

'Thank you for the cigarettes,' he said to Arjun. 'Chinese ones are the best.'

'I agree. Glad you like them.'

'Yes, he came to see me, this boy.' The elderly man's

speech had traces in it of Anglo-Indian English and Bengali. 'You showed me his photo last time. He took out the wallet, said he wanted to know where he could order more.'

'What did you tell him?'

Mr Leong shrugged. 'I told him to get lost. Long time since I did that business. It's true.'

'Do you know Anil Sinha? From the Kolkata Customs?'

Mr Leong shook his head. 'Why was this fellow killed?'

'That's what I'm trying to find out.'

'You're a ... detective?'

'Yes. Rohit Vats' wife hired me. Otherwise, she might not get a life insurance policy.'

'And how is my nephew connected to this?'

Arjun told him of the connections between Rohit, Vivien and Sheng Li. In between the waiter returned with a flask of herbal tea, and Mr Leong gave him further directions.

'Crazy fellow,' he said, sipping his tea, when Arjun finished. 'No wonder he ends up dead in Garfa.'

'I know Sheng Li deals in wildlife products, and I know he visits Kolkata. He must be visiting you too?'

'He comes sometimes, whether I invite him or not. He has some friends here.' Mr Leong suddenly spat on the floor. 'Useless fellows.'

'How is he related to you?' asked Arjun, lighting a cigarette of his own.

Mr Leong poured himself some more tea first. 'He's my cousin brother's son. Our fathers were brothers—there were three of them. My father and Sheng Li's father left Canton after the Communists took over, my grandfather told them it was safer that way. My father came here, to Calcutta, while Sheng Li's father moved to Hong Kong.'

'Where he had a restaurant in Quarry Bay?' Arjun asked, remembering what Vivien had told him.

'Yes. But Sheng Li ...' Mr Leong shook his head. 'He was a no-good fellow.'

'*Jianghu*?' Arjun asked.

Mr Leong nodded. '*Char sau bees admi*,' he said in Hindi.

'Who is his supplier here in Kolkata?'

'I don't know.' Mr Leong looked at Arjun and drank his tea unhurriedly. 'But ... ask me about wildlife product suppliers here in Calcutta, and I'll tell you what I know ... do you understand?'

Arjun understood. 'If I were a rich fellow from South-East Asia looking for animal products, who would I get in touch with here?'

'Let me tell you a story. When my father was running the shoe business in Tiretti Bazar, he had all sorts of *friends* coming to him. From Sikkim, Bhutan, Arunachal, Assam, Shillong. With all sorts of animal products. For a commission he would find buyers for them. Even overseas, Hong Kong and Taiwan. The wallet you saw, it was supplied from Taiwan. One of Sheng Li's suppliers. There was one fellow who came from Guwahati once with tiger bones. He was a Muslim, from Rajasthan. He was in Guwahati then, supplying beef to the zoo there for the tigers. Anyway, this fellow later moved to Calcutta to pursue this line of business. From what I hear he's very big now, and his relatives have come from Rajasthan to work for him. Only what I hear, understand, I have no contact with that sort of business nowadays.'

As if on cue the waiter entered with a tray.

'I understand. What's his name?'

'Muhammad Khan. Now for the rest, use your own intelligence.'

The food was laid out: clear soup, dumplings, noodles, and a pork dish.

'This is our special,' Mr Leong said, indicating the pork with a pair of chopsticks. 'Pork cooked with rice wine sediment. You can use chopsticks?'

'I can, yes.'

'Let's start then.'

They ate. The food was lightly flavoured and delicious: Hakka cuisine. The pork had a malty taste which Arjun loved.

'The three brothers,' Arjun asked as they ate. 'Any of them alive now?'

Mr Leong shook his head. 'They're all gone, even the youngest one. My father and Sheng Li's father used to send him money, and he built a large house in our old village in Guangdong. It was called Canton back then. Then during the Cultural Revolution they came looking for him. They took him to the fields and shot him. Afterwards they even sent a bill to my grandfather for the cost of the bullet. So that is our story. Here, have some more tea.'

The elderly man came out to the lane to see Arjun off.

'Can I ask you something?' said Arjun. 'What's that shiny stuff over there?'

He pointed to the open drain on the other side of the road ahead of them.

'Chromium, used in tanning,' Mr Leong said. 'Highly polluting stuff. The tanneries are supposed to have moved from here, but there are still some who do it. With the help of the police,' he added.

They came to the end of the lane and Mr Leong stopped.

'Thank you for your help,' Arjun said.

'What will you do now?' Mr Leong asked him.

'Work with the Kolkata Police to find out who killed Rohit Vats.'

'What about Sheng Li?'

Arjun shrugged. 'From here I go back to Delhi.'

Mr Leong looked at him for a moment, then said, 'A lot of overseas Chinese come to Tangra during Chinese New Year. Revisiting their roots. Do you understand?'

'I do. Why tell me that?'

'That too, you might understand.'

With that Mr Leong turned and walked back towards his restaurant, and Arjun walked to where Prasenjit had parked the taxi.

38

At the Garfa police station there were two men sitting inside the men's lock-up. When Arjun walked past the thick bars, he recognized one of the men as Biman Bose, Section Officer under Anil Sinha. The other man was slim and neatly dressed and wore glasses. In the IO room SI Munda was stretched out in his chair talking to a colleague working at another desk. He sat up when he saw Arjun entering.

'How did it go, Arjun ji?'

The sub-inspector's white uniform was grimy by now, with patches of sweat under the armpits. Arjun felt a pang of sympathy for the man, remembering his words at their first meeting: *it is in these kind of things that my life is getting spent.*

'*Bhalo*,' he said in Bengali, and both policemen beamed in appreciation.

'Kolkata seems to suit you,' the sub-inspector said. 'What did you find out from Leong?'

'He gave me a name.'

SI Munda looked at him expectantly.

'But first,' Arjun said, 'who are the two you have in the lock-up? I thought one was Biman Bose.'

'Biman Bose and Anil Sinha, I managed to get a warrant

for both,' SI Munda said, and grinned. 'I was just about to go and start their interrogation.'

'Together?'

'Separately. My colleague Dipankar will handle Bose.'

Arjun looked around, and the other policeman nodded at him.

'The name Leong gave you...' said SI Munda.

'Why don't you talk to them first? I wouldn't want to prejudice you in any way.'

SI Munda thought about it, then nodded. 'Okay, that's fine.'

'Could I be present at the interrogation?'

'Sorry, that's not possible, you know.' SI Munda stood up and tugged at his pants. 'But wait here. We'll go and try some local food afterwards. Ok? Dipankar, come.'

After they had left Arjun made himself as comfortable as he could in the chair and took out his phone. To his surprise there was a reply from Poppy Barua to his message: IT'S OKAY. CALL ME WHEN YOU'RE FREE. He told her that he was in Kolkata, and said he would call her when he got back to Delhi. He felt pleased: the lines of communication were open once more. He messaged Rhea; she was out for a movie with friends, girls all of them. SI Munda's colleagues came in and went out, one settling himself at his desk to laboriously write out a report. Arjun scrolled through some news on China on his phone.

Finally, after a little more than an hour-and-a-half, SI Munda reappeared.

'Arjun ji, let's go.'

Following the sub-inspector out of the station, he

stopped at the lock-up, where Biman Bose and Anil Sinha had been returned to. He heard Bose say in Bengali to the neatly dressed man that this was the crime branch person who had also come to the Customs office. Anil Sinha stared at Arjun coldly, no emotion displayed on his face. Arjun wondered what the two had told their interrogators.

'Yes, they both gave us one name,' SI Munda said, before adding scornfully, 'government officers, they open their mouths even if we just *describe* torture.'

'Even Anil Sinha?'

SI Munda laughed. 'He was first. When I said I would take him to the canal where we found Rohit's body and push his face into the black water. If he drowned, we would say he tried to run away.'

It sounded to Arjun not too different from how the Delhi Police might have handled the interrogation. They were sitting in a dimly-lit restaurant in Dhakuria waiting for their dinner. The sub-inspector was in civil dress, first having taken Arjun to Haltu, where he had waited in the Gypsy in a narrow street while SI Munda had entered a building—in which he stayed on the first floor with his family—and come out a while later having changed. A waiter now came up to them with two fresh lime sodas.

'What was the name?' Arjun asked.

SI Munda smiled. 'You first.'

'All right. Muhammad Khan.'

The sub-inspector nodded. 'They took that name too.'

'He's from Rajasthan and used to supply the zoo in Guwahati with beef for their tigers before moving to

Kolkata. He has several family members working for him.'

'Then he shouldn't be hard to track down,' SI Munda said, and took out his phone to make a call.

Arjun sipped his lime soda: it wasn't bad, but an aperitif before the Bengali meal the sub-inspector had ordered for them would have been even better.

'Sorry I didn't take you for any drinks,' SI Munda said, 'but I really cannot be in any such place.'

'You don't drink?'

'Stopped. There was an incident. After that I never drink. Also I don't like to go to places where people are drinking—I'm afraid I might start again.'

'What happened?' Arjun asked.

SI Munda studied his large hands for a moment. 'There was a boy in the lock-up, eighteen or nineteen. Arrested for theft. He threatened me, said he had connections. One of our officers from the thana had given a party. I drank there, several pegs. When I got back to the thana I went into the lock-up and beat up the boy. Later he died, internal haemorrhage.' The sub-inspector took a deep breath and exhaled before resuming. 'Nothing happened to me, I was lucky. My superiors saved me. The boy's connections didn't bother about him. But his parents ... when they came and met me, and asked me what had happened ... I couldn't say anything to them. From that time I stopped. More than a year now.'

Arjun nodded. The sub-inspector's story reminded him of something in his past, something he had spoken about only once in his life so far. He wasn't going to mention it again.

'You feel remorse for what you did, and have tried to change, that's what is important.'

'You really think so?'

'Yes. Cheers.'

Arjun raised his glass of lime soda, and SI Munda did the same.

'So, Mr Leong told you about Khan's life story?' the sub-inspector asked.

'Yes. Sounds very likely that he's Sheng Li's supplier.'

'We'll find out where he is. After that ...'

'A raid?'

The sub-inspector nodded.

'Could be a big case for you.'

'I'm thinking about that too.'

Their food arrived: prawns cooked with taro leaves using mustard oil, fish curry, rice. They started eating, using their hands.

'Dhakai cuisine, from East Bengal. You might find it bit heavy.'

'It's delicious,' Arjun said, helping himself to more of the prawns.

He wondered how to broach the subject of Agent Zhang's offer, and decided to wait till after dinner. A waiter came by with a kadhai of rice, and both men were served more. SI Munda told the waiter that they would have mishti doi after their meal.

The sweet curd over, both men sat back in their chairs, sated. For once Arjun had no desire for a drink, now he just wanted to climb into bed after a last cigarette.

'You know, something interesting happened to me on

my last day in China,' he began, and proceeded to tell SI Munda about his encounter with Agent Zhang and the offer he had made Arjun.

The sub-inspector listened quietly, his frown deepening. It didn't seem like a good sign to Arjun.

'So that is what he proposed, basically,' he said at the end.

'And you agreed to it?' SI Munda asked, disbelief in his voice.

Arjun shrugged. 'I've considered it.'

'Are you crazy! How can this be allowed?'

Arjun felt a twinge of irritation. This was the man who had got Anil Sinha to cooperate by threatening to drown him in a canal.

'Think about how it can be made to happen. It could benefit us both in the long run.'

'Those people are our enemies, Arjun ji.' He shook his head. 'I'm sorry, I can't allow this to happen.'

Arjun felt a slow deep anger rising within him. After all that he'd been through. Before he could say anything though the sub-inspector's phone rang. SI Munda picked it up and listened, saying *acha* and *thik ache* several times. He hung up and looked at Arjun.

'Muhammad Khan has been located.'

39

The following evening Arjun found himself in the back of one of Garfa police station's white Gypsys with two constables and an inspector for company. SI Munda and another constable who was driving were up-front. They moved slowly through the clogged traffic on Sealdah flyover, exhaust fumes swirling through the open back of the Gypsy and vehicle horns blaring around them. Arjun saw, through the cars and buses, discoloured old buildings to one side of the flyover, while on the other side were the lighted tracks of the Sealdah railway yard, where a couple of blue-coloured coaches of the Eastern Railway waited for an engine.

When SI Munda had called Arjun in the afternoon and asked him if he wanted to accompany them on the raid he had agreed, and, turning down the sub-inspector's offer of being picked up on the way, had taken a taxi to the Garfa thana. SI Munda had spent the day organizing the raid. Arjun was surprised to find that he hadn't bothered to inform the local thana where the raid was to take place, till he found out that it was because of reasons of secrecy and, even more important, SI Munda had the backing of an influential ACP at police headquarters. Which was why he had possibly gotten off in the lock-up death case.

The constables and the other inspector, a slim Bengali youth by the name of Saurav Sanyal, treated him politely once they were in the vehicle headed north across the city. It was a first for Arjun; the Delhi Police had never offered him this courtesy, but then, he tried to keep himself at arm's length from them. He was filled with a vague tension: the upcoming raid, the sub-inspector's reaction the previous night when he had brought up Agent Zhang's offer.

They came down the flyover, and some distance ahead at a crossing the driver turned right onto a smaller road. SI Munda started talking tersely on his phone in Bengali, possibly with his source. Their surroundings grew darker, with crumbling housing blocks set back from the road—they looked like government property. The Gypsy took a couple of turns on the narrow road. A mood of tense expectation had settled upon the men inside. They came out to a slightly larger road, and now there were more lights and more people, some of them wearing skullcaps.

Arjun saw, from his rear seat, a modest-sized but shiny new mosque, followed by a couple of parked trucks and then a line of raw-brick buildings with what seemed like workshops at the ground level. There was a musty animal-like stench in the air. He guessed they were somewhere in the vicinity of Rajabazar. SI Munda said something to the constable driver, and the Gypsy came to a halt on the roadside. Across the road, on which scooters and pedestrians hurried past, was a biryani restaurant with its pots and pans on a table on the road while inside people sat on benches and ate. They got down from the Gypsy. Already there were stares being directed their way. SI Munda came up to Arjun.

'Stay at the back, ok?' he said. 'And be careful.'

'You know his exact location?' Arjun asked.

The sub-inspector nodded, and then indicated with a movement of his chin towards the raw-brick buildings. Arjun looked, and his eye was caught by a short, bearded man walking towards them talking on his phone. SI Munda made a movement of his palm, and the three constables and Inspector Sanyal fell in behind him. The bearded man reached the biryani restaurant, looked inside as though searching for someone, then turned around. The policemen started moving. The bearded man slipped into an alley, and SI Munda dropped in behind him.

Arjun followed Sanyal who was just before him. SI Munda was resourceful, no doubt about that. Following the rest of them into the alley, Arjun saw that the people squatting on the ground floor rooms of the buildings and working were making shoe brushes, from what looked like heaps of goat hair. The alley was narrow and turned left and right past small houses and general stores, kebab sellers fanning coals on tables or stands set into nooks and corners. People coming from the opposite direction turned to look at the file of policemen. From up ahead Arjun could hear snatches of the bearded man's conversation. A musty smell of too many people crowded into too little a space was in the air.

Suddenly they were in front of a large black gate, with a whitewashed building rising up behind it. The bearded man had stopped beside the gate, still talking.

'I was looking for him in the biryani place just now,' he was saying loudly in Bengali. 'He's there? With you? The bastard. Wait, I'm coming there now. Wait.'

With that he hurried off. Arjun looked as he passed: it wouldn't be a surprise if there was no call in the first place. A scrawny man in a guard's uniform who had been sitting on a stool before a nearby shop came up to the group and asked them what they wanted.

'You're the guard?' SI Munda asked. 'Open this gate.'

'Yes, I'm the guard, but who are you to just come and...'

SI Munda slapped him hard, then caught him by the scruff of the neck.

'Who am I?' he roared. 'I'm your bloody father! Open the gate!'

The guard did as asked: he opened a smaller gate set into the large gate. SI Munda stepped inside, dragging the guard in after him. The rest of the team followed, with Arjun bringing up the rear. The constables had their lathis, the inspectors had their pistols, but he had nothing in hand. He bent himself slightly and went through the open gate. There was a small open courtyard with piles of boxes and cartons, and he could see Sanyal going into the building through the high and narrow front door. Something caught his eye: he stopped and picked up a rusted piece of a thick iron construction bar. Then hurried in after Sanyal.

It was dim and stuffy inside, and Arjun could hear voices being raised up ahead. Women's voices shouting, and passing an open door, Arjun could see them: two middle-aged women in salwar kameez, standing inside a small kitchen. He moved on. The corridor opened out and a staircase came into view. A stout man in a lungi came running down the steps, while a few other men had emerged from rooms on the ground level, and were trying to obstruct SI Munda, their voices rising up in unison. Why were the police inside the house? Where was their warrant? Who were they looking for in a private residence?

'Step back all of you!' SI Munda yelled, his adrenaline flowing in him now. He raised his pistol. 'Where is Muhammad Khan? Where is he?'

'There's no one by that name here!' shouted the lungi-clad man, his eyes bulging out.

'We'll see about that!' SI Munda said. 'Sanyal, get all the rooms searched.'

Two constables started looking into the rooms on the ground floor, while another followed Sanyal—who had his pistol drawn too—up the stairs. The lungi-clad man followed them, yelling abuses now. SI Munda pushed past two young men blocking the corridor. Arjun was about to go up the steps, when a whiff of something like rotten meat made him stop. He moved along the corridor, and the smell grew slightly stronger. One of the two young men shoved him back, and he came forward and punched him hard, raising the iron bar to ward off the second man.

Then he heard something, a cry. He started running. An open door to his right: he had an impression of a large room with stacks of boxes and a strong stench emanating from it. There was no one inside, and Arjun headed for the open door at the end of the corridor. A gunshot rang out just as he jumped across the threshold, and he had only a moment to figure out what he was seeing: a small stretch of courtyard with a water pump at one end and lit by a high lamp, a youngster on the ground with blood seeping out from what looked like a bullet wound in his thigh and a meat cleaver beside him, a middle-aged man in trousers and a half-sleeve shirt pointing a pistol at SI Munda who stood with his arms half raised.

'Arjun!' the sub-inspector cried out, and as the man holding the gun turned to look, Arjun threw the rod at him in an underhand throw, striking him in the face. The sub-inspector took two strides, wrenched the hand holding the gun aside and grabbed the man's throat with his other hand. Arjun ran forward and caught hold of the other man's wrist too, and prised the gun free. SI Munda, one hand still on the man's throat, pushed him back till he came up against the back wall. Standing with the gun in his hand, he could smell the gunsmoke in the air.

'Muhammad Khan?' Arjun asked.

'Yes, this is the bastard,' SI Munda growled. 'Thought you could shoot me, ha?'

The rest of the men in the house appeared in ones and twos, followed by Sanyal and the constables. Arjun glanced down at the wounded youth, and picked up the meat cleaver.

'Put your hand on the wound and press on it,' Arjun told him.

Sanyal came up to SI Munda. The other men were being kept at a distance by the constables, but things could turn ugly at any moment, they knew.

'Should we get out of here?' he asked. 'Or...'

SI Munda looked at him, then shoved Khan aside and took out his phone.

'Watch him carefully,' he said, and Sanyal pointed his pistol at Khan, who seemed like a cool customer. Arjun shifted the cleaver from his left hand to his right and picked up the iron rod. If there was going to be a showdown in close quarters he was prepared. SI Munda was talking rapidly on the phone now, asking for men to be sent straight away, it was an emergency.

'The local thana?' Ajun asked him. 'You're letting them know?'

SI Munda shrugged. 'No problem. We have our man now.' Then to Sanyal, 'Handcuff this fellow!'

The sub-inspector came closer to Arjun and laid a hand on his shoulder.

'Thank you for saving my life bhai,' he said.

Arjun just nodded. He hadn't even thought about it till then. The two women came out now, and, upon seeing the youth on the ground, started wailing out loud. Sanyal, who had handcuffed Khan, looked at the men being held back by the three constables, then at SI Munda.

'Sir, are they coming soon?'

'They should be here any moment, Sanyal.'

40

Three months later, on a pleasantly chilly February evening, Arjun was at a table in Oly Pub on Kolkata's Park Street with a large Blender's Pride for company while on his phone he went through the latest draft e-mail for Sheng Li composed by himself and SI Munda. It was his third visit to the city in connection with the Vats case; Muhammad Khan and his nephew were behind bars following the Rajabazar raid, while Anil Sinha and Biman Bose were out and cooperating with SI Munda's investigation.

It hadn't taken long for the sub-inspector to get the truth out of Khan and his nephew. Not having got anything out of Mr Leong, Rohit Vats had picked Anil Sinha's name out of the Kolkata Customs website and given him a call; Biman Bose had picked up and, worried by what he heard from Rohit Vats about wildlife trafficking, had informed his senior officer Sinha, who had passed on Rohit's number to Khan, 'just to give him a warning'. Sinha told SI Munda that he had no knowledge of what had happened next: Khan and his nephew had called Rohit to a meeting at Kasba industrial estate at night on the pretext of providing him information, then strangled him and dumped the body in the Garfa nullah. According to Khan, he had taken the extreme step out of alarm: his most important customer Sheng Li had called him just a few days before that and mailed him a screenshot of Rohit Vats, saying that there was an Indian looking into his business.

SI Munda had contacted Rohit's office and the insurance company on behalf of the Kolkata Police to let them know that Rohit had been murdered and a case to that effect had been filed in his thana. Both SI Munda and Kadambari Vats had thanked Arjun for solving the case. The insurance pay out for Rohit's wife had been cleared by the company. It was all settled, except for Sheng Li. This was Arjun's personal project now. SI Munda had grudgingly agreed, unable to refuse the request of a man who had saved his life.

'Think of it as fulfilling Rohit Vats' last wish,' he had told the sub-inspector, even as he wondered whether *he* was doing this for Vivien's sake.

With the approval of SI Munda's protector, the ACP (who himself hadn't been told the full story; he thought it was something to do with Khan and his nephew's upcoming trial), SI Munda had made Khan use his phone to call Sheng Li and say that due to increased surveillance by government agencies he was switching over exclusively to encrypted email via VPN. Khan had been made to send an opening mail, and then Arjun and SI Munda had taken over. An elaborate story had been created—with the help of photographs supplied by Anil Sinha—about a large consignment of yarsagumba, the caterpillar fungus, a few kilograms of it, which had been seized on its way from Sikkim to Kolkata and was now in the safekeeping of Kolkata Customs. Arjun and SI Munda (writing on behalf of Khan) told Sheng Li that the consignment would be replaced with dried herbs with the help of an insider in the customs department, and that he was welcome to come and inspect the quality of the goods before purchase.

Sheng Li had taken the bait, and, as Arjun had calculated, agreed to come over during the Chinese New Year. No news of Khan and his nephew's arrest had appeared in the press, so Sheng Li accepted it when he had been told—over email—that the police had forgotten about Rohit Vats' murder. Even Khan and his lawyer didn't make much of the phone call and email; they presumed it had something to do with the chargesheet being prepared by the police. Arjun and SI Munda were the only people who knew about Agent Zhang and his offer (besides of course the employees of Nexus Security).

Now Arjun sipped his whiskey and went through the e-mail again. It was a weekend, and around him there were loud voices and laughter, but he concentrated at the task on hand. What was of utmost importance was preserving Khan's tone and style, which seemed to have been wrought by essay and comprehension books at school and possibly the tenders for beef he had submitted to Guwahati zoo. *Greetings, and hope you are in good health. Kindly inform as to date of travel, so necessary arrangements for replacing the stock can be undertaken. Interest in the consignment is high, and I urge you to finalise matters at the earliest.* Sheng Li's replies on the other hand tended to be brusque and to the point. From his last e-mail: *Noted. Sample looks good, I've already told you. I will come and check the stuff myself. Follow all precautions in the meantime.* Arjun sighed, and pressed the send button, then drained his glass and signalled to one of the red-jacketed waiters for a repeat. The mail had been sent: now it was up to Sheng Li to confirm that he was on his way.

At a nearby table a pretty short-haired woman in a dark saree and a cardigan laughed out loud; Arjun glanced in their direction, and she held his eye for a moment. His thoughts turned to Poppy Barua, as they often had during the past few weeks. They had messaged and spoken on the phone after Arjun had got back, but hadn't met yet; she was swamped with work, she said, but that would change by the time he was back from this trip. He was looking forward to it. A waiter with a small pail in hand approached, and Arjun motioned for some ice to be put into his drink. He had finished half of it when SI Munda appeared, in plainclothes, with both a sweater and a jacket to keep him safe from the cold.

'Arre, not feeling cold, Arjun ji?' he enquired as he sat down across the table.

Arjun was in an old pair of jeans and a light sports jacket.

'Come to Delhi and you'll know what the cold is. Want a drink? It'll warm you up.'

SI Munda smiled and brought his palms together.

'Don't tempt me. Acha, so you've sent the mail?'

'Yes. Once he replies we're set. Or not.'

'He'll come, don't worry,' the sub-inspector said, looking around the place. He turned to Arjun and shook his head. 'But I'm still worried. What are we doing, Arjun ji?'

Arjun looked at him for a while, then drank up his whiskey and stood up.

'Come on, we better get going.'

Half-an-hour later a taxi dropped them off near a popular restaurant in Tangra. Arjun paid the driver, and after the taxi drove off both men walked ahead and then down a smaller lane flanked by brick walls. They stopped at an iron gate and knocked; a small shutter opened and closed, and the gate opened. Mr Leong stood there in a light-blue tracksuit, reminding Arjun of a PT master of theirs from a school in Arunachal Pradesh decades ago. He closed the gate and asked SI Munda and Arjun to follow him.

It was a large structure, with a family shrine just inside the main entrance; there was a car and a motorcycle parked in the open ground floor, a badminton net strung between two posts, and some old machinery.

'This was a tanning unit before, now closed,' Mr Leong said, seeing Arjun looking.

They climbed up a flight of steps and into a sitting room which seemed to be out a Hong Kong movie from the '80s, right down to the patterned iron grilles on the windows. Mr Leong led them through to the kitchen where he asked them to sit at a round table. An elderly woman stood at the gas stove stirring something in a pot, while in a spacious inner storeroom two young men were swinging about what looked like lengths of dough. Mr Leong said something to the woman, then opened a cupboard and returned to the table with three small glasses and a bottle of what looked like rice wine. He poured out three glasses, and the woman brought them a plate of prawn crackers. She remained standing there looking at the two guests.

'Excuse me, what they are doing?' SI Munda asked Mr Leong, pointing toward the storeroom. He had met the restaurateur twice before, after Arjun's second trip.

'Making noodles for our lunar new year,' Mr Leong said. 'Three days away.'

Arjun looked at SI Munda. 'I thought you had left drinking.'

The sub-inspector smiled sheepishly. 'This is rice wine, I can have a little.'

The woman said something to Mr Leong, cackled with laughter, and went to the storeroom. The three men clinked their glasses together and sipped the wine. It tasted smooth and sweet and familiar to Arjun. Mr Leong noticed him looking at the bottle.

'Shaoxing rice wine,' Mr Leong said, 'you might have had it in China?'

'Yes, in Shaoxing,' Arjun said. 'So, whose place is this? The tannery?'

'My brother-in-law, my wife's cousin brother,' Mr Leong said, pointing a thumb toward the storeroom. 'They left for Canada some years ago. We'll be leaving too, after we sell this place and the restaurant.'

'Your children?'

'Already in Canada. Where are the cigarettes now, let me see.' Mr Leong got off his stool and rummaged in a wooden cabinet.

From China to Calcutta to Canada, Arjun thought. There was something sad about it, but something affirmative too: the ceaseless flow of life. Mr Leong came back to the table with a packet of Double Happiness.

'I saved a packet,' he said to Arjun, and offered him a cigarette. The two men lit up. From somewhere came the beat of a drum and chanting.

'They're practising the dragon dance for the new year,' Mr Leong told them.

Arjun savoured the flavour of the oven-baked Virginia tobacco. SI Munda cleared his throat. He was a bit flushed from the wine already.

'We sent the e-mail to Sheng Li,' he told Mr Leong. 'Now he just has to let us know if he's coming for the Chinese new year.'

Mr Leong nodded. 'He'll come. And he'll let you know on that day itself.'

'Anyone he would like to meet here in Tangra?' Arjun asked.

Mr Leong snorted. 'He'll come here. And meet some friends of his.'

'If he comes, which I'm hoping he will, where would be a good place to ... get hold of him?'

Mr Leong considered the question for a while. In the storeroom strands of noodles were appearing out of the roll of dough. SI Munda lit himself a cigarette as well.

'There is a festival, like a mela, in the grounds of the Chinese school here. I'm sure he'll turn up there to have a look. Once he leaves...' Mr Leong spread both his hands apart.

Arjun nodded. 'Why the school though?'

'Almost ten years now, no classes there. No more Chinese students. But Sheng Li studied there for a while.'

Arjun was surprised. 'I thought he grew up in Hong Kong.'

'He did. But for two years he and my brother were living here. There were some ... problems in Hong Kong. Then they went back. But when he comes he visits the school.'

SI Munda looked at Arjun, nodding his head.

'What does he look like?'

'Tall, muscular, short hair. He has a scar on his right cheek. Well dressed.'

'Anything or anyone we should keep an eye out for?' Arjun asked. 'His friends?'

'Not really. But there's a fellow he knows, from Kalimpong or Darjeeling, Tenzing. He's dangerous. A criminal.'

'What does he look like?' Arjun asked.

'You'll spot him easily. Tall, like Sheng Li. Has a ponytail. And only one eye.'

Mr Leong drained his glass, made them do the same, and refilled.

'We didn't say a toast,' he said, and lifted his glass.

Arjun and SI Munda raised theirs as well.

'To the coming new year,' Arjun said. 'Gong hei fat choy!'

Mr Leong smiled, and took a large gulp of his wine.

'One last question,' Arjun said. 'Why are you doing this? When I asked you the last time, you told me I might understand. I haven't. Isn't he family?'

'He is, but he is also a disgrace to the family,' Mr Leong said fiercely. 'Now, let us stop talking about him and enjoy the wine. *Ki bolen*, Sub-inspector Munda?'

SI Munda smiled tipsily and raised his glass.

41

As Mr Leong had predicted, Sheng Li replied (to Muhammad Khan) three days later, saying he would be arriving in Kolkata that afternoon, and would like to meet the following day to check the merchandise, in some out-of-the-way place where they wouldn't attract any attention. Arjun, who was at the same guest house in Gariahat as the first two times, and who hadn't signed out of his mail app on his phone, saw the mail straightaway. He then replied, setting up a meeting at a transporter's office in Posto Bazar the afternoon of the next day, adding that he would mail Sheng Li the exact address the next morning, after checking out the place once again. Then he called SI Munda with the news. The sub-inspector, who had grudgingly agreed to the whole operation in the first place, sounded less than happy.

'Posto Bazar? Why there?' he asked Arjun.

'Why not? It's out-of-the-way and a transporter's office sounds perfect.' He didn't tell SI Munda that his father had lived in the area as a child.

'How to pick him up there? Very crowded area.'

Arjun sighed, not knowing if the sub-inspector was being deliberately dense. 'Not there, we'll be waiting for him in Tangra. At the Chinese school. Today's the new year.'

'Oh ok. I see.'

'Yes. And I'll see you in the evening.'

He hung up, and opened a can of beer: he had bought a couple from the nearby wine shop the previous evening. As before, the doubts began gnawing at him. Why was he here? What guarantee was there of Sheng Li showing up? What if the smuggler stayed somewhere else, and decided to come to Posto Bazar from there? In the end he smoked a cigarette and went to have a shower, but not before sending a mail to the ID Agent Zhang had given him, saying that Sheng Li was landing in Kolkata that afternoon.

At 8 p.m. that night he was back in Tangra with SI Munda, this time in a Gypsy of the Garfa thana. The sub-inspector was in plainclothes, and in a slightly sullen mood, making his disapproval clear. Arjun noticed, but didn't say anything. With any luck the operation would be wrapped up by midnight. He went through the reply from Agent Zhang on the mail app on his phone once again: a WeChat number had been provided; Arjun was to message it once visual contact was made.

They passed a closed restaurant, near which a couple of young men were being helped into red and white dragon costumes for the customary dances. Then came a group of people letting off fireworks before a house lit up with stringed lights and earthen oil lamps, after which the street was dark and quiet again. Arjun tried to imagine how it must have been two or three decades earlier, or even when Sheng Li had gone to school here. It was a community and a place dying out, slowly but surely. Like me, he thought. He turned to SI Munda.

'You remember the description, right?' he asked.

'Yes.'

'Tall, well built, short hair, scar on right cheek. Dresses well.'

'Yes.'

'And his friend. Tall, ponytail, one eye?'

'Yes, I remember!'

'All right.'

Arjun turned away. The Gypsy took a turn, more lights and crackers again, some children too, a rare sight, but only some of them were Chinese. They passed a Kali temple that looked both Indian and Chinese, a few devotees inside. Then dark and quiet again. Arjun lit a cigarette.

'Stop here?' he said.

SI Munda brought the Gypsy to a halt on the side of the lane, and they got down. The drain running beside the vehicle glinted with chromium run-off. They went ahead on the dusty lane and took a turn. Up ahead were the high whitewashed walls and decorated gate of the Chinese school. People, mostly Chinese, were going in and out, while a Chinese pop song played on loudspeakers behind the wall.

'So, here we are,' Arjun said, putting off his cigarette underfoot.

'What do we do?' the sub-inspector asked.

'Let's take a round inside first,' Arjun suggested.

They went in past the arched gate with Chinese characters atop it; on a large lawn flanked by a basketball court and lit up by lights were several makeshift stalls selling mostly snacks of all sorts, but also new year's souvenirs as well as packaged foodstuff. Families and friends, and locals too, milled about. Beyond the lawn was the large three-storied school building in the shape of an upside-down block letter U. Here and there Arjun could make out American and Australian accents from the children running around. No sign of anyone like Sheng Li or Tenzing as yet.

SI Munda meanwhile had stopped at one of the food stalls, and asked the woman what sort of momos she was selling. The shiny-faced woman replied back, also in Bengali, saying those were siu mai, and not momos. Arjun and the sub-inspector had two plates of the open dumplings with pork filling along with green chilli sauce poured onto their plates by the woman.

'Nice, they are holding on to their culture,' SI Munda observed, looking around.

With food in his stomach he seemed to be in a more agreeable mood.

Arjun threw his empty paper plate into a dustbin, wiped his hands with a paper napkin, and took out his phone.

'Let me call Mr Leong,' he said.

The restaurateur was at home, he said, he didn't like crowds. He would have the special noodles with his wife and some relatives later at home. But he had news for Arjun.

'He's here, Sheng Li. He should be visiting his old school.'

'That's where I am. Let me know if you hear anything else.'

Arjun asked SI Munda to wait outside the gate, to keep an eye up and down the lane and also on who entered, while he took a few more rounds of the place. Walking around, he touched the slim plastic container in his jacket with a filled syringe inside. Even if everything went off well, he was still entering dangerous territory here. He would be glad to be back in Delhi, maybe meet Poppy Barua after that.

He decided to go have a look at the school building. The Canto pop from the loudspeakers rigged to the school walls rang louder. The classrooms were all closed, had been for a long time now according to Mr Leong, and the people—many of whom might have studied here as children—were all chatting and laughing as they went up the broad staircase, with their children and teenagers. Arjun followed them.

On the third floor was a large empty hall in the central part of the building, with decorations hung up and a few people and children at a couple of tables; maybe they had had some sort of dance performance earlier. But all the people were carrying on to the terrace, and he went along. At the top of the empty building was a large covered structure open on three sides, its inner walls painted maroon and bright yellow; on the fourth side was another smaller room with two deities—fierce-looking bearded men—housed in box-like shrines behind red curtains. People were praying before them and lighting incense sticks and sticking them into large sand-filled urns.

Arjun went over to one of the sides of the building and lit a cigarette; down below were the lights of Tangra, firecrackers going off here and there, while the old tanneries stood dark and deserted. Towards the outer boundary roads of the area tall apartment complexes were coming up. He lit a cigarette and looked back at the temple; there was a statue of a man in maroon pants and a yellow shirt with a horse beside him, possibly some Cantonese tradition, and large mounted drums, while elderly men and women were resting on maroon-painted benches after the climb. A procession of dancing dragons came along the school lane to the beat of drums, followed by a line of people, and halted at the school gate.

Sheng Li, returning to have a glimpse of his old school (even as he mixed business with it), thinking about it somehow touched Arjun: it could have been him, returning to one of the many schools he had studied in across the North East, thanks to his father's construction job. He put out the cigarette after smoking half of it, and walked over to the inner room. Under richly embroidered pendants hanging from the ceiling were tables full of offerings: fruit, chocolates, dumplings, juice. He helped himself to an incense stick from a packet lying on one of the tables, lit it, and made his way through the devotees to one of the deities. Folding his palms together he prayed for his departed father, and for the other people in his life. He didn't know what the temple or the deities exactly stood for, but the formal setting lent sanctity to the occasion. He stuck the incense stick into an urn, and then made his way down the stairs.

Going down past more people who were coming up, he wondered if this—saying a prayer for his father—had been the whole point of the case. As he came down to the second floor, a man with a blue baseball cap pulled low over his face and his hands in the pockets of his leather jacket crossed him on his way up. Arjun glanced up: the cap and the stairs had, for a split second, taken him back to Bhikaji Cama Place and DCP Prem Tanwar lying on the floor of the corridor and the girl in the red sari. Then it struck him. The man wearing the cap had moved ahead and disappeared. Arjun turned around and went back up.

Once he reached the terrace and took a few steps forward, Arjun saw the blue cap moving in towards the shrine. The man was tall, well-built, and well dressed. Arjun threaded his way past a large family group who were leaving, and moved forward. From the open outer room he could see the man lighting several incense sticks and praying. Suddenly the man turned his head, as though he had heard something, and looked straight at Arjun, who could now make out the scar on the other man's right cheek. Sheng Li held his eyes for a moment, then turned and buried the incense sticks in an urn and hurried out of the temple.

Arjun followed him, then started running down the stairs after him, taking out his phone at the same time and calling SI Munda.

'He was here, at the school temple!' Arjun yelled. 'He's coming out now! Be ready!'

42

As Arjun ran out onto the forecourt of the school, he could make out Sheng Li hurrying towards the main gate. He continued running, banging into people who staggered or fell and yelled after him. A group of young volunteers at the gate made to stop him, but Arjun pushed his way through them and out into the lane. He looked right and left, and saw near the corner of the lane—from where he and the sub-inspector had come—two men grappling with each other in the dim light. He made a dash for them, panting with the exertion now. At the corner of the lane was parked a black SUV, and a tall man was approaching Sheng Li and SI Munda from its direction.

Arjun got to them first, and tried to separate both men, so that he could land a clean blow on Sheng Li. Out of the corner of his eye he saw the tall man approaching him, and turned. The other man had a ponytail, and something glinted in his hand. Instinctively Arjun raised his left arm, and felt the blade slice across his jacket sleeve and forearm, followed by a burning pain. It was instinct too that made him ignore the pain and slam his right fist into the man's face, following it up with a knee to the groin; the man groaned and fell, and Arjun for a moment stared at the skin grotesquely folded over one eye socket, before scooping up the knife. He turned towards the other two, and partly registered SI Munda on the ground as well, before a fist slammed into his jaw and sent him reeling to the ground.

The next thing he knew Sheng Li was above him, two large strong hands around his throat. He raised the knife, but it was in his left hand, and the pressure on his throat was already making him lose consciousness.

'Who are you?' Sheng Li growled. 'Who sent you?'

Then there was a dull thud, and he fell, and Arjun saw SI Munda standing above him with a large stone in one hand. He looked to his left, and saw Tenzing, the one-eyed man, getting to his feet. Arjun forced himself to get up, and tossed SI Munda the plastic container from his jacket pocket.

'Fast, open it!' he said, 'open it and inject him!'

Tenzing came at him again, and this time Arjun was prepared. He side-stepped and tripped the other man, and as Tenzing fell on his knees, slammed the butt of the knife into his temple. He collapsed on the ground face-down, and only then did Arjun become aware of the people standing away from them and staring.

'Go, go away,' he said to them, staggering a little. 'Just a fight. Come on, get away!'

SI Munda was kneeling over Sheng Li with the syringe in one hand, hesitating.

'His neck, inject him in his neck,' Arjun said to him.

The two of them dragged the smuggler to the Gypsy around the corner and put him in a sitting position in the front seat—Arjun said he would be less noticeable that way. Then they came back and carried the still-unconscious Tenzing to the SUV and dumped him in the back seat. Arjun could hear the peppy Canto pop coming from the school grounds as he took Tenzing's cell phone, and took out the keys from the ignition and put them into the unconscious man's jeans. His jacket sleeve was sticky with blood now, and he took it off and tied his handkerchief around the gash. Then they went back to the Gypsy, and Arjun got into the front seat, the senseless Sheng Li between him and SI Munda.

The sub-inspector was grim-faced as he started the vehicle. Arjun looked at him.

'This time you saved my life. Thank you.'

SI Munda nodded slightly, then asked, rather coldly, 'Where to now?'

'Let's get out of here first,' Arjun said, 'while I check.'

He took out his phone and sent a message to the number Zhang had provided: *Target spotted and engaged.* The reply came straightaway: *Condition of target?* Arjun replied: *Sedated.* He made Sheng Li lean against him so SI Munda could drive more easily. Again came the reply: *Good. Head towards Bidhannagar. Further instructions will follow.*

Arjun put away the phone and sighed, feeling both tired and wired now. He said to SI Munda, 'Head towards Bidhannagar. Salt Lake City, isn't it?'

'Yes.'

'Wait ... is the Chinese Embassy there?'

'Embassy means ... it is a consulate. Residential building only. Four storeys, white and red. I remember it.'

'So the handover will be somewhere near there.'

SI Munda squeezed past a group of people getting ready to burst crackers, then headed towards one of the exits. He looked at Sheng Li, half-leaning against Arjun.

'What was in the injection?'

'Just a sedative. Not dangerous, it'll put him to sleep for a while.'

The sub-inspector shook his head. 'I don't know what we're doing.'

Arjun gritted his teeth. 'Yes, you told me that before.'

He could say a lot of things, but he held his tongue. The operation above all, just as he had learnt while in the army.

'Which way will you go?' he asked, partly to change the subject.

'From the inside roads. There might be checking on the main roads.'

SI Munda drove out of Tangra, then through narrow roads and crowded tenements, Dhapa and Beleghata, no one paying the slightest heed to the vehicle or the seemingly asleep man inside. Arjun kept checking his phone, and after about fifteen minutes another message: the handover was to take place near Bidhannagar College on 1st Cross Road. Arjun told SI Munda, and the latter nodded. They rode in silence, crossing over the main road into the neater environs of Salt Lake City. SI Munda drove faster, took a left and then a right. They were driving along a wide road now, traffic speeding along on either side of the divider. Then the sub-inspector swore softly in Bengali.

'What is it?' Arjun asked.

SI Munda slowed down the vehicle, and then Arjun saw it: a police barricade.

'They won't stop you, will they?'

'They might. Just to have a chat.'

'Fuck.'

He saw now under the yellow glare of the sodium lights three staggered barricades with 'Kolkata Police' painted on them and constables checking the papers of motorcyclists, and a car. A stout man with a police cap raised his baton and waved them down, walking over when SI Munda had stopped just before the barricades. To their right, cars continued to speed past. Arjun swore again: just their luck. He put his shoes over the jacket on the floor of the vehicle and lowered his bandaged arm. The police officer came over to SI Munda's side, a sergeant with two stars on his shoulders like the sub-inspector (but a slightly different stripe pattern).

'Where are you headed?' he asked in Bengali, and without waiting for an answer went on. 'Bidhannagar Police got a tip-off. So doing some checking. But we'll be leaving in a while.' It was then that he noticed the inanimate third passenger.

'Hey, what's the matter with him?' he asked.

Arjun could feel his heart hammering, but SI Munda just chuckled lightly.

'This is my friend Lt Col Arjun, posted in Assam,' he said, pointing a thumb at Arjun, 'and this is his friend Jimmy. Had a bit too much at Park Street, so I'm going to drop them both.'

The sergeant moved his head closer to look at the two men. Arjun could feel the dryness in his throat but forced himself to smile what he hoped looked like a drunken grin.

With a stern look on his face the sergeant straightened up, glanced towards his constables, and then broke out into a laugh.

'Go, go and drop them,' he said, and tapped the vehicle with his baton.

'See you,' SI Munda said with a smile, and started the engine and drove through the barricades on the roadside.

Neither man spoke for a while. Arjun appreciated the sub-inspector's presence of mind: one or two of the North Eastern states had their state houses in Salt Lake City.

'You handled that well,' he finally said.

'No problem,' said SI Munda. Up ahead was a large roundabout. 'Which way now?'

Arjun took out his phone to check: a phone number had been sent in a message; it would call him very soon.

'Slow down,' Arjun said.

SI Munda slowed down, and moved left towards the side of the road. Arjun's cellphone started ringing: it was the same number. He answered, and was surprised to be addressed by a voice speaking rough Hindi.

'Where have you reached?'

Arjun looked out and saw a signboard.

'There's a big gol chakkar ahead and Bidhannagar College is straight ahead,' he said in Hindi.

'You're close. Keep coming straight. Opposite the college, you'll see a Toyota Innova under some trees. Stop behind it.'

'What's the car number?'

The voice told him, and hung up. SI Munda looked at him as he took a half-circle of the roundabout.

'Chinese speaking in Hindi?'

'Just drive,' Arjun snapped, suddenly jumpy.

They were crossing apartment blocks and office blocks now, then the trees of the college campus to their right. Up ahead, in the shadow of a spreading tree between two large buildings, was the Innova. Arjun pointed, and SI Munda slid in behind it. Two well-built men got out of the back of the vehicle.

The sub-inspector leaned across and took out his service pistol from the dashboard compartment, and held it down in his right hand.

'I'm not getting out,' he said.

Arjun opened the door and got down. The men had sharp noses, one of them was bearded. The clean shaven one spoke, in rough accented Hindi.

'Is that the fellow?'

'Yes,' Arjun said. 'Let's get him out.'

He held the door open while the two men took the unconscious Sheng Li out of the Gypsy's front and carried him between them to the open back door of the Innova. Arjun saw a third man in the driver's seat of the Innova. Only the clean shaven one came back.

'Tell them we've collected him,' he said.

Arjun nodded.

'Are you police?' the man asked.

Arjun shook his head, and asked in return, 'Where are you from?' but the man only raised a hand in a gesture of farewell, turned, walked back to the Innova and got in. The large vehicle sped off; Arjun kept looking till it disappeared in the yellow sodium haze before going back to the Gypsy.

'Who were those people?' SI Munda asked him as he took a U-turn up ahead.

Arjun didn't say anything as he typed out a message: *Target delivered.* In return came a thumbs up emoji: two of them. He sighed and put his phone away. It was all done.

'You know what they looked like to me?' SI Munda continued, 'They looked like Pathans to me.'

Arjun didn't answer, looked out of his window at the passing buildings.

'Could they be Pakistanis? What have you done, Arjun ji? We had got Rohit's murderers, why couldn't you just leave it at that?'

Arjun shrugged. He wanted to be angry, at this man who was responsible for a custodial death and was now lecturing him, but he just felt a deep resignation.

'I don't know,' he said.

'Who did you do it for? Rohit? Or was it for that Chinese bar girl you met?'

This time he lost it.

'I don't know! Stop the car, I'll get down here.'

SI Munda shook his head. 'I'll drop you. Then please leave Kolkata tomorrow. I could raise a look-out for the Chinese fellow, airport, train station, highways. But I gave you my word.'

'Thanks,' Arjun said, and thought to himself: too old, I'm too old to make new friends.

SI Munda had him back at the guest house in Gariahat in under half-an-hour. Arjun got down, then went across to shake the sub-inspector's hand.

'Take care and thank you,' he said, determined not to show bitterness.

'You saved my life that day, and today I saved yours. So we're even now. Goodbye, Detective Arora.' With that the sub-inspector drove off into the night. Arjun slowly climbed up the steps to his room, where he poured himself a large whiskey and lit a cigarette, but then got into bed and started shivering: the moment when he had been on the ground, Sheng Li's big hands choking the life out of him, returned to him, and he felt an indescribable fear and panic. He felt like a small child again, having run home after yet again being tormented in some small town for being an outsider, waiting for his mother or his father to comfort him—but he was all alone now.

43

The doorbell rang, and Arjun went to the front door and opened it. Kadambari Vats stood there in a white salwar kameez, her face scrubbed and shiny, a large black bag slung on a shoulder. Unlike the first time she had visited, Arjun was dressed and clean shaven: he had been waiting for her. She smiled at him.

'Hello Arjun.'

'Hi, Pinky. Come in.'

The sitting room had been cleaned and there were even flowers in a vase on the centre table. The balcony door and windows were open: outside it was one of those rare perfect afternoons that sometimes stole upon Delhi in November and in February. Shouts came up from the park below where both a football and a cricket game were going on. Pinky sat down on the sofa and Arjun went to the kitchen to make some tea.

When he returned with two cups and a plate of biscuits on a lacquered bamboo tray she half rose and handed him an envelope.

'It's a cheque. I hope it'll do?'

'Sure.'

He set out the tea and biscuits and put the tray aside.

'And I'm sorry it took so long,' she said, 'but I was waiting for the insurance payment.'

'No problem, Pinky,' Arjun said with a smile. 'Here, your tea.'

She looked inside her bag and took out a hip flask with a leather cover.

'This was Rohit's, he had got it from London. I wanted to give it to you. As a memento ... to say thanks ... if I hadn't got the insurance money ...' she sniffed and wiped her eyes.

Arjun took it from her and turned it around in his hands.

'It's very nice. Thank you so much for it.'

Pinky sniffed and nodded, drank some tea.

'One thing I don't understand,' she said, after recovering her composure, 'is why he was doing it? Why was he after this Chinese smuggler? I mean ... for what?'

Arjun placed the hip flask on the table, then looked at the back of his hands.

'I don't know,' he said finally, 'maybe there was some old rivalry between them.'

'How did you find out about him? In China? The smuggler.'

'Someone ... Rohit knew from London told me about him.'

'A girl? Or a guy?'

'A girl.' He couldn't go on lying.

'Did he meet her when he was there?'

Arjun leaned forward, and took her hands in his. 'Listen, Pinky, your husband loved you and the children very much. He said so to his work colleague in China. Now that you have the insurance money, try and put the past behind you and make a new life. Think about your children.'

She nodded, bowed her head, and sniffed again.

'If he had only said goodbye to me that morning when he left,' she said, looking up at him. 'Do you understand?'

Arjun nodded, thinking about his father, thinking about Rohit and Vivien. After Pinky left, he went out to the balcony and lit a cigarette. He could see her walking by the side of the park, then getting into the driver seat of a grey-colour Alto and driving off. It was over, and he felt a curious emptiness within himself.

That evening he was at a Kashmiri restaurant in Pamposh Enclave, just across the Outer Ring Road from CR Park; Arjun had walked there across the overpass. There was a Kashmiri society next door, and Arjun had always supposed there was some connection between the two; the restaurant had a 'Members Only' sign at the entrance, but anyone could enter. It was a spacious hall with the bar at the back, and crowded with regulars from the society and other people looking for an unpretentious place to drink.

Keeping Arjun company was Bunty Chawla, and there were chicken kebabs and fish tikka on the table between them besides two Blender's Pride whiskies.

'Hmm, I had forgotten how good these kebabs were,' Bunty remarked through a mouthful.

'I've come after a long time too,' Arjun said, his eyes scanning the crowd from their small corner table. 'I think they mix ghee with the mince in the kebabs.'

'*Jo bhi ho*, they are tasty,' said Bunty, now helping himself to a fish tikka. 'Has the fellow you wanted to check out arrived yet?'

Arjun shook his head. 'Not yet.'

'Who's he again?'

'Basheer Drabu, a Kashmiri politician.'

'Hmm. Don't tell me he's connected to that Kolkata incident? Those Pakis?'

'No no, his son is going around with Rhea. Sonali asked me to check out the father.'

'Oh ok, like that. But really *kancha*, I don't understand. Why try to get that Chinese fellow. What will you get out of it? That Bangali policewala was correct.'

Arjun shrugged and ate a piece of kebab. 'Maybe I was wrong. But also, maybe, it might be of help to me in the future. Don't you think?'

'Maybe,' Bunty said, and finished his drink and stopped a passing waiter and asked for two more large whiskies.

'Small for me,' Arjun told the waiter.

Bunty peered at him suspiciously. 'Small? Are you okay?'

'Yes. Just going slow.'

Bunty studied him now: clean shaven, wearing a blazer over a clean dress shirt.

'There's something fishy, you know. Where are you going from here? Why are you grinning? Oh wait ... you sly bastard ... who is she?'

Arjun grinned and told him.

'Well, she's a good piece of ass,' Bunty said reflectively. 'So you'll desert me then?'

'Go home early to your family.'

'Arre family I take care of everyday. How often do we meet? But I understand,' Bunty said, and winked. 'Looks like fireworks will go off tonight, my dear.'

Arjun laughed and raised his glass. He looked around, and saw Bashrat enter behind a tall, good-looking man with thinning hair and a gentle belly, followed by some more Kashmiri-looking men. They took their places at a reserved table and Arjun noticed a waiter hurrying over to them and making a slight bow.

He had had Ujjwal Negi look up Basheer Drabu, and one of the things Negi had come up with was that Drabu was in Delhi, where he visited this particular restaurant most nights for drinks and dinner. So Arjun had contrived to be there: he wanted to see Drabu for himself, and show him *his* face too. Deep down he agreed with Sonali: he didn't want Rhea to be collateral damage in any way.

After they had finished their drinks, settled the bill, and visited the washroom, the two of them approached Basheer Drabu's table on their way out.

'Bashrat, hi!' Arjun called out. 'What are you doing here?'

The teenager looked surprised, then uncomfortable.

'Hello, Uncle,' he said, getting up slowly, 'just came for dinner ... with Dad.'

He indicated with his hand to Drabu senior sitting beside him. There were drinks and plenty of snacks on the table. Basheer Drabu looked up at Arjun quizzically. The other men at the table went on talking in Kashmiri. Bashrat turned to his father and said something, and he stood up to shake Arjun's hand.

'Arjun Arora. Your son Bashrat is friends with my daughter Rhea,' he said, in Hindi.

'Nice to meet you, Arora ji,' the other man replied

in accented Hindi, a thin smile on his face. 'My name is Basheer Drabu.'

'You live in Kashmir?' Arjun asked.

'Yes. You've visited?'

'No, never.'

'You should come sometime.'

'Thank you. I'll keep it in mind.'

Arjun bid farewell to the two Drabus. Once outside he lit a cigarette.

'That was the boy's father?' Bunty asked him. 'Shifty-looking fellow.'

'That's what I thought too.'

'Keep an eye on Rhea.' Bunty unlocked his car. 'Come on, I'll drop you.'

'It's ok, I'll walk. You'll have to make another unnecessary round.'

'Ok lover boy, as you wish! See you later.'

Arjun walked back to CR Park via the overpass. Vehicles streamed by below, mostly from the Nehru Place side. Nearing the steps going down he turned to look, and saw a young man with a satchel slung across one shoulder hurrying towards him. Taking out his phone he pretended to browse through it as he slowly went down the steps to the right, and as he did so kept to the left, so that he could see the feet of anyone behind him. He almost stopped after taking a turn of the steps, and the youth hurried past him onto the footpath below. Arjun came out of the overpass, lit a cigarette and looked around: the paranoia which had come upon him in the Kolkata guest house following Sheng Li's handover was still with him.

He got home, checked himself in the bathroom mirror, then put on an EPL game and settled down to wait. The doorbell rang, twice, just after 9 p.m. He went to open the door. Poppy Barua stood there in a pink hooded sports jacket over a black sari, and a bottle of wine in her hands. Arjun grinned.

'Getting younger by the day.'

She handed him the bottle and came in.

'Don't laugh, I was in a hurry getting ready,' she said as she took off her jacket.

'At least you're not wearing sneakers,' he observed, spotting her black heels.

'What's this, you haven't cooked?' she asked, looking into the kitchen.

'I thought I would, but I was at the agency, then meeting some people ... we'll order, anything you want.'

'That'll do. Now open the wine, I'm thirsty.'

Arjun opened the bottle of Australian red wine, but poured himself a Blender's Pride. He also switched off the television.

'About the last time,' Poppy said when they were sitting down on the sofa. 'I'm sorry. It was just that...'

Arjun raised a hand. 'It's ok, let's forget about it.'

She nodded. 'Anyway, Vani Shetty has quit. Problems with management. And apparently *I* might take her place.'

'Oh ... that's ... wonderful. Really great!'

'Nothing's finalised yet, so let's see how it goes.'

'Cheers to new beginnings,' Arjun said, and they clinked their glasses and drank.

'And you cracked that Kolkata case you said last time. Congratulations.'

'Thanks.'

'So what did you find out in China?'

'Well, that's a long story.'

'I have all the time in the world,' Poppy said.

She sank back into the sofa, tousled her hair and smiled at him, and he knew he wouldn't be able to keep his hands off her much longer. He shifted a little closer to her on the sofa, and said, 'After I landed in Shanghai, I went to the service apartment where Rohit Vats had stayed and got myself an apartment for...'

He woke early the next morning, his stomach growling with hunger. Fast asleep beside him under the blanket was Poppy. They hadn't even ordered dinner the previous night, having ended up in the bedroom with their glasses. Now he ran his hand over her body and she purred like a cat and moved closer to him.

'I'm getting something to eat,' he told her, 'you want anything?'

'No. Come back soon,' she mumbled into her pillow.

He made himself a cheese sandwich in the kitchen, and as he ate it made a cup of coffee which he took out to the balcony along with a cigarette. In the park the joggers and walkers and meditation practitioners were out, enthused by the comfortable coolness of the morning. The fine weather, Poppy in his bed—he felt a deep sense of contentment as he drank his coffee and smoked his cigarette. The newspapers hadn't been thrown up as yet.

Arjun checked his phone: no further messages on WeChat since that night in Kolkata, but there was a new mail for him from the email ID Zhang had given him, titled

'Shanghai news'. He opened the mail: there was just a link, followed by 'Thank you.', followed by a capital 'A' and 'Z', which Arjun took to mean 'Agent Zhang'. He clicked on the link: it was a story on the website of an English-language newspaper Arjun had seen in China.

'Fugitives Brought Back to China' said the heading, with a photo under it showing a line of hooded men walking down a boarding ramp from a plane at night, under bright lights, while helmeted security men waited for them on the ground. The caption below the photo said: 'Several more fugitives from justice were brought back to Shanghai last night from Myanmar as part of the ongoing "Operation Fox Hunt" programme of the Chinese government.' Arjun increased the size of the photo to look at the men wearing black hoods, seven of them in all. The last one was tall, and wore a stylish leather jacket and jeans and sneakers: Sheng Li.